DAWN
OF THE
ASSASSIN

BILL BREWER

Bill Brewer

THRILLEX Publishing

Dedicated to you the reader.

Thank you for choosing this book.
I hope you enjoy the story

Praise for Bill Brewer

"Diversity, the polarity of wealth, strong female leads—Brewer delivers a contemporary, socially relevant thriller with whiplash pacing and an eye for detail. Unputdownable."

- K.J. Howe, International bestseller of THE FREEDOM BROKER and SKYJACK

"The action starts on page one and never stops. David Diegert blasts on to the thriller scene like a hollow point from a Beretta. You're going to love this book."

- Wayne Zurl, Author of the Sam Jenkins Series

"Action, adventure, intrigue, daring escapes, an unjust court-martial and a dose of redemption - *Dawn of the Assassin* has it all. Don't miss an instant of this heart-pounding thriller, the latest in the *David Diegert* series. Pick up your copy by the eminently talented author Bill Brewer now!"

- Lt Colonel Rip Rawlings (USMC), Co-Author of RED METAL

1

Tattered boots found unstable footing in the snow as David Diegert trudged two miles to his night-shift job at the mini-mart. *Without money, life sucks,* he thought as the chill penetrated his coat and the snow-impeded walk numbed his toes. Normally he passed the time checking e-mail, reading the news, or playing Mobile Strike. On this trip, he was left with only his thoughts since his service had been cut off for nonpayment.

His job was lousy, but with only a high school diploma in the rural economy of northern Minnesota, Diegert was lucky to have it. Minimum wage sapped his efforts at financial progress. He hated living at home with his parents and older brother, but he hoped the raise he was due would give him enough to get his own apartment. He also hoped to save some money for college, although right now a car would be nice.

Scuffing the snow off his boots on the doormat, which he would later have to clean, Diegert stepped inside. He smelled the pizza cooking and heard the hot dogs sizzling, but his senses had grown numb to it all and it only served to dull his appetite. Barbara, his heavyset coworker, looked up from the counter she was cleaning and gave him a nod. The store manager, Barley Cummings, eyed him quizzically from the door of his messy office. Barley was proud to tell anyone who asked, and even those who didn't, that he was named after the main ingredient for making beer. Cummings beckoned him over with his fingers.

"Hey, didn't you get my e-mail?" asked the rotund manager.

"No," said Diegert, breaking eye contact. "My phone's dead."

"Well, we're downsizing."

"You're making the store smaller?"

"No, I'm making the staff smaller, and I had to let you go."

With a sense of having just been insulted, Diegert replied, "And you told me with an e-mail?"

"Yeah, thought I'd save you the walk. Look, your pass card has been deactivated, and unless you're gonna buy something, you gotta go. You don't work here anymore, Tonto."

Diegert absorbed the news with disappointment, anger, and embarrassment rising up at Barley's use of his nickname from high school that he hated.

"I'm due for a raise, and so now you fire me."

"It's called corporate cost control," said Cummings matter-of-factly as he put a hand on Diegert's shoulder, nudging him toward the door. Diegert slapped the thoughtless boss's hand away and shoved him up against the soda machine.

"Don't fuckin' touch me."

Cumming's huge belly shook as Diegert pressed him back against the soda fountain. The store manager's wide ass activated the dispensers, which soaked his pants.

"Don't do anything crazy," pleaded the overweight imbecile, who'd never realized that the muscles that bound Diegert's six-foot-two-inch frame were so strong.

Releasing his grip on Cummings and stepping back, Diegert thought about "crazy." He looked at the shelves of chips, the stacks of soda bottles, the cardboard displays of cookies, as well as the refrigerated cases full of beer. He wanted to smash them all, clear the shelves with a sweep of his arm and toss the soda behind the counter where it would crash on the sandwich boards and the pizza oven. Then he would shove a shelving unit right through the glass, bursting the bottles of beer. He wanted to destroy the entire shitty little store where he had wasted so much time. But he did not.

Stepping away from the frightened man, Diegert said, "I'm walking outta here on my own." He turned and left, dropping his employee pass card on the floor.

As he walked away from the store, down a dark country road, Diegert heard the acceleration of an engine and saw his tall shadow cast on the road by flashing red-and-blue lights. He peered over his shoulder at the county sheriff's car, watching as it passed by and pulled in front of him, nose to the snowbank, blocking his path. Officer Paul Tate stepped out of the car and walked back to Diegert.

"Dave, I'm placing you under arrest."

"Oh, come on, Tates."

"Don't give me any shit. Barley called it in, and you have the right to remain silent."

Officer Tate handcuffed Diegert and put him in the car.

At the police station, locked in a processing room, Diegert sat alone for a long time, which allowed his thoughts to wander back to his childhood.

He remembered sitting on the couch—which was really a foam mattress on top of an old door held up by cinderblocks—huddled under a blanket in the cold house while his mother, Denise, read to him from *Harry Potter and the Goblet of Fire*. She cleverly created a distinct voice for each character. David loved the adventures of Hogwarts and was magically transported there by the imagination of his mother.

"God damn it, there's not enough beer in here," bellowed David's father, Tom, as he pulled his head up from inside the fridge.

"I told you to have at least a twelve-pack in here all the time," he shouted as he slammed the fridge door. Denise stopped reading, rose from the mattress, and went to the kitchen.

"You fuckin' injuns can't count past five," Tom said as he shoved the tall, dark-haired woman into the cupboard door. David's fourteen-year-old brother, Jake, quickly left the kitchen and closed the door to his upstairs bedroom.

"Leave her alone," demanded little ten-year-old David. Dressed in pajamas, he stood defiantly between his parents, facing his father with a look of determination.

His father laughed. "Look at the little bastard standing up to protect his slut of a mother. Come on, little man, let's see what you're really made of."

Tom Diegert put up his fists and so did David. Tom flinched his left hand and smacked David's face with his right, snapping the young boy's head and spinning him onto the floor. Blood oozed from David's lips as his mother screamed for Tom to stop. Tom turned his rage on her, slapping her face and shoving her up against the counter.

"This is my house, and you're my wife, and I'll do whatever I goddamn want."

David stepped behind his father, kicking him in the knee. Tom spun and backhanded David across the face, sending him tumbling over a kitchen chair.

"You think you're a tough little guy, eh? Let's see how you like this!"

Tom opened the kitchen door and threw David out into the snow of a Minnesota winter night.

The door slammed, jolting David Diegert out of his recollection of that night over ten years ago.

Sheriff Michael Lowery crossed the room and stood before the chair to which Diegert was handcuffed. "It's your lucky day, son. Oh, I know you lost your job at the mini-mart and you beat up your boss for firing you."

"I didn't beat him up, Mr. Lowery," protested Diegert.

"He says you pushed him into a soda machine, but I convinced him not to press charges. You've been arrested, but you're not being charged. You're free to go."

Diegert looked at him untrustingly. "This is the lucky part?"

"Yup, it is," the lawman said as he unlocked the handcuffs. "But that's not all."

As the sheriff of Broward County handed Diegert a business card, he said, "Major Carl Winston, US Army recruiter. I suggest you go see him and consider serving your country instead of assaulting its citizens."

Sheriff Lowery took a seat next to Diegert. "Ya see, I know you've had it rough. I've responded to some of those domestic disputes at your house. But I also remember when you won States in wrestling. You were the first kid from Broward to ever go to States. I felt very proud down at the tournament."

Diegert looked at him, surprised to learn that he had made the trip all the way down to Minneapolis for the State Wrestling Tournament six years ago. His father hadn't bothered.

Lowery continued, "I want to see you do well in life. Tell Major Winston I sent you, and he'll be very understanding. But, David, if you piss away this opportunity, you will not be walking out of here the next time you're arrested."

Diegert stood up and put the card in his shirt pocket. He hesitated before extending his hand to the sheriff. They shook hands and Diegert walked out into the cold winter night.

The walk home was windy, but the frigid, piercing air was not nearly as uncomfortable as the dynamics of the Diegert household. David had grown tall and strong, so his short, fat father now used his words rather than his fists to hurt him. Stepping straight into the kitchen of the small house, Diegert encountered his father's scorn before he'd even taken off his boots.

"Hey, dipshit, Jake told me you got fired from the mini-mart."

"Well, then, I'm glad I don't have to tell you."

"Don't you give me any of that wiseass shit. If I stop getting calls from them to tow away illegally parked cars, I'm blaming you."

Putting his coat on a hanger in the closet, Diegert replied, "The failure of your business is not my fault."

"Your maternal bitch isn't here to defend you, so you'd better watch your mouth."

Jake interjected, "Barley says you assaulted him, and he had you arrested."

"I didn't beat him nearly enough. The charges were dropped and Lowery let me go."

Diegert passed by the kitchen table where his father and brother sat with their brown bottles of beer, a bag of chips, and two cigarettes smoldering in the ashtray. As David opened the fridge, Jake said, "Don't take any of our food."

With a disdainful smirk, David said, "I've got my own."

David stood at the kitchen counter making turkey sandwiches.

"What are you going to do without a job?" asked Tom.

"I don't know. Maybe Jake will let me help him sell drugs," David replied sarcastically.

Jake looked up, sneering at him as he raised his middle finger from his doughy fist.

"Now, dipshit," began his father, "it usually takes a person about two months to find a new job. So I want the next two months' rent up front."

David turned to look at his father with an incredulous expression of disbelief.

"I'm also raising the rent, so you owe me two thousand dollars."

Pounding the kitchen counter and extending to his full height, David spun to face the table. With a sharp kitchen knife in his hand, David said, "What? A thousand dollars a month to shit in your toilet and sleep in the barn? No fuckin' way."

"Hey, you're lucky to have a roof over your head, and I hate the way your shit stinks, so if you want to live somewhere else, you go right ahead."

Pointing the knife at Jake, David barked, "What about him? He lives in the heat and eats whatever he wants. Why the hell doesn't he pay rent?"

"Look, don't make your problems seem like someone else's." Nodding toward Jake, Tom continued, "He has a very different financial situation from you, so fairness is not the issue."

Jake sniped in, "You ought to try running a business rather than being an employee."

"Yeah, well, most of the time I was with Sheriff Lowery, he was asking me about meth, oxy, and heroin. I don't think your secrets are safe anymore."

"What did you tell him?"

"I told him you're so fucking stupid that it would be real easy to set up a buy and have you show up with enough drugs to put you away for twenty years."

Jake's chair screeched across the floor as he bolted up from the table. David advanced quickly, pinning his brother backward over the sink. He brought the knife to Jake's throat. Jake grabbed his forearm, saying, "Really, you're going to cut me right here in front of Dad?"

Pressing the blade against the skin, David said, "Gladly."

The snap of a hammer being drawn back pulled their attention to their father, whose .38 revolver was pointed at David.

"Let him go. Get your food and get the fuck out of here."

David stepped back, drawing the blade across Jake's throat just enough to scare him. He moved to the counter to finish making his sandwiches.

Jake rubbed his neck, checking for blood, but remained at the sink. "If you snitch, you're dead, you little punk bastard."

The intensity of David's glare conveyed the complete absence of love between them. He put away his food, then slammed the fridge door. His father kept the gun trained on him while he put on his boots and coat. With his dinner in a plastic bag, Diegert left the house and headed for the barn.

David had a small bedroom up in the loft of the old barn out back on the property. The room was defined by two exterior walls and two hanging tarps, which together formed a small rectangle. Since his father used the building as a garage for working on cars, the odor of oil and gas permeated the floor and walls. A thermal sleeping bag and extra-thick blankets insulated Diegert on his single bed. Illumination was provided by a floor lamp, but there was no source of heat. Wearing a wool hat to bed, he often shivered himself to sleep, but it was better than sharing a room with his brother under the same roof as his father.

2

The next morning, Diegert arrived at the Armed Forces recruiting center in Bemidji. Standing at the counter, Diegert observed a tall, strong-looking African American man dressed in fatigues approach.

"Hello, son, I'm Major Carl Winston," the man said with confidence as he offered his hand.

"David Diegert," was the simple reply as the two men instinctively assessed one another's strength while gripping hands.

"Oh, Sheriff Lowery gave me a call about you. I'm glad you're here."

Diegert cracked a slight smile as the major directed him around the counter and brought him into the recruiting center. The major's crisp, spicy cologne made Diegert wish he had showered that morning.

"Son, let's address my first question right now. Do you think you're strong enough to be in the US Army?"

"I think so."

The major stepped over to an open area with a metal bar suspended from the ceiling.

"The army standard is ten pull-ups. Why don't you show me how many you can do?"

Diegert removed his coat, took off his heavy boots, and jumped up, grabbing the bar, pumping out twenty-two pull-ups.

"Well, that's a good place to start," said the major, whose look of surprise revealed he was truly impressed.

The two walked into an interview room and sat down on comfortable chairs. The Major offered Diegert bottled water and then asked, "Why do you want to join the Army?"

"Whoa, I never said I did. The sheriff told me to come, and I knew he would call you."

"Alright, so Sheriff Lowery told me you lost your job at the mini-mart."

"So?"

"So what was your mission at the mini-mart?"

The major let the question linger. Diegert looked at him suspiciously.

"Whaddya mean, like exceptional customer service and bullshit like that?" asked Diegert.

The major smiled knowingly, nodding his head, and then asked, "And what is the mission of the US Army?"

Diegert looked at him but wasn't going to answer with something stupid.

Winston continued, "The mission of the US Army is to uphold and defend the Constitution of the United States and to protect this country from all enemies foreign and domestic."

Diegert was underwhelmed; everybody knew that. Why the question, he wondered.

"We achieve this mission through the actions of soldiers who go from being lost young people to dedicated military professionals capable of learning, achieving, and leading." Winston stood up and walked over to his desk. "All men need a mission, and there is no better training experience in the world than that of the US Army. We help you find within you the best you can be."

Diegert watched as the major turned from his desk with a picture frame in his hands.

"The Army challenges your sense of self and allows you to bring out the brave person who resides within you."

The major sat back down next to Diegert with the picture frame facedown in his hands.

"David, is there a brave person inside you?"

"Yeah."

"How do you know?"

Diegert stayed silent.

"How do you know what bravery is?"

Diegert stifled a quiver in his lips as he held the major's eyes and sought his answer.

"I'm not afraid."

"OK, you're defining what it is not, but do you possess the courage and resilience necessary to persevere in the face of physical and moral adversity?"

Diegert angled his face to Major Winston but held his gaze.

"I've seen young men like you, David, grow into capable, powerful warriors with integrity and values that represent the very best of our country. These men sat in the chair you're in and then became members of the most formidable fighting force in the world."

Winston spun the frame in his hands and showed Diegert a group of a dozen young men all dressed in combat uniforms with helmets and rifles. He saw the smiles on their faces and the spirit of union apparent in their camaraderie.

"These men are all members of the 1st Cavalry Division out of Fort Hood. This picture was taken upon their arrival in Afghanistan. It was sent to me by this man." Winston pointed to one of the guys whose broad smile conveyed the pride he felt for what he was doing. "That's Joe Bortle. He came through here after being in a drunken bar fight and getting arrested. He was headed to jail until a judge gave him the same kind of choice Sheriff Lowery gave you. Now he's the sergeant of this squad, and they are one of the best units in Afghanistan. He sent me the picture, and on the back, he wrote, 'Major Winston, thanks for helping me make the right choice with the most important decision of my life.'"

The major looked squarely at Diegert.

"If there's a warrior in you, David, and I believe there is, then there's only one safe way to let him out, and that's to grow and develop within the US Army. Guys like you make the very best soldiers. You'll become a man of high character."

A smile spread across the young man's face; the recruiter had coaxed out a sprout of pride from the compost of Diegert's dreary life.

"Have you ever considered going to college?"

The question yanked Diegert from his thoughts of becoming a soldier. "Yeah, but it's too expensive."

"After serving two years of active duty, you'll be eligible for the GI Bill, which can pay your college expenses while you earn a bachelor's degree."

"Really? I serve two years, and they pay for four years of college?"

"Well, you have to complete basic training, then begin active duty. You also have to qualify for the tuition payments. But if you're smart and serve well in your MOS, I'm sure you'll qualify.

"What's an MOS?"

"It's a military occupational specialty. It's basically a job in the Army. You said you were getting paid minimum wage at your retail job, right?"

"Yeah."

"As a soldier, you will not only earn more than that in a salary, but you'll also receive a full compensation package that covers housing and healthcare, so you get to keep all the money you earn."

"How much will I make?"

"I would estimate your total compensation package would be worth thirty-five to forty thousand dollars."

"Really? That seems like a lot."

"If you're willing to serve your country, then it's worth it for your country to pay you. If you enlist in the next two days, there's also a fifteen-hundred-dollar signing bonus."

Diegert looked at him with suspicious but excited eyes.

"You can start filling out your information on this tablet."

Diegert went to work typing all his personal information into the small computer. As he typed, he started to feel the excitement of moving forward with his life. This was going to be exactly what he needed. When he was done, he handed the tablet back to Major Winston.

"Look, son," said the major calmly and clearly, "you go home and discuss this with your folks. You don't need them to sign anything. You're of legal age to make this decision yourself. But you are volunteering your life for several years, and I want you to talk to them. Call me in two days. If you tell me it's OK, I'll have you processed to Fort Benning, Georgia, to begin Basic Combat Training."

"How long does that take?"

"Basic is ten weeks, then you'll have fourteen weeks of Advanced Individual Training before you'll join the 1st Cavalry Division at Fort Hood in Texas."

"That's a lot of training."

"Wanting to become a soldier may feel natural to you, but it definitely takes a lot of training."

Diegert shook the major's hand with enthusiasm and left the office excited that he was going to become a soldier intheU.S.Army.

3

Standing outside the Triple Crown Diner, Diegert braced against the cold. His mother's shift ended at eleven p.m., but the single-digit temperatures made each minute as long as the icicles hanging from the gutters. Diegert was too excited to wait at home for her, and he wanted to tell her about the Army without his father and brother around. When her five-foot-eleven-inch frame stepped out the diner door, David approached as she wrapped her scarf around her neck and pulled a wool hat over her lustrous black hair.

"Hey, Mom."

"David, what are you doing here?"

"I wanted to surprise you and walk you home."

"Alright. I just never expected to see you here."

"That's why it's called a surprise."

They started to walk down the road.

"How was your shift tonight?" he asked.

"Same as always. Everyone talking about how cold it is, but they all want ice cream on their pie. I never expected to find you waiting out here for me."

"I've got something to tell you, Mom."

"Something good, I hope."

"I think it is. I'm going to join the Army."

Denise Diegert looked straight ahead, making no reply as she continued striding forward.

"Well, what do you think?"

"I can see why you'd think that's a good choice, but I hate the thought of you going to war."

"Just 'cause I'm joining the Army doesn't mean I'm going to war."

"We are at war all over the world. If you're in the Army, you're going to war."

"Oh, come on, Mom."

They turned the corner onto the dirt road on which they lived.

"I've got nothing to keep me here and no chance for a good job. The Army is going to pay me forty thousand dollars."

"I know there isn't much for you here, but I'll worry about you."

"There's just as much for you to worry about if I stay here. I'm going to call the recruiter tomorrow and commit. Then I'll be shipped out to Georgia for training in two days."

"Two days?"

"It's coincidence. A training class begins next week. It's OK. I'm ready to go."

David stopped walking and held his mother's mitten-covered hands.

"I'll worry about you, Mom."

She sniffed back tears, turning her head away.

"I'll worry about leaving you with Jake and Dad."

"Don't worry about me," she said as she released one hand and held on to the other as they resumed walking. "I have a wife's way of handling him, and even though he and your brother are criminals, I'm not worried about them."

"They're both pathetic jerks who don't deserve to have you in their lives."

"I love our home, David. I've put so much work into it, and it is the only home I've ever really known. When they're not around, it is such a lovely place for me to be."

"Yeah, thinking back on how it used to be and how much you've done to it, I can see why you love it. It's just too bad those two idiots live there too."

As they approached the small two-story house with its snow-covered roof, Denise said, "This house is where my heart lives."

Standing outside between the snowbanks of the driveway, David said, "I'm not saying anything to either of them. Please don't tell them about the Army, but will you take me to the bus station when I leave?"

She looked at him, her dark irises bathed in liquid emotion, then hugged him tightly. "Of course, David. Besides, I have a doctor's appointment in Bemidji on Thursday, so I'm going anyway. Your secret's safe with me, but I'm afraid my heartache may betray me."

"I trust you, Mom, and I love only you. What's with the doctor?"

"Oh, just some routine women's health checks, nothing to worry about."

David let her go and walked back to the barn as she opened the door and stepped into the kitchen.

* * * *

The next morning, Diegert borrowed his mother's phone and got excited when he heard it ringing.

"Major Carl Winston speaking."

"Major Winston? It's David Diegert."

"Well, hello, son. I'm glad to hear back from you. Did you have a talk with your folks?"

"Yes, sir."

"And they're OK with your decision?"

"Yes, sir, they are."

After a brief pause, the Major said, "OK, then I will process your application and have a bus ticket waiting for you at the Bemidji station to take you to Fort Benning day after tomorrow."

"Excellent, sir. Thank you, and I'm very much looking forward to getting started."

"Very well, David. Congratulations, and I look forward to hearing about your successful career in the US Army."

"Thank you, sir, thank you for giving me this chance."

"You're very welcome, but it's your country that'll be thanking you for the gift of your service."

After he hung up, Diegert thought about the gift of his service. He would be serving his country, and for the first time, he realized he would be helping others, not just doing things for himself. He felt a flash of pride, and a smile rose from his lips as he thought of himself as a patriot.

* * * *

On the morning of his departure, Diegert had the car warming up as he waited in the driveway for his mother. When the kitchen door opened, his father stepped out into the zero-degree weather wearing dirty sweatpants, a gray T-shirt, and fuzz-lined moccasins. His eyes squinted as he descended the steps and moved toward the car. He rotated his fist and arm, and David pressed the button to lower the window.

"What the fuck you doin' in the car?"

"I'm taking Mom to a doctor's appointment in Bemidji."

"Get the fuck out. I never said she could use the car."

"Look, Dad, I'm taking her. She asked me to, and that's all there is to it."

"Fuckin' bullshit. You can't just use the car."

"Dad, you're gonna freeze out here."

"Fuck you. You sound like your mother, like a scared little bitch."

Denise Diegert stepped out of the house and was intercepted by Tom as she attempted to cross the driveway to the car.

David exited the car and stood by the driver's door.

17

Squeezing Denise's arm, Tom said, "I didn't hear anything about a doctor's appointment. What's wrong? Why are you going to the doctor?"

Without struggling against Tom's grasp, Denise stood with stoic resolve and said calmly, "I have to see the gynecologist. It's very typical for women to have examinations from time to time, and I would appreciate it if you would let me go."

"Fuck that. You're not going anywhere. We don't have health insurance to pay for this, and unless you're really sick, you're not going."

David grew angry listening to his father's foolishness. He crossed the driveway, grabbed his father's hand, and pulled it off his mother's arm. Tom Diegert swung, striking David in the jaw with a solid right. David's head snapped, and he stumbled back against the car. Tom took a fighter's stance, but his self-confidence evaporated since he had just picked a fight with the 180-pound State Wrestling Champ of Minnesota. In spite of his misgivings, Tom's bravado ruled the moment. "Come on, you pussy, let's see what you're made of."

David stepped away from the car and moved toward his pathetic opponent. With lightning skill, David shot low, going to one knee, wrapping up his father's legs and putting him on his back in two seconds. He flipped his dad's legs, holding them perpendicular to the ground so that Tom was stuck on his back like a turtle. With an arm lock, David retained control of both legs, which allowed him to see the fear and the fury in his father's eyes.

"Let him go."

The command came from Jake. Turning, David looked right into the barrel of a Ruger SR22 pistol.

"Let him go and stand up."

David complied, letting the turtle's legs fall to the snow. He stood up with his hands in the air.

"Dad, are you OK?" blurted Jake.

Tom Diegert had to roll over onto his stomach, struggle to his hands and knees, and pull on Jake's outstretched arm in order to stand up.

Jake was so pissed he started shouting at David while pointing the pistol. "You fucking bitch, you little fucking bastard, how dare you treat him like that? You are such a prick. I can't believe you have the balls to treat Dad like shit."

Jake's movements were as unhinged as his words, and he was handling the gun as if it were a toy. He stepped closer and closer, continually waving the gun in David's direction. Backed up against the car, David struck his brother's arm and pushed him hard in the chest. As Jake awkwardly fell back, a shot rang out from the Ruger. The unaimed bullet went wild, striking Tom Diegert in the left hip.

Tom fell to the ground, shocked by the pain and the sight of his own blood. Jake stared with horror at the blood splatters in the snow. He looked at the gun in his hand with utter disbelief. Getting up, he shouted at David, "You goddamn, fucking idiot! Look what you've done. You fucking shot Dad."

"You're holding the gun, genius."

Jake swung his arm into full extension, pointing the gun at David's head. "Die, fucker."

Denise Diegert stepped in front of the gun, putting herself between Jake and David. "Stop it, Jake." She turned to David and said, "Get in the car." David stepped around to the driver's door. Denise lowered Jake's arm, calmly looking him in the eye. "You need to help your father. Take him to the firchouse and have one of his buddies patch him up. I'm leaving with David, and I'll be back in two hours. You need to act now."

Nodding his head, Jake turned to his father, who was groaning in the driveway and clutching his bleeding hip. In spite of his condition, he shouted out at David, "You fucking son of a bitch. You're the son of that bitch!" He pointed at Denise as she opened the car door and climbed in. "You fucking shot me, you shithead."

David, looking over the roof of the car, shook his head at the stupidity of the two idiots as they struggled to get up and make their way into the house. He opened the car door, got in, and backed the car out of the driveway.

4

On the drive to Bemidji, Denise shook in her seat, reacting to the violence that had just exploded in her family.

"Is he going to be OK?" she asked David.

"He's a tough old lump of shit; he'll be OK. Besides, the gun was only a .22."

"What about the police?"

"I think it's pretty unlikely either of those pseudo felons are going to call the cops."

"But they could do it just to make things difficult for you."

Diegert did not reply as he considered that Jake and his father might very well try to use this against him. He took comfort in the fact that they had no idea where he was really going.

"Mom, you've got to promise me you won't tell them anything about the Army."

"I won't, but eventually they're going to ask about you."

"Don't wait for them to ask. Tell them something stupid, like I was so upset that I ran away. Don't let them know that you know where I am."

"You think they'll buy that?"

"I'll write a note, and you can tell them you found it in the car. It'll keep their anger on me. I'm also going to leave my phone in the car."

"But I want to be able to talk to you."

"I'll get a new phone in Georgia, and we can text."

"We can't talk?"

"We'll see, but I'll text you as soon as I get a new phone."

Parking the car in the lot of a convenience store, David scowled at the sight of the Bemidji bus station. In any other city, the station would only be considered a bus stop. Using the back of an envelope he found in the glove box, David wrote a note. He left his mom in the car to read what he'd written to his father and Jake as he walked toward the convenience store.

> *Dear Dad and Jake,*
> *I'm so sorry for the way I've acted lately, and I apologize for the incident that led to Dad being shot. I know forgiveness is hard, but I ask you to search your hearts for some measure of understanding of how bad I feel about the way things have turned out. I'm going away. I don't know where, but I won't be seeing any of you again. Good-bye.*
> *David*

David picked up his ticket at the store, then came back to the car to find his mom crying.

"David, your note made me so sad. I can't believe our family has disintegrated like this."

"Mom, I just wrote the note to keep them from figuring out that I'm in the Army. I'll see you again, and when I do, I'll be a soldier in the US Army. Now give me a hug." She leaned over and embraced him, but the finality of his note left her feeling like this goodbye was for a lot longer than either of them knew.

They didn't have much longer to wait before the bus pulled up to the curb in front of them. Only two other passengers were waiting to board. After getting his duffel bag out of the trunk, David embraced his mother with all the strength of his love.

"I'm trying to be brave for you, David, but I'm gonna miss you."

"Mom, you just did the bravest thing I've ever seen. You stepped in front of Jake, willing to take a bullet for me."

Denise gasped as she averted her gaze to the ground, saying, "David, I did what any loving mother would do."

"You did a lot more than that, and I will never forget it. You saved my life. You also did a great job raising me, and now it's time to show the world who your son is."

"I'm so proud of you, David. I love you so much."

"I love only you, Mom, and I will carry that with me everywhere I go."

Diegert saw the bus driver waving his arm. He kissed his mother on the forehead, slung the bag's strap over his shoulder, and walked backward to the bus. Through the window, Diegert saw his mother still standing at the rear of the car as the bus pulled away and moved down the road.

5

Twenty-four weeks of training in Fort Benning Georgia earned David Diegert the rank of private first class. He distinguished himself by achieving expert marksmanship on the firing range with rifles and handguns, as well as mastery of Level IV in Modern Army Combatives. Diegert paid attention to his instructors and not only learned to become an effective and efficient fighter, but he also embodied the Army's creed of selfless service and teamwork. Now stationed at Fort Hood, outside Austin, Texas, he was a soldier in the 1st Cavalry Division. An enlisted infantryman, whose skills and abilities were broad enough to fulfill many different roles in the Army's vast network of needs.

Through texts with his mother, he learned that Tom did not see a doctor, and although the wound had healed, the slug remained in his hip. The limp in his gait was worse in the morning, but whenever he was in pain, he had David to blame. Surprisingly, Tom did not let Jake burn the note that David had written them; instead, he folded it carefully and kept it in a drawer. David wondered if it was sentiment or hope for vengeance that caused his father to keep it.

"Private David Diegert," shouted Sergeant Jesse Rodriguez from the entrance of the barracks.

"Yes, Sergeant," snapped Diegert as he jumped off his bunk and stood at attention.

"Get over here, Diegert. I've got something important for you."

Diegert quickly hightailed it over to his sergeant, who led him through the barracks door.

"Captain Corcoran wants to see you. Head over to his office right now."

Bursting with excitement, Diegert briskly walked to the captain's office. He had applied for Ranger School and was hoping the captain was going to tell him that he'd been accepted. In the captain's office, Diegert stood at attention.

"At ease, soldier," said the dark-haired thirty-something captain. Looking up from a file on his desk, he continued, "David...Diegert, you've been here at Fort Hood for four weeks. How do you like Texas?"

"I like it, sir. I love the 1st Cavalry."

"Good, that's what you're supposed to say, and I appreciate a man who knows his role."

"Yes, sir."

"Do you know why I've called you here today?"

"No, sir."

"Care to guess?"

"Well, sir, I did apply to Ranger School, and I'm hoping you're going to tell me I've been selected."

The captain stepped from behind his desk and paced over to Diegert.

"Private Diegert, I'm afraid that is not the case. You are being deployed to Afghanistan."

What? When? Why? The questions raced through his brain, but he had learned not to give voice when receiving orders from an officer.

"You're shipping out tonight, and it's just you."

"Just me? Why...?" The statement burst forth before Diegert could restrain it. "Sorry, sir."

Captain Corcoran stepped closer to Diegert.

"We're the rear detachment for our company in Afghanistan. One of our squads suffered a loss, and through the individual replacement program you are being sent to backfill the open position."

"Yes, sir."

Stepping out of Diegert's personal space, the captain continued. "You'll be joining a squad from the 1st Cavalry. Fellow soldiers who've trained here at Fort Hood just like you. You are the only one going, but don't make it sound like we're abandoning you like a lost puppy. Get your shit together and report to transport at 1600."

"Yes, sir."

He sent a text to his mother, letting her know he was being deployed to Afghanistan.

Thirty-six hours later, the hot, dry environment of central Texas seemed like an oasis compared to the even hotter, drier, dustier conditions at Kandahar International Airport in Afghanistan. The heat was oppressive, and the fine sand in the air started to clog David's nose with silica snot.

6

Private First Class David Diegert reported to his support squad in Afghanistan, where he was immediately treated like the Fucking New Guy and given the shittiest jobs of this unique MOS. Led by Lieutenant Alvin Prescott, this group of enlisted general service soldiers supported the operations of a Special Forces unit referred to as the Syringes.

Opium is to Afghanistan as corn is to Iowa. Right away Diegert became aware of the squad's role in the effort to sustain the progress that had been made in Afghanistan. The squad ran ten tons of opium a month. They moved it onto base, packed it in mislabeled crates, and smuggled it to the United States on return flights of supply planes privately contracted by the Department of Defense. The organization went right up the chain of command, although none of the activities would ever appear in an official report. Little green men like Diegert and the rest of the enlisted just followed orders. Hush money kept their mouths shut, while all the cargo was being transferred to private contractors. The flights didn't return to military bases but to corporate fulfillment centers where the illicit contraband found its way to market.

The Special Forces guys, in spite of all their combat capacity, realized you couldn't build peace if you keep shooting people. So they'd set up the opium network to appease the local tribal leaders. The opium gets to market, the locals get paid, and the Syringes make money as the middlemen. The Afghans who are helped become allies. The illicit trade keeps the peace, which was the primary objective of the entire mission. The rise of heroin on American streets should surprise no one.

For Diegert, the whole thing was such a disappointment. All the training in the Army focused on the mission as defined by combat objectives and enemies overtaken. This was illegal bullshit, appeasing the enemy rather than defeating them. He hated his role as drug mule supplying opium to the US, which would end up as heroin being sold by dealers like his brother Jake! As Diegert contemplated this dissonance of purpose, he heard his name.

"Hey, Diegert," shouted Lieutenant Alvin Prescott.

Diegert stopped packing a crate with burlap bags of fresh opium to see his jerk of a superior officer standing by the entrance of the hangar in which they processed the Afghan's most important export. Prescott motioned for Diegert to come over to him.

"Yes, sir?"

"I just got done inspecting your weapon."

"I'm not due for inspection for two more days."

"Shut up, I can inspect anything at any time, and your weapon was insufficiently cleaned and lubricated."

"That's bullshit."

Stepping forward and looking up at Diegert, Prescott emphasized his point.

"Don't you get insolent with me or the shit you're in will just get deeper. I'm fining you three thousand dollars."

Diegert couldn't believe his ears. This little idiotic officer was using his power to make up for his shortcomings as a person. His latest gambit was to extract outrageous fines from his soldiers' drug hush money for infractions of military protocol. Mixing the "business" and the military was totally wrong, but his greed knew no bounds. Several guys had paid the fines, and this had emboldened their hollow leader to expand his extortions.

"You can't do that," replied Diegert.

"You want to make it five thousand? I know exactly how much money you've got, and if you can't meet minimum "Army Strong" standards, then a monetary sanction will get your attention."

Diegert stuck his finger into Prescott's thin chest, saying, "You can't mix the business with the Army."

Slapping Diegert's hand aside, Prescott launched into a tirade. "You do not speak to me like that, and how dare you touch me? I'll have you in the stockade so fast you'd think one of those sandstorms sucked you into your cell. I'm your superior officer, and you will submit to my orders and abide by my discipline."

Diegert's boiling temper was not extinguished by Prescott's salivary spray. He pushed Prescott's chest with both hands, forcing the surprised lieutenant to stumble. Diegert grabbed the man by the front of his shirt and punched him twice in the face as he swung the lieutenant's body and tossed him to the ground. Prescott's torso skidded to a stop in the sand, and he struggled to rise.

"Hey, you can't..." Diegert didn't wait for the rest of the statement before he front kicked him in the chest, sprawling him onto his back. Grabbing him again by his shirt, Diegert hauled him up off the ground. Prescott swung his fist, striking Diegert in the head with such little force it stunned Diegert how weak this man was. Diegert spun Prescott around, kicked his legs out from under him, and slammed his face into the sandy ground. A group of soldiers started to gather.

Diegert brought his face down to Prescott's and growled, "You are a prick, and I will not take your shit."

Standing up and walking away, Diegert was tackled by four MPs, who cuffed him and took him immediately to the stockade. Prescott stood up and brushed himself off while limping to medical. None of the soldiers under his command stepped up to help him.

* * * *

Captain Dylan Reeves from the Judge Advocate General's Corp was assigned to serve as Diegert's lawyer. He conducted the requisite defendant interview in Diegert's stockade cell.

"So, reading this report doesn't reveal much for me to use in your defense. You wanna tell me why you beat the shit out of your commanding officer?"

Diegert looked at the clean-cut captain, but the tone of the question made him feel like he was not talking to someone who was on his side. Diegert knew that ratting on the opium operation was not an option. If he spoke against them, the Syringes would see to it that he was KIA in a couple of days. That's what happened to Emmitt Stilchus, the guy he replaced. The official report listed his death as the result of an improvised explosive device, which was true, but the Syringes set up that IED when Stilchus stupidly told everyone he was going to blow the whistle if he didn't get more money.

"The situation between Lieutenant Prescott and me was a personal issue."

"Were you and your superior officer having an inappropriate sexual relationship?"

"No!" replied Diegert, bristling at the accusation within the question.

"If you're not going to tell me about the incident, then how about you tell me a little bit about yourself."

"Like what?"

"Well, I know you're from Broward County in the northern part of Minnesota, you have a black belt in karate, you were a state champion wrestler, and you've earned skill level four in Modern Army Combatives. You're assigned to the 1st Cavalry Division out of Fort Hood, and back in high school you were referred to as 'Tonto.'"

Diegert's annoyed expression suddenly turned more agitated at the use of his hated nickname.

"Back in the day, you didn't like that name, did ya? Now you'd beat up anybody who called you that, wouldn't ya?"

Diegert felt the pain of his heritage once again tearing at his heart. His mother's mix of white and Native American blood made her an outcast of both the white and Ojibwa cultures of northern Minnesota. Even though his mother had married a white man, making Diegert only a quarter native, he was still referred to as an Ojib-white by the kids in school. They constantly taunted him, reminding him to stay in his place.

Reeves continued. "It's amazing what you can find out about someone with a Web search. How about you tell me a little bit more about your family? What was your father like?"

Diegert's contempt was hard to hide as he recalled the fool who was his father. Tom Diegert was short, fat, bald, perpetually dirty, and regularly drunk. He ran a tow-truck business in a rural area where everyone had four-wheel drives. He treated his wife like shit, making worse their mismatched marriage. She was taller than he, lean with long black hair and an exotic face. To Tom Diegert, she was the squaw he married so she wouldn't be homeless in the dead of winter. Tom Diegert had been in the Army as a young man, and even though he hadn't done shit with the rest of his life, he was proud of his military service. For Diegert to tell his father that he'd been dishonorably discharged was really going to suck, especially since Tom didn't even know he was in the Army.

"My father is a proud military veteran; he'll be angry with me if I'm dishonorably discharged."

"I could see that being uncomfortable. What branch of the service was he in?"

"The Army."

"Where was he stationed?"

"I don't know."

"What was his rank?"

"I don't know that either."

"So did you and your dad discuss your commitment to serve?"

"No."

Reeves sat quietly, waiting for more information, which Diegert did not provide.

"How about your mom?"

Diegert's mother was the person he admired most in the world—the one person he truly loved. She was hardworking, dedicated, and thoughtful. She had issues with fear and lack of self-confidence, remnants of growing up in foster homes after her own mother committed suicide when Denise was twelve. Despite her difficulties, she showed David a mother's love and made sure the house was a comfortable sanctuary for her second son.

"My mom is a beautiful, loving woman who always puts others before herself."

"Sounds lovely. Was the marriage between her and your Father a happy one?"

"Not really."

Again, Reeves let the silence linger, but Diegert added nothing.

"You know the process of getting to know someone benefits from explanations that are longer than just two words."

"Oh really?" was Diegert's only reply.

Reeves grew impatient. "Any brothers or sisters?"

His brother, Jake, was just like his father, short, loud, and focused on himself. He played football, which his dad loved, followed, and supported. He, too, was a half-breed but crossed the line and hung with the cool kids by being their drug dealer. At first, he'd sold stolen beer, then pot and pills, and then heroin and crystal meth. He made sure David's life remained miserable. Often when Diegert was working at his job at the mini-mart, Jake and his friends would smash jars and make a mess in an aisle just so they could laugh at him while he cleaned it up.

"My brother, Jake, is a jerk. I don't talk to him very often."

"Sibling rivalry?"

"He doesn't have anything I desire."

"How about growing up was he someone you could trust and confide in?"

"Definitely not."

"I see. Why did you join the Army?'

"For the college benefits. I want to do my active duty, get out, and go to school on the GI Bill."

"Wouldn't a student loan be a better idea?"

Diegert tilted his head back and cast an unappreciative look upon his lawyer.

"Anyway—I don't see a sense of patriotism in you, a desire to serve your country, or the motivation to fulfill a family tradition. The Army is simply a means to an end for you, and I think you're now finding that the role of a soldier requires a lot more work and sacrifice than any semester in college. What do you want to study in school?"

"Math. I'm pretty good at math."

"I'm glad to hear it, but I have to tell you that your defense is not adding up to an acquittal."

Reeves watched Diegert's face as the statement sank in.

"You will most likely be convicted of this crime and dishonorably discharged. I don't believe Lieutenant Prescott is pressing any additional charges, and the final sentencing is up to the Judge."

"As my lawyer, what do you advise me to do?"

Reeves tapped his pencil on the table while contemplating his reply.

"I don't think you're committed to the military life," said Reeves as he slid his papers into his briefcase stood up and placed his JAG officer's cap securely on his head. He crossed the small space of Diegert's cell, then looked back as he stood in the doorway to say, "I see your future outside the US Army, but I'll see you at the court-martial on Monday."

7

The courts at the military base at Kandahar Airfield in Afghanistan were located in the commandant's area, where legal proceedings were only conducted on Mondays and Fridays. After an uncomfortable weekend in the stockade, where the ventilation was so inadequate that the body odor rivaled that of a bag of hockey pads left in a hundred-degree car trunk, Diegert sat quietly with Captain Reeves as they waited for the court-martial proceedings to begin. The earlier consultation with his lawyer did nothing to raise Diegert's confidence; nevertheless, he had to move forward with this unfortunate conclusion to his short military career.

Diegert shuffled in his seat and quietly ground his fist into his palm, feeling the regret of his actions as his thoughts moved on to what lay ahead. At first, being in the Army had been so cool, training at Fort Benning and being stationed at Fort Hood were both good times, but in Afghanistan, everything was totally fucked up.

"Private David Terrance Diegert," shouted the MP serving as court bailiff. The lawyer and the accused entered the room, which was used for many functions but today served as a court of military justice. Seated behind an eight-foot folding table was Colonel Reginald Hayes, fulfilling the role of judge. Next to him was the plaintiff, Lieutenant Alvin Prescott, with his lawyer, Captain Patricia Stokes.

At Judge Hayes's direction, Captain Stokes presented her case, which implicated Diegert as insubordinate to his superior officer before violently assaulting him and causing bodily injury. Captain Dylan Reeves's presentation recounted the incident and concluded with an admission of Diegert's guilt and an apology. With nothing more from either member of counsel, Judge Hayes pronounced Diegert guilty as charged and commenced with the process of dishonorably discharging him from the US Army.

Returning to the stockade, Diegert had time to think about how much it sucked to be powerless in a system that allowed the Special Forces personnel to do what they wanted while sidelining the enlisted who spoke out, took action, or threatened to disrupt the status quo. Diegert thought about how the Army had been a new beginning where people didn't judge him for what they heard about his family or thought about Indians. But now he was learning that it didn't matter who or what you were if you were one of the powerless. People in power would fuck you over without even meaning to. He had no idea what he was going to do now.

* * * *

Back at Fort Hood, Diegert completed the processing of his discharge by being informed of all the privileges he would not have. No GI Bill, no outplacement employment assistance, no veteran's benefits. He was also disallowed to own a firearm, take a position teaching in a public school, and he could not become a police officer or security agent. A dishonorable discharge was almost as bad as a felony conviction. He took a bus from the base with his stuff in a duffel bag and got a room in a cheap place on the outskirts of Austin called the Single Star Motel.

In the motel room, Diegert dumped out his duffel bag, put his clothes in the dresser and closet, set his toothbrush and shaving stuff in the bathroom, and returned to the bed. Lying there were three items he had received from his mother a few years back. She had acknowledged his eighteenth birthday as his coming-of-age day, and to her it signified him becoming a man. She marked it by presenting him with three gifts that were part of the ritual for young

Ojibwa men who were coming of age. A ritual Diegert had never heard of or expected.

The first gift was a leather amulet on a leather necklace. The necklace was beaded with colors that signified the seven values of the Ojibwa: wisdom, love, respect, bravery, honesty, humility, and truth. The amulet was a circular piece of leather. On the front, the top half was white and the bottom dark black. In the center, spanning both the top and the bottom halves, was the imprint of a human foot. The back contained an Ojibwa inscription, which stated: *A man must travel through darkness to find the light.*

The second item was a hunting knife. The knife had an antler handle, a six-inch blade, and a leather sheath. The blade had a razor-sharp edge and point. The back side of the blade had serrated teeth extending from the hilt for an inch and a half, and the rest was a sharpened edge designed for scraping and planing. Inscribed on the blade in Ojibwa was the phrase: *The blade is both a tool and a weapon; let it work for you and defend you.*

The final item was a woven wool blanket his mother had made for him on her loom. Its intricate pattern of stripes and diamonds were in tones of brown, yellow, and red. In the top corner of the blanket, she had embroidered an Ojibwa mother's prayer: *Your mother's love will be with you always, covering and comforting you no matter where you journey in life.*

She'd presented these gifts to him at home while his father and brother were out getting drunk at the Moose Jaw Inn. Of the three gifts, Diegert thought the knife was really cool. The amulet and blanket were nice, but he really didn't care about them. After presenting him with the gifts, his mother had begun to tell him about Ojibwa customs for young men coming of age. She said, "David, these gifts symbolize the transition you are now making from a boy to a man. They can help you on your journey to find your purpose in life. You can find your spirit through a vision quest." Diegert had never heard his mother speak of the Ojibwa customs before, and it freaked him out that she suggested he find meaning in life by communicating with a spirit. She continued, "Ojibwa young men let the spirit in, and it guides them to their life's destiny. As an Anishinaabe, one of the good beings, you can let the spirit help you live a full and rewarding life."

Diegert's brow furrowed and his eyes narrowed, an Amish-nobby? What was she talking about? Diegert looked at his mother with a sidelong glance as he thought that maybe she had gotten into some of Jake's drugs. His mother smiled at him as she placed a mocha maple chocolate cake on the table, his favorite. Her baking was exquisite, and Diegert's smile returned as she cut a piece of birthday cake, saying, "I want you to have the very best life, and a vision quest seeking your Ojibwa spirit will get you there."

"Thanks," said Diegert as she handed him the cake.

His mother, who was always the most practical and down-to-earth person in his life, was now speaking of spirits and journeys and the meaning of life. She was also saying that happiness lay in his Ojibwa spirit. In fact, Diegert felt the Ojibwa part of him was the root of all his problems; the ostracism, the taunting, and fighting, the just plain being ignored by all the cool kids was because of being an Ojib-white.

He looked at his mother. "Thanks for the cake and the presents, I really like the knife, but an Ojibwa spirit quest, I don't think so. Why are you dumping all this on me now?" Denise Diegert slid the fork out of her mouth and began to chew a bite of cake. She placed her gaze directly on the eyes of her son, who continued speaking. "Having Ojibwa blood in me is the worst part of my life. People in town, kids in school, and even the Indians on the reservation all hate me and you for being half-breeds. I hate the Ojibwa part of me, and I'm certainly not going to seek out any Indian spirits to guide me. I want them to stay the hell away from me."

Swallowing her cake, Denise began, "You're young, and you need time to realize the importance of accepting who you are and embracing those things which make you unique."

Scoffing, Diegert said, "Did you memorize that from a lousy self-help book, because it sounds like psychobabble bullshit. I don't need a spirit to guide me, and I'm sure not impressed with where the spirit led you. So if this is the best an Indian quest can do for me, you can fucking forget it."

Diegert never swore at his mother, but the sudden infusion of Ojibwa culture and the lifelong pent-up frustration at the bigotry and prejudice he lived with brought out feelings he had long suppressed.

His mother replied, "I'm sorry you feel that way, but if you don't seek the spirit with respect, it will find you in your darkest hour, where you will then be compelled to face the spirit's wrath."

"Oh yeah, right. Now the spirit is a great big threat." Diegert grabbed the knife off the table. "If the spirit is going to come get me, I'm not going to be unarmed." With his new weapon in his hand, Diegert walked out of the house and into the night.

Recalling all this discourse with his mom, Diegert found his motel room a claustrophobic cell. He caught a bus for downtown. Austin was a city alive with diverse young people, techies, bikers, college students, musicians, artists, and especially weirdos who kept the city as it wanted to be. Whoever you were, there was a bar for you in Austin. Diegert entered the Dark Horse feeling like the name reflected his place in life. The ten-dollar cover got you all the honky-tonk music you needed from the band at the back of the bar. The bouncer was huge, six eight, and had to weigh over three hundred pounds. The big man smiled and told Diegert to have a good time. At the bar, Diegert took a stool, spun around, and leaned against the bar, looking at all the country western people. Guys were wearing Stetsons, Wrangler jeans, and Frye boots. Diegert wondered if the bar had a stable out back for their horses. The women did the big-hair thing with the tight, checkered blouses, and several of them had barely enough denim to cover their asses. Having not seen any women while in Afghanistan, Diegert literally couldn't avert his eyes from the feminine beauty on display at the Dark Horse.

"Hey."

He nearly fell off his stool when a female voice startled him out of his staring. She spoke as he turned his head.

"The ten dollars covers the band. If you want a titty show, you're going to have to go down the street to one of the strip clubs."

Diegert spun his stool around, placing his forearms on the bar. She was cute and feisty, and since it was still early, she was energetic and ready for a busy night of tending bar.

"You want a Star?"

Diegert looked at her like she was a third-grade teacher handing out stickers.

Realizing he didn't comprehend, she asked, "You want a Lone Star beer?"

Chuckling at his foolishness, Diegert replied, "Sure, thanks."

Placing the tall brown bottle on the bar, she said, "I haven't seen you here before."

"I've never been here."

"You don't seem like a cowboy. What kind of pickup do you drive?"

"I don't have a truck."

"You're definitely the only guy in here who'll say that."

Diegert tilted his head and smiled at the precocious brunette who held his eye contact with confidence. "What's your name?" he asked her.

"I'm working, and I'm not here to flirt."

"Of course not, I just asked for your name?"

"Taurus...like the bull."

"That's your last name?" Diegert asked hesitantly.

"Uh-huh," she said with a nod to the obvious.

"Well, what's your first name?"

"Collette," she said.

"Collette Taurus." The instant he said the name, she burst out laughing, and several patrons at the bar started cracking up at the guy using such an intimate term in such a public place. Diegert, realizing he had just been played for a fool, retorted, "My name's Mike."

The bartender replied, "Well, I wasn't asking, but if you're going to tell me that your last name is 'Hunt,' then you really are a cunt, and that makes me especially disinterested in you."

The embarrassing rejection was abruptly interrupted when furniture and bodies crashed to the floor at the entrance of the bar. All attention turned to the fracas between the bouncer and some rowdies at the front door.

The big man, who had been so friendly to Diegert, had pushed one of a group of four guys to the floor, knocking over a table and chairs. Two of the others were punching and kicking the giant with each blow to the face producing a spray of blood. The bouncer went down, the guy who was pushed was helped up, and the four leather-clad men entered the bar led by the tallest man, who wore a sleeveless black leather vest over a white T-shirt. The leader sported a gray

Van Dyke around his mouth and chin. Like the others, he looked a little too old for such delinquent behavior.

The commotion brought the manager from an office behind the bar. A thin man with wide eyes and a nervous look surveyed the scene and muttered, "Not again." Diegert watched as the uptight man struggled to help the bleeding bouncer to the kitchen.

People were filing into the bar without being checked or paying the cover. The four rowdies took a table in the back corner of the bar, and the feisty bartender was now playing cocktail waitress and taking their orders. When she returned behind the bar, Diegert said to her, "I bet you wouldn't have come to get my order if I sat over there."

"Damn right, you're not Igor Dimitrov...Russian mobster," she said while mixing the drinks and opening the beer bottles on her tray.

Diegert gazed over, observing the muscular silver-haired man, dressed up as a biker with his gang of goons, and remarked, "You'd think he owns this place."

"Better than that, he owns the loan that got this place started." The bartender, whose name Diegert still didn't know, hefted the tray to her shoulder and left to deliver the Russians their drinks.

Through the kitchen door came the nervous manager. He smoothed his shirt and adjusted his glasses as he stepped toward the bar. Diegert called out to him.

"Excuse me."

The manager stepped over to Diegert.

"I know things are happening fast here tonight, but it looks like you could use a man at the door."

They both turned to see a crowd of confused people entering the door while not paying a cover charge. Diegert turned to the manager and offered his hand.

"David Diegert."

Taking his hand, the manager introduced himself.

"Terry Buscetti. Do you have any experience?"

"Yup."

"If you steal any of the cover money, I'll have those guys who roughed up the other guy beat the shit out of you."

Diegert didn't avert his eyes as he said, "I won't steal from you, but you've got to pay me thirty dollars an hour to sit at that door."

"That's a lot."

"What happened to that other guy will never happen to me. That door will be secure."

"Come on back, and I'll give you a shirt, and you can get started."

Back in the kitchen, the big guy's facial wounds were still bleeding. Buscetti said, "His ride is on its way."

The manager pulled a black polo shirt from a hanger with the bar's horsehead logo. "Put this on and remember its ten dollars per person."

As he was leaving the kitchen, Diegert stepped over to the injured man and patted him on the shoulder. "Those are some nasty wounds."

"That fucker had brass knuckles."

They looked at each other as they searched for words they could not find. Diegert gently slapped him on the shoulder again before he left the kitchen.

At the door, Diegert did the job and collected the money without incident. At one point, the bartender, on her way to the Russian table, swung by the door to say, "You've got to be brain damaged to be taking this job."

Diegert just smiled and thought she was probably right, but he needed a job, and this one would do. For the next two weeks, he was at the door every night and eventually learned that the bartender's name was Tracy Vandersmith.

She was a pre-med student at UT and never lingered when her shift was done. She gave Diegert a ride home one rainy night, and when she saw he was living in a cheap motel, she shouted at him out the car window, "We work together, that's it. That's all it will ever be. You got that?"

Diegert's legs were soaked by the spray off her tires as she pulled away.

8

The High Note Drifters commanded a fifteen-dollar cover charge at the Dark Horse. Igor Dimitrov and three guys from his entourage were not charged as Diegert cleared the way for them to enter the bar. As Dimitrov passed, he stopped and told Diegert, "Uri Pestonach was supposed to meet us here. You know which one he is, right?" Drawing his finger across his forehead, Dimitrov continued, "The guy has just one eyebrow." Diegert nodded. "Since he's late, I do not want you to let him in."

Diegert's gaze centered on the big Russian's eyes. Dimitrov produced a hundred-dollar bill and handed it to Diegert, repeating, "Don't let Uri in."

Diegert signaled his compliance, accepting the hundred.

Thirty minutes later, Uri Pestonach arrived, pushed his way through the line, and proceeded to enter. Diegert had to place his hand on the guy's chest to impede his entrance. The furrowed forehead and narrowed eyelids were overshadowed by his unibrow, but they projected the man's displeasure with being handled. Standing in front of Uri, Diegert tried to explain.

"Sorry, man, you can't come in tonight."

"What the fuck is this?" bellowed the insolent Russian.

"Tonight you are not allowed in. Perhaps another night would be better for you."

Slapping Diegert's hand from his chest, Uri's incredulous expression found its voice.

"You can't stop me from coming in, and if you're worried about the fifteen dollars, you can fuck yourself."

Diegert saw Uri's hand slip into his pocket, and he watched as the angry man withdrew his hand in a fist. The dull yellow of the brass caught Diegert's eye as the fist was thrust at his head. Diegert tipped his head back as the fist blazed by. He grabbed the man's forearm, twisted it behind his back, and pressed on the radial nerve. The pressure on the nerve forced Uri's fist to open. Diegert swept the man's hand, stripping the brass knuckles off his fingers. He shoved the man forward into a cigarette machine. The angry man awkwardly spun around to face Diegert, who now had the brass knuckles on his fist and a *fuck you* smirk on his face.

Diegert dropped into a balanced stance and gave no sign of retreat as he squared off against the Russian, who was now armed with only his skin. The patrons at the door formed a ring around the two combatants, Diegert said, "You can leave now and come back another night."

The Russian's angry expression showed the fear of embarrassment as his situation had become the center of attention for a growing crowd. He circled Diegert, seeing the brass knuckles were on his enemy, who seemed to be without fear.

Diegert stood up out of his fighting stance. "You are free to go." He extended his hand in front of him, motioning toward the door.

Uri's brow formed into a *V* as his angry eyes peered at Diegert. Realizing the Russian wouldn't be taking the gentleman's way out, Diegert dropped his right foot back and brought his left hand up. Uri put his weight into a swing with his right. Diegert leaned back and grabbed the big guy's arm, pulling him off balance while delivering a bone-crushing strike with the brass knuckles to the temple of the belligerent bar crasher. Uri's consciousness vacated his brain as his bulk fell to the floor. Diegert grabbed the back of the big guy's leather coat and dragged him outside.

Igor Dimitrov was stunned to see how quickly his best muscle had gone down at the hands of Diegert. The economy of movement and the lethality of force the young man displayed impressed the mobster. He couldn't recall ever seeing a one-punch knockout in a bar fight. Skills like that could be very useful, thought the boss of the local Russian Bratva.

The next day when Diegert showed up early for his evening shift, Tracy Vandersmith told him, "Hey, slugger, Terry told me to send you to his office when you got here."

"Thanks."

"Don't thank me, he didn't look happy."

Knocking on Buscetti's office door, Diegert called out softly, "Hello."

"Yeah, get on in here."

Buscetti got up and closed the door as he directed Diegert to sit down next to his cluttered desk. "Listen, about last night—"

"Hey, he had it coming."

"I'm not worried about fucking Uri. No, Mr. Dimitrov has asked that you...rough up a guy here tonight."

"Rough him up?"

"Yeah—put a beating on a guy who's been encroaching on the business, you know."

"The business?"

"Come on...you know Dimitrov runs the Russian Bratva. He's pushing meth and heroin into Austin, and he's putting the squeeze on the Mexicans."

"Oh... Yeah."

"Well, he wants you to beat up the spic the Mexicans send here every night to spy on 'em. I sent his picture to your phone. Keep an eye on him, and when he goes outside, put a beating on him. Dimitrov has a thousand dollars for you when it's done."

A quizzical look crossed Diegert's face as he thought about assaulting someone for money.

"Come on—come on, I need you to do this, and you need the money," said Buscetti impatiently.

"Alright…but I get the money up front."

Pulling a thick envelope from his desk drawer, Buscetti said, "I got the money right here. When the job is done, it's yours. Now go get ready. The High Note Drifters are playing again tonight, so it should be busy at the door."

As he left the office, Diegert checked his phone to see a picture of a medium-size Mexican guy smoking a cigarette while leaning against a Camaro.

As Diegert walked out into the bar, Tracy shouted, "Hey, Mr. Tough Guy, if you can go beating up people for the entertainment of the bar, how about you help me by stocking the fridge with beer?"

"If it entertains you, I certainly will," said Diegert as he opened the case and began filling the shelves.

The High Note Drifters' loyal following filled the bar by the end of their first set. Diegert noted that the Mexican guy's name was Miguel Lopez, or at least that's what his Texas driver's license said. Lopez had paid the cover without incident and eventually got a stool at the far end of the bar. From time to time, Diegert would observe the guy, and it really appeared like he was doing nothing. He drank his beer slowly, smiled at people, but didn't talk much and was otherwise easily forgotten.

As the evening wore on, Lopez crossed the bar, exiting right in front of Diegert while shaking a cigarette out of his pack. Buscetti appeared at his side and told Diegert, "I got the door." He nodded toward the exit, and Diegert followed Lopez outside.

Lopez had his cigarette burning as soon as he stepped onto the sidewalk, the nicotine sending a wave of relief to his stimulant-deprived nerves. Exhaling, the tension from his craving dissipated as fast as the cloud of smoke. He was shocked when Diegert shoved him into the wall.

Diegert slapped the cigarette out of Lopez's hand. He pushed the Mexican around the corner and into the alley back by the bar's dumpsters.

"Hey, what the fuck?" shouted Lopez.

Diegert said nothing as he pushed the medium-size man again, this time knocking him against the wall between two dumpsters.

"What the fuck you doing, man? I know who you are, you're the bouncer."

Diegert's first punch was lightning fast, striking Lopez on the cheek. The Mexican stumbled backward but remained standing.

"Fucking A," said Lopez as he put his hand to his face. "You don't know who you're fucking with. The Quinoloans are going to hunt you down and—"

Diegert's next combination struck Lopez three times in the face, leaving him with a bleeding nose. Using the dumpster for balance, the man still stood but was dazed. The smeared blood from his nose on the back of his hand made it clear he was not going to talk his way out of this. Straightening himself, he tried not to wobble as he put up his fists. Diegert saw the vulnerability and exploited the guy's weakness by throwing a fake. The instant Lopez reacted, Diegert struck with a combination that included a second punch to the bleeding nose. The Mexican crashed into the back wall, falling to the ground in an awkward pile. Diegert stepped to him and kicked him twice in the ribs. Lopez coughed up blood and desperately extended his hands to fend off the next kick.

Seeing the man defenseless and covered in blood, Diegert stepped back and watched him struggle. He felt powerful in a primal, dominant way. He had beaten his enemy so swiftly and completely, he felt like the king of the pride. He also felt foolish. He had assaulted this man for money, with no indication that Lopez deserved this. Even Lieutenant Prescott had deserved what he'd gotten. Diegert had to admit to himself that he had violated the ethics of martial arts and had used his skills to instigate violence. He could feel the point turning. *Fuck it*, he thought, *I need the money, and this fucker is a drug dealer playing a dangerous game.* He snapped a picture of the defeated Lopez, who gurgled through his bloody lips, "You're gonna get yours." Diegert walked away, listening to the defeated man, who raised his voice and said, "I'm gonna kill you, motherfucker. I know who you are."

After washing the blood off his hands, Diegert showed the picture to Buscetti and collected his envelope of cash. He resumed his post at the door and soon found himself opening it as Igor Dimitrov and his crew departed. As he passed, Dimitrov stopped to shake Diegert's hand. Clapping his big paw on Diegert's shoulder, he said, "*хороший удар.*" Good punch. It was an unusually friendly gesture, which Diegert didn't understand and to which he did not reply. Strangely, he felt both a sense of camaraderie and revulsion. After the group left, a feeling of foreboding crept over him.

The next morning was a bright, dry Texas beauty with the fragrance of bluebells and oleanders mixing with the diesel exhaust that hung in the air around the Single Star Motel. The flowers made him think of home, and Diegert recalled how his mom had always put so much effort into keeping the house neat, tidy, and attractive. She did all the gardening, and although he had mowed the grass, she made the place look real nice with flowers and her well-tended berry bushes. She kept the chicken coop secure, repairing the damage from attempted incursions by foxes and coyotes. She painted the house, washed the windows, and pulled the weeds. His mom took pride and pleasure in keeping their small, simple home, which was fronted by a dirt road, looking like a place that was loved and appreciated.

At this time of day, she would be home since she worked the evening shift at the diner. He smiled as he waited for her to answer his call.

"Hello," she said.

"Hey, Mom."

"David, I didn't expect a call from you."

"Yeah, well, they finally gave us phones over here. How ya doin'?"

"Fine, I'm fine. How about you?"

"I'm doing OK, although the Army isn't everything the recruiters tell you. I'm supposed to be home in eight months."

"Eight months? That long?"

"Yeah, I might get some leave for a week or two, but I don't know when that's going to happen." Diegert turned out of the wind so he could hear better. "I tell ya, Mom, Afghanistan is really hot this time of year."

"Oh, that's too bad. I miss you, David."

"Yeah, I miss you too, Mom."

"Without you, I have to do everything around here."

"How are Jake and Dad?"

"They're fine. Usually drunk. Jake's still dealing drugs. I don't let them bother me."

"But you're OK, right?"

Through the phone, Diegert got only a muffled response. He listened carefully, and he could hear the soft gasp of a cry escaping from his mother.

"Mom, what's wrong? Tell me what's going on."

Her sobs were being stifled, and he could hear that she was struggling to speak.

"Come on, Mom, talk to me; tell me what's happening."

"I'm scared."

"Is Dad hitting you?"

"No, no, no, it's not that."

"Then what? What are you afraid of?"

"I'm afraid we're going to lose the house."

Diegert thought about the house and property and figured it wasn't even worth a hundred grand. They'd been living in it for more than twenty years, so surely it should be close to being paid off.

"What do you mean, lose the house?"

"The bank is threatening foreclosure."

Diegert's thoughts flashed through his head. Although she was smart with money, his father had bought the house before he'd met his mom, and Diegert had no idea how the mortgage was being financed.

"Tell me what the bank said."

"A man came to the door and gave me some papers. They said Dad hasn't been paying the mortgage, and he took out an equity loan some time ago. We owe a hundred and sixty-seven thousand. David, I don't know what to do," sobbed his mother.

Diegert dropped the phone from his ear as the number passed through his mind. The small house and his father's beat-up old barn were worth nowhere near that much. Blinking his eyes, Diegert slowly shook his head as the problem became clear.

"How much money do you have?"

Snuffling back her tears, Denise Diegert said, "Fifteen hundred in my checking account, that's it. I've no idea what Dad has. He's never told me about how he handles his money, but it obviously hasn't been good."

"Mom, how much time did the bank give you?"

"Two months, but the entire amount is due by then. Apparently, they've been sending Dad notifications for a while, and they're now at the point where it's pay it all or lose the house."

As the predicament settled into Diegert's thoughts, his mother continued.

"David, I don't want to lose the house. This is the only home I've ever had and, you know, I do all the work, keep it nice, and I feel safe here. If I have to leave, then the fear starts all over again. Please help me."

Imagining her there in the small, tidy kitchen, tears flowing over her high cheekbones with a feeling of desperation and abandonment welling up inside her, Diegert wanted to reassure her.

"Mom, I will help you get that money, and I will keep you from losing the house."

"How, David? How are you going to do that?"

"I'll find a way. You just hang in there, and I'll find a way. My time is up. I've got to get off the phone. Bye, Mom."

"Good-bye, David. I love you."

When the call disconnected, Diegert gazed across the parking lot of the Single Star Motel and realized he had no idea how he was going to get that much money.

9

The Austin Police Department encircled the alley behind the Dark Horse in yellow tape as soon as the bullet-riddled body of a Mexican man had been reported between the dumpsters. They confiscated Buscetti's video surveillance recordings and began the long process of interviewing all the patrons and employees who had been working the previous night.

Buscetti texted Diegert: *Tune into the news.* Diegert brought up a local news app and saw the video of himself pushing Lopez through the alley to the dumpsters. The view of what happened between the big trash bins was blocked, but after a few minutes, the video showed Diegert walking out of the alley, alone. The grainy image made it hard to identify the man on the screen, but Diegert certainly recognized himself.

Diegert replied: *I need a place to hole up.*

Buscetti texted back: *1370 Valencia Drive. Go there and stay put.*

The address wasn't too far away. Diegert pulled his hood over his head and walked to Valencia Drive, which was located in an upscale suburb. The house had a winding drive leading to a nice house set back thirty yards from the road. When he knocked on the door, it opened right away, surprising Diegert, who looked up into the heavily bearded face of an impressively large man who introduced himself as "Peotor Vladak." Diegert was nearly yanked through the door by the powerful man, who didn't release his hand until the front door had closed.

"I know your name, and I know your crime," said the man who stood six foot five inches tall and weighed over two hundred fifty pounds. "But you are safe here. This is a safe house."

Peotor nodded his head and gestured for Diegert to follow him into the next room.

Diegert remained rooted in the foyer. "I didn't kill that guy."

Peotor's smile crept out from under his beard. "I saw the video, and you wouldn't be here if you didn't earn your entrance with a murder. Come. Follow me into the kitchen."

Peotor trained his gaze on Diegert's face as he held his arms out and proceeded into the kitchen.

"Sit here, friend."

Diegert sat on a stool at the raised counter as Peotor called out, "Sam, come down here, we have a guest."

Rapid footfalls on the stairs preceded the entrance of a thin, wiry young man with close-cropped blond hair and wide-set hazel eyes. From the bottom of the stairs to the kitchen the guy checked his phone screen twice. He finger stroked the screen until satisfied with the effects before looking squarely at Diegert. Peotor spoke, "This is the guy from the video who killed the Mexican."

The wiry man's eyelids narrowed as a slight sneer distorted his otherwise inexpressive lips.

"I didn't kill him," offered Diegert. "I only beat him up. When I left him, he was alive and shouting." Diegert felt like he was pleading to the police. The thin man raised his sleeve, revealing a tattooed bicep depicting a combat dagger from which four distinct drops of blood fell off the blade toward his elbow. Leaning forward, the man said with clarity, "Don't let anyone take credit for what you've done."

Diegert swallowed hard as the proud murderer stepped back, dropped his sleeve, extended his hand, and introduced himself. "I'm Sam Klemczar. How long will you be with us?"

Diegert felt the cold of Sam's hand pass into him like a winter's draft.

"I don't know." The question forced Diegert to face his situation and realize he had no idea what to do. His answer passed by the ears of Sam without being heard, since the thin man's phone had buzzed, and the screen once again had his full attention.

As the young man's climb up the stairs drummed through the house, Peotor told Diegert, "You can use the refrigerator but don't take anything from the bottom shelf or the one above that. You can use anything in the door."

So it went for two days, with Sam almost never coming downstairs and Peotor constantly talking about Russia and all the exploits of the Russian mob all over the world. At one point, Sam had returned to confiscate Diegert's phone for "safety reasons." Without communication, Diegert began to get paranoid. He wanted to talk to Buscetti and check in on his mom, but Sam's insistence that his phone could be tracked, and the safe house blown forced him to be incommunicado. Not being able to do what you want for even the most basic things can make anyone edgy. Diegert, however, had the Austin Police Department, the Quinoloan cartel, and probably the FBI all looking for him. Not knowing if he was really safe or just being set up to be turned over was very aggravating.

Peotor's laptop became the only conduit to the outside world, and Peotor's worldview was dominated by the exploits of assassins as depicted on the darknet. The underground Internet required the installation of Tor software which rerouted digital signals so they couldn't be traced. It presented a means of worldwide communication that couldn't be tracked or controlled by law enforcement. Peotor told Diegert the original software was designed by the US Navy. It had been adopted by criminals and served the needs of drug dealers, human traffickers, fences for stolen merchandise, and contract killers. The killers fascinated Peotor. Assassins seeking employment posted their exploits, including graphic pictures of the people they'd murdered. The more audacious assassins posted GoPro videos that not only showed the kill but the process of breaching security to execute the target.

Watching all this with Peotor at first shocked Diegert, then intrigued him, and finally numbed him as the bloody images became routine and the videos that were just simple shaky shots of dead bodies were no longer entertaining compared to the more complex depictions of the entire process. Diegert, though, was amazed by the money; the going rate was about a hundred thousand dollars USD for a human life. In addition to the assassins' postings, there were several pages of contracts to kill being advertised.

"One day, you will see my page on the darknet, and I'll be the most sought-after assassin in the world." Peotor's boastful statement did nothing to impress Diegert, but what he said next was more chilling.

"An assassin must commit to the kill. When the pistol is pointed, the trigger must be pulled, and then the assassin must walk away." Diegert's doubt of Peotor's capacity to kill was weakened by his lethal pronouncement. The big guy continued, "I can do this. I can shut my emotions down in order to become as cold as Sam. He has four kills, you know."

"Yeah…he showed me his tattoo."

After a rapid flurry of keystrokes, Peotor brought up a screen to show Diegert.

"Look at his website; you can see his kills."

On the computer, Diegert saw four grisly posthumous portraits, all with entrance wounds in the forehead.

"One day I will have many more tattoos than that guy," said Peotor as he gestured upstairs to an unconvinced Diegert.

"Then why are you just sitting here babysitting me?"

"Babysitting? There are no babies here. What do you mean?"

"What are you waiting for? There are contracts right here with all the information you need to carry them out. Why aren't you doing one of these jobs?" asked Diegert as he tapped his fingers on Peotor's screen.

Peotor's round face turned to Diegert. "I need to lose weight, and I need to get my knee fixed." Peotor slapped his right knee. "I hurt it playing rugby, and I need surgery to fix the ligaments. I can't run on it. Hey, since you killed the Mexican, we can use him to set up your profile."

"No way, I don't want a profile."

Later, for dinner, Sam cooked himself up a soup with sausage, noodles, lard, and butter. It looked to Diegert like a liquid heart attack with several different layers of fat fighting to remain separate from the broth. Peotor stared enviously at the fatty meal while he peeled back the foil on his cup of lite yogurt. Diegert finished fixing a turkey sandwich, but before he bit into it, he asked Sam, "Can I use your phone to call Buscetti?"

Sam's gaze snapped at Diegert, and he instinctively snatched his phone off the counter. "No, you can't."

"When am I going to get to speak with Buscetti and get out of here?"

Sam replied, "According to Mr. Dimitrov, you're to stay here. He specifically said you aren't to leave."

An unnerving chill trickled down Diegert's spine as Sam's revelation of who was in charge registered within him.

"You're to remain as our guest," said Peotor, the smiling bear.

"I appreciate the hospitality, but I would like to move on and get back to my life."

"Your life," said Sam coldly, "is safer here than out on the street. You will remain until I hear from Dimitrov."

Peotor added, with a smile that included yogurt at the corner of his beard, "I'm glad you're staying here with us."

Diegert wondered if Peotor was really as dumb as he looked, but he felt the cold from Sam's icy stare and realized his predicament might have far more dire consequences than he'd initially thought.

* * * *

On day four, Peotor asked Diegert to fire up the laptop, telling him the password was "RUSSIA." When Diegert signed in, the screen immediately opened to a site displaying gay porn.

Diegert sensed Peotor's bulky body coming up behind him.

"Hey, let's watch some of this…together."

The scene on the screen of one man fellating another turned Diegert's stomach, but it turned Peotor on.

"No, that's not my thing," Diegert said as he stood up, handed Peotor the computer, and moved to the other side of the room.

"Come on, I thought you'd like it."

"You thought I was gay?"

"What's wrong with being gay?"

"Look, I'm not saying there's anything wrong with it, but I'm not gay. I don't want to watch gay porn."

"What…you're too good for gay sex?"

"No, man, I'm just not interested."

Peotor's face became a hard scowl as he turned his attention to the screen, watching the porn with the sound up high. Diegert distracted himself with a magazine, but it was like trying to find peace and quiet at a Dionysus orgy. As Peotor's excitement intensified, he undid his pants and pulled out his erection. "I want your wet lips on my cock.

Get over here," he commanded in an authoritarian tone Diegert had not heard him use before.

The Russian reached to his right, taking his Makarov 9 mm pistol off the table and pointing it at Diegert. The incredulous American got up and walked over to the couch.

"That's right, kneel down and suck it." With the gun in his hand, Peotor proclaimed, "Power and pleasure."

On one knee in front of the big guy, Diegert encircled the man's cock with his fingers and gently stroked it up and down. Loving the pleasure, Peotor leaned his head back and closed his eyes. The instant the big guy's lids fell, Diegert crushed the erection in his grasp and grabbed the gun from the stunned man's hand. Peotor's painful holler alerted Sam, who bounded down the stairs into the living room. Keeping the squeeze on the big guy's dick, Diegert pivoted and put two bullets into the skinnier guard as he entered the room. Letting go of the guy's prick, Diegert plunged his knee into the bellowing man's crotch. Diegert pulled Peotor's head back by the hair and put the barrel in his face. He pulled the trigger, shattering Peotor's cranium, splattering the carpet with blood and brains.

10

With two dead bodies and a bloody mess in the Russian safe house, Diegert was stunned at what he'd just done. Shooting two men so quickly left him gasping for breath. The adrenaline rush was like none he'd ever felt, and he was afraid he was going into cardiac arrest. With his heart bashing against his sternum, he stepped back and fell into a chair on the opposite side of the room. He sat there realizing his life would never be the same. The eerie quiet was unsettling, but it was broken by the sound of blood dripping to the floor from Peotor's head. Being trapped, not communicating, and worrying that he'd be killed by these mobsters, Diegert had reacted with a survival reflex.

The sound of thumping and dragging drew him into the kitchen. Sam had two bullet holes in his chest and was sucking air through pursed lips as he reached back with his elbows to pull himself across the floor. The blood exiting the wounds in his back smeared across the floor as he struggled to make his way toward the stairs. Diegert stood by the granite-topped island looking at the pitiful four-time assassin as he desperately sought to escape.

When their eyes met, Diegert saw the fear and felt a jolt of power he hadn't expected. This man, who had struck Diegert as so cold and ruthless, now had fear radiating from his face. This man, who had killed several others, now displayed the weakness and desperation of wounded quarry about to be killed. The powerlessness and the abandonment of hope for mercy played across Sam's face and filled the vector between his and Diegert's eyes. Diegert felt triumph. He felt like he did after beating Miguel Lopez in the alley, but this sensation was even more powerful and primal.

This man was going to die, and Diegert was going to look him in the eye as he shoved aside his humanity to end

Sam's pathetic little life with explosive violence. Sam's eyes widened until his irises were ringed by the bright-white sclera as Diegert raised the pistol, squaring the sight bead on the point between the eyes where the nose began.

Sam stopped shuffling and pleaded, "Please don't." The bullet imploded the nasal and frontal bones producing an immediate splash that spread across the hardwood floor when the back of Sam's skull was pulverized by the force of the close-range projectile. Diegert did not flinch after firing the weapon. He gazed upon the dead man while the anger and frustration of his being a captive mixed with the sudden liberation he felt now that there was no one to hold him hostage. The feeling was more than that, though. The capacity to inflict death by his will and hand heated his blood, engorging his muscles with an animalistic sense of power. The adrenaline was huge, and Diegert felt so alive and energized for having shot these men to gain his freedom.

If Diegert were to become an assassin, then a killer he would be. The abuse he had endured from his father and the servitude of his lousy old job as well as the disappointment of his service in the Army all left him feeling weak, lost, and rudderless. In contrast, here now was something that made him feel powerful, in control, and free of himself.

In the Army, he was trained as a soldier to kill enemies for the sake of the mission as well as to protect his fellow soldiers. He had done that today. His willingness to cross the line, to become the killer, grabbed his thoughts and expanded his sense of self with an unexpected realization. He enjoyed the kill. This moment, this internal experience, extended from his head to his muscles to his soul, filling him with an unprecedented sense of personal power.

After washing the blood off his face and hands, he gathered up useful things: guns, ammo, some cash, car keys, his phone, as well as his Ojibwa knife. He was wearing his amulet while he looked at the blanket his mother had made him. Using the knife, he cut out the embroidered prayer folded it up and stuck it in his pocket. From Peotor's computer, he downloaded the Tor software and verified that he could access the darknet on his phone. Exiting the back door, he came around where the cars were parked and drove away in a big black BMW 738i.

A stolen Bratva vehicle would quickly become a liability. Diegert found refuge on the interior of the third floor of a downtown parking garage. He accessed the darknet and read through a number of contract offerings for assassinations. He figured he was accused of one murder he didn't commit, and now was guilty of taking two lives, so if convicted he was going to jail for life or a spot on death row. He reluctantly realized that the best thing to do was go all in. It was scary and messy, but he admitted to himself that he felt charged by the power of the experience. Shooting those two guys had left him with a strangely liberating sense of relief. This was a feeling he would never admit to anyone, but he couldn't deny to himself. His emotions were raw, confusing, and powerful.

Out of all the advertisements he reviewed, he was attracted to one that was a two-part job. A successful hit in Miami got you a private jet out of the US to perform a second job in Paris. This seemed like just what Diegert needed, the money was good, a hundred thousand dollars, but the flight was more important. If he could escape the US, he would be able to establish himself in Europe and remain free and unpursued.

* * * *

His reply to the ad went secretly to the computer of Aaron Blevinsky. Blevinsky was employed as a special operations manager for an elite group known as

Crepusculous. All of Blevinsky's communication was sent blindly. No one knew the real identity of the person with whom they were communicating when that person worked for Crepusculous.

This elite organization, comprised of four men, represented the smallest percent of the world's wealthiest people. Their combined wealth encompassed 75 percent of the world's resources. Their ability to influence governments, markets, and the global economy made them the most powerful people on earth. All four of the men were practically unknown in the media, largely because they owned most of the media outlets in the world and made sure that tawdry gossip and investigative news stories were focused on the few competitors they had. Crepusculous meant "in the shadows," and from their clandestine positions, these men controlled the world.

As director of special operations, Blevinsky was tasked with ensuring that Crepusculous had a private military. From battle-hardened commandos to stealthy assassins, Blevinsky kept ready a group of men and women who could carry out missions deemed necessary by the four Board members of Crepusculous.

With the ad that attracted Diegert, Blevinsky was fishing for a fresh operator, someone young yet confident and ready to prove himself. A prospect for the future who had very little past and could be groomed for a special mission he was planning for the Board.

* * * *

Blevinsky read Diegert's message, which was sent under the online ID, Next Chance: *I'm interested in the opportunity you're advertising.*

He replied under the online ID, Darkmass: *What experience do you have?*

Next Chance: *I have three recent completions against narcotic organizations.*

Darkmass: *Were there complications from law enforcement?*

Blevinsky's questions kept Diegert on the line, which was essential for the success of a reverse tracking worm designed in a Crepusculous tech lab that was able to move through Tor and identify the source of a signal. Each message Diegert sent led Blevinsky closer to identifying him.

Next Chance: *I was never arrested or clearly identified.*

Darkmass: *You're free of convictions?*

Next Chance: *Quite.*

Darkmass: *Do you have a profile on the darknet?*

Next Chance: *No, I do not, but the recent completions are news in the Austin area.*

Blevinsky kept Diegert waiting while he looked for news stories on the Web, allowing the worm more time to work. Once the worm was able to find the signal's path, it was able to move through the various servers the Tor software had hopped between. Within minutes, Blevinsky had Diegert's phone under surveillance. From it, he was able to identify him as David Diegert, extract his e-mails, and locate him by GPS. He learned that Diegert was twenty-five years old from Broward, Minnesota; had been dishonorably discharged from the Army; was a reasonably handsome guy with dark hair and features; had $2,604 in credit card debt; and was currently located in Austin, Texas. If he kept mining, he would find more, but for now, he had what he needed.

Darkmass: *I see the news from Austin, a Mexican outside a bar and two guys in a suburb. Be in Miami in two days. When you arrive, you will receive instructions.*

* * * *

Diegert was surprised how quickly Sam and Peotor's deaths had made the news. The bus station was only two blocks away. In the trunk of the car, he found a black reusable shopping bag into which he placed his useful items, tied the top of the bag, and walked to the station.

After a twenty-two-hour bus ride through most of which Diegert slept, he stepped into the blazing sun and heavy afternoon humidity of Miami. While walking away from the bus, his phone buzzed, and the text from Darkmass instructed him to take a cab to the Blue Pearl Restaurant and Nightclub in Miami Beach. En route, his screen revealed a photo of a large, mustachioed Hispanic man named Victor Del Fuentes. The accompanying text read: *This is your target. Send a message when the job is complete. Make it look like an accident.*

"An accident," muttered Diegert after he paid the cabbie and approached the Blue Pearl. As he got closer, the expensive nature of this club became obvious. Dressed in casual clothes and carrying his shopping bag, Diegert simply passed by while gathering visual intel. The outdoor diners enjoyed a fabulous view of the ocean while an army of waitstaff attended their every need. Through the windows, more tables could be seen, along with a bar and a large open dance floor.

Diegert surmised that when the dinner crowd left, the Blue Pearl transformed into a partying nightclub. Farther down the street, he came upon Ocean View Park with its quiet public space next to busy Ocean Drive. From a food truck, he got a chicken fajita. It felt good to eat, and he sat looking out at the water waiting for darkness to fall.

* * * *

Unknown to Diegert, Blevinsky tracked Diegert's phone signal across a map of Miami.

* * * *

During the long bus ride and now sitting through the setting sun, Diegert thought about what he had done and what he was going to do. Killing the two Russian guards was self-defense. A reactionary act anybody would have done, given the threat. Beating up Miguel Lopez was different; getting paid meant instigating the attack. There was no threat, no need, just an opportunity, and a greedy reward. Whoever killed Lopez, and it was obviously Dimitrov, had set him up, and that bad choice pinned him with three murders. Without intending to, he had become a killer of men and was now being hired to do it again. The experience of killing was thrilling, but now it was also guilt-inducing.

Do I just walk away from this and forget it? Diegert thought. *I can't really do that, because I'll eventually be caught, convicted, and executed. If I complete this job and leave the US, I will have enough money to live in Europe and get away with this. I'll live cheap, earn more money, and send it back to Mom. God, this sucks! I can't believe I'm in this shit.*

His mind went blank as contemplating the intractable situation failed to produce a better solution. His thoughts turned to how he would kill Victor Del Fuentes and make it look like an accident. Making a plan and thinking about the future as only a matter of hours was far more comforting than worrying about the rest of his life. Focusing on the Del Fuentes mission kept him from being paralyzed by the consequences of his earlier actions.

Darkness fell as the sun set, and he left Ocean View Park. Passing through the pools of light projected on the sidewalk by the streetlamps, Diegert could hear the sounds of a party coming from the Blue Pearl. He was attracted to the thump of music, the din of a hundred conversations punctuated by bursts of laughter and the kinetic waves of a crowd in motion. He knew the transient sense of camaraderie that formed as people were relaxed by alcohol and tacitly agreed that they were all having a good time.

Twenty bucks got him inside the party, and he began his reconnaissance. Del Fuentes was not hard to find. The big, handsome gentleman sat at a corner booth with a beautiful young woman beside him and several couples surrounding the table. He was gregarious and animated and clearly in control of the evening. The waiter would approach him from behind, speak directly into his ear, and then walk briskly away when Del Fuentes waved his hand. He looked like the king of this court and someone who relished the servitude his money and power was able to buy. His bodyguard stood off to the side, likely with a gun under his summer-weight suit coat.

From his seat at the bar, Diegert was able to observe his target. As the evening progressed, Del Fuentes eventually rose from his seat and forced his considerable bulk out of the booth and down the hall. The bodyguard was instructed to stay put with a wave of the hand. Diegert followed, observing as the big man bypassed the men's room where all the rest of the guys went and entered a room farther down the hall marked "Private." The king certainly wasn't going to piss with the pawns, and Diegert knew he had found his opportunity to stage an accident.

Diegert got a cheap motel room in Overtown for which he paid cash and falsified the registry. He showered and slept, but he was buzzing on adrenaline now that he had a plan to kill Victor Del Fuentes. In the morning, he went to a hardware store and acquired a screwdriver with multiple heads, needle-nose pliers, electrical wire, and an aerosol can of ignition starter fluid. From a consignment shop, he purchased black pants and a black shirt. Combined, the two garments dressed him like all the waitstaff at the Blue Pearl.

After passing the day avoiding being burned by a sun that was almost as hot as Afghanistan, he entered the kitchen of the Blue Pearl looking like a new guy on the waitstaff. Del Fuentes was in his booth with a different young lady and a new set of couples enthralled with the king's every word.

Diegert stepped out of the kitchen in his waiter's attire, went straight down the hall, and entered the room labeled "Private." The toilet was to the right, the sink to the left. The room had soft lighting, which gave the space a gentle glow in which to complete your business. Stepping to the sink activated a sensor that illuminated an overhead unit. The brighter light conveniently lit the sink for the washing of hands. Diegert smiled as his plan had found the perfect situation for execution.

Using his tools and the canister of engine-starting fluid, Diegert turned the overhead sink light into an automatically activated explosive device in a matter of minutes. Stepping out of the room, he heard, "Hey, you're not supposed to be in there." The young waitress had a tray of meals in her hands and cast Diegert a scornful look as she continued out to the dining room.

Diegert just looked at her, smiled, and shrugged his shoulders.

For thirty minutes, Diegert blended in with the staff while observing the booth. The young lady with Del Fuentes was very disinterested in the paunchy man and seemed to be much more enamored with the cleavage of the wife sitting next to her. Del Fuentes's bladder eventually asserted itself, and the big guy exited the booth.

Diegert moved toward the restaurant's exit. The explosion was immense, blowing the door of the private bathroom right off its hinges and across the hall. Del Fuentes's dead body lay in the doorway as a grisly decapitated corpse. The crowd grew hushed for a second, contemplating that perhaps there was an accident in the kitchen. The situation turned into a panic when a waitress, seeing Del Fuentes, screamed like a victim in a horror movie. By this time, Diegert had already taken his leave and was walking down the street turning the corner and leaving the scene of his first "accidental" assassination.

The text Blevinsky received from Diegert had only one word: *Completed.*

Checking the news a few hours later, Diegert read a post from the *Miami Herald* announcing the death of Victor Del Fuentes in what appeared to be a freak accident in the men's room of the Blue Pearl. Obviously, Blevinsky had also read it as his reply gave Diegert the address of the Miami Executive Airport southeast of Miami. The text included the tail number of the plane and a boarding code to show the plane's crew.

When Diegert arrived, the sleek design of the Gulfstream G650 made him feel out of his element yet eager to move forward. As he boarded, his initial impressions were surpassed by the luxury appointments of the interior.

"Welcome aboard, Mr. Diegert," came the voice through the cabin speakers. "I am your captain, Edward James, and your co-captain for this flight is Robert Allen. We are ready for departure as soon as you're comfortable. Our flight time to Paris is seven hours and forty-three minutes. Amber, your cabin attendant, will be serving you as soon as we reach our cruising altitude of thirty thousand feet. Please press the green button on your armrest when you are ready to fly. Thank you."

Sitting in the broad, soft leather seat, Diegert's smile revealed his pleasure to be receiving such service and respect. Amber was a gorgeous young woman whose continuous smile told him she was ready to please. After one last satisfying breath and a look at the cherry wood trim of the cabin, Diegert pressed the green button and left America behind.

The comfortable seats, the serene sky, and the sense of secure quiet, lulled Diegert into contemplation. His reaction to killing Sam and Peotor was so intense he realized that the time he felt most powerful was when he was fighting. In high school, the only place he felt competent and confident was on the wrestling mat. The intensity of the matches had cleared his thoughts, allowing him to detach from his regular life and use his skills on the mat to gain a sense of power. The success of thrashing guys into submission filled a void in his day-to-day life. The minute practice was over, returning to the hallways or the bus, and pretty much everywhere else, he was filled with doubt and self-conscious judgment.

In the Army at Fort Benning, he'd felt good when training. The full-pack marches, low crawling through the dirt and practicing Modern Army Combatives had given him a sense of accomplishment. He was able to detach from the pain of the struggle and push through whatever was asked of him. But in the barracks, the mess hall, or the PX, he'd felt empty, hollow, and without purpose. These recollections came back to him with unsettling clarity. He had just killed three men while emotionally detached from the experience.

To kill was a powerful catharsis, a forceful expression of his anger, and frustration finding a release in a spasm of violence, but he did it out of a necessity to survive. He experienced an adrenaline rush during the action, but it was followed by a deep crash, and soon Diegert felt like shit. He was doing the work of others, who, through their power and money, were forcing him to comply with their demands or suffer the consequences. In spite of the luxurious surroundings, Diegert realized he was in a cylindrical jail cell financed by those who were ordering him to kill. How far was he willing to go to fulfill his employer's requests for death?

He willed himself to hold on to the feelings of guilt and recrimination that surfaced after killing. He didn't want to become someone addicted to violence, a junkie seeking a kill to get a thrill. He held the guilt in and nurtured it, swallowing its poison. He would crush any kill thrill with the guilt of having killed. Caught between the power of taking a life and the emotional consequence of having committed the ultimate sin, Diegert hurtled forward at six hundred miles per hour into an uncertain future.

11

The stairway of the Gulfstream opened at Le Bourget, a private airport in Paris. David Diegert descended to the tarmac, where he was met by a chauffeur who did not introduce himself before ushering the American into the rear compartment of a Renault. A smartphone, on the seat beside David, chirped when the car door closed. Instructions on the phone indicated the target was named Gunther Mibuku. There were no other details about the man, but in his photo, he looked biracial. Diegert was to meet one of Mibuku's female consorts, whose cooperation was making this mission possible. Next to him was a gray fedora, which he was to wear while sitting at a table in a street-side café. The nameless chauffeur dropped Diegert at the sidewalk.

Wearing the hat, drinking coffee, and seated at a sidewalk table, Diegert took in the view of Paris. The lively movement of people and the strange lack of tall buildings seemed a bit incongruous for a large urban city, not at all like Minneapolis and definitely not like the small town of Broward, Minnesota. "May I join you?" asked a strikingly attractive Asian woman. "Certainly," said Diegert as he looked up at the surprisingly tall, dark-haired beauty.

As she sat down, she placed her smartphone on the table. The screen displayed an alphanumeric code, "A12B14C18," and the pretty woman said, "Please confirm."

Diegert was confused for a moment and sat still just looking at her. "With your phone," the lady urged.

Pulling out his phone, he saw the same code and showed it to her: "A12B14C18."

"Chateau Lambert Room 316. I will be meeting him at seven p.m. You'll receive a text from me when the time is right. The guard in the hall is your problem."

"OK."

She got up and left, and David's eyes were not the only ones gazing at her lovely feminine form as she walked away. Before he could take another sip of coffee, the chauffeur in the Renault pulled up, and Diegert was whisked away.

As they drove, the nameless chauffeur pointed out the Chateau Lambert and took Diegert to an apartment that he referred to as a safe house. In the apartment, Diegert found the equipment he would need. A hotel photo ID, which was also a room keycard, an MK 23 pistol with a suppressor and two extra clips of ammunition, latex gloves, and a rubber mask. He put the mask on and looked in the mirror. The rubber panels covered his cheeks, forehead, chin, and nose. He still had good visibility, and the thing was not uncomfortable, and it would fulfill its role of distorting his face for the surveillance cameras. There was also a paper map of the neighborhood with indicated routes to the hotel, one to walk there and a different one for coming back. Diegert put both on his phone. In the kitchen, there was bread and cheese, and on the television, a soccer game.

As seven p.m. approached, Diegert took the longer route to the hotel. Dressed in black so he would blend in with the service staff, he attracted no attention on the street. At the hotel, he found a linen closet and acquired a set of towels.

Diegert walked the halls and rode the elevators, carrying his towels and looking like he belonged. One British chap on the elevator, heading to the pool, took one of the towels and gave Diegert a polite nod. At seven forty-five p.m. he received the Asian woman's text.

Withdrawing his pistol and attaching the suppressor, he placed it between the first and second towel. As he walked down the hall approaching Room 316, he stopped perpendicular to the guard, pressed the barrel into the man's chest, and fired a muffled shot. The failed protector slumped forward with Diegert breaking his fall. Using his keycard, Diegert opened the room, dragged the man inside, and laid him on the floor. A second bullet to the head assured the guard would no longer be an obstacle.

Locking the door behind him, Diegert saw the Asian beauty getting dressed and pointing the way into the suite's bedroom. The target was on the bed. A magnificent specimen of a man, very fit looking, all muscle covered in smooth skin. He was sexually spent and contently stretched out on the king-size sheets. Diegert stepped to the side of the bed, and the slightest look of confusion crossed the man's face as he opened his sleepy eyes before two bullets entered into his head. Aside from the slight moment of surprise, it seemed to Diegert like he died a happy man having just had sex. As instructed by his employer, Diegert used his smartphone to send video confirmation of the hit. He received an immediate reply, which acknowledged the completion of the mission, but the message had an additional component, stating: *$100,000 has just been placed in your account, for an additional 5%, take out the girl.*

Checking his account, he could see the money was there. Diegert thought of helping his mom, and even though five thousand dollars wasn't much, every dollar he earned got her closer to paying off the house.

The girl was throwing the last of her belongings in a shoulder bag and beckoning him to hurry so they could leave together.

He didn't know this woman. Maybe she wasn't an accomplice but a criminal like Mibuku. Maybe she was going to turn him in as soon as they stepped out of the room. Why would the employer want her dead? Was she an ally or an adversary? As she approached him, Diegert raised his MK 23, placing the laser sight on her chest. She stopped in her tracks and looked him squarely in the eye.

"Really, you're gonna shoot me?"

Waving his phone in his hand, he said, "Our employer is asking me to. Why would he do that?"

"Fucking cheap bastard."

"Or maybe I'm being warned not to trust you."

"Oh, come on. I'm just a girl with habits in a town full of customers. I'm no threat to you."

Gesturing toward the dead body on the bed, Diegert asked, "What's the story with this guy?"

"We don't have time to play kill and tell. Let's get out of here."

Killing Mibuku was easy, it was intended, it was the plan. Killing her was not. His employer had given him no explanation, and she didn't feel like a threat. Diegert definitely did not want to kill a woman. He hadn't really thought it through, but facing the issue right in front of him, he could not bring himself to shoot her.

"Alright, but you're coming with me."

"That's stupid."

"Stupid is not controlling the situation, and until I feel it's right, you're staying with me."

Diegert put on his facial distortion mask and a black baseball cap.

"What, no disguise for me?"

"Sorry, you're leading the way."

They exited the back of the hotel and took the short route to the apartment.

The streets were not too busy, and with a fast pace, they made quick progress on the sidewalks. Rounding a corner, they came upon the scene of a car accident. A Peugeot driven by a mom with two small children had rear-ended a

Fiat that belonged to a middle-aged couple. The man yelled at the police officer as he pointed at the damage to his car while gesturing about the mom's distracted driving. Diegert kept his head down for fear the distortion mask might attract attention. The tall prostitute put a little more sway in her hips, exaggerating her stride, drawing glances from both the cop and the irate motorist. Diegert placed a tight grip on her arm as they continued down the street, turning the corner onto the final lane and into the apartment building. Climbing the stairs, Diegert kept looking behind him, fearing that the cop might follow them into the building. He knew it was paranoia but killing someone can bring that out in a person.

The apartment was small, but Diegert realized just how cramped it was when the prostitute had to sit on the bed while he occupied the one kitchen chair.

"How did you get this job?" asked Diegert.

"Through an e-mail, I never spoke to anyone. All instructions...electronic," she said, cocking her head to the side and drawing out her last word.

"So tell me about Mibuku."

"Aren't killers supposed to do their homework before they pull the trigger?"

"It was a short-order contract, and I was given very little information."

"And now you're questioning your actions. I do that all the time after I fuck somebody I probably shouldn't have."

"What about Mibuku?"

"What about him? He was a drug dealer and always had the best stuff. The kind I like. He had a big, hard cock and an arrogant personality. He liked Asian women because he thought our cunts were smaller...tighter. What a narrow-minded fool."

"You had a regular thing with him?"

"We had an occasional recurring thing, but as you can see, I sold him out for a big payday. Your employer has promised me good money for helping you."

They sat quietly contemplating their places in life. Diegert thought about how they were both hired to provide a service. She provided the pleasure of the flesh, associated with the creation of new life, and he deliberately and violently brought lives to an end. Their occupations cast them outside of society, their work, unacceptable. Yet there was no shortage of demand for their services. Realizing that a prostitute was his closest ally made Diegert shake his head. The woman broke his reverie.

"If you want to fuck me, it's five hundred, otherwise I'll be leaving."

He could see her hands twitching in a soft but constant tremor; she needed a fix.

"Where are you meeting for your payoff?"

"We're not meeting. The money is going into an account."

Diegert nodded knowingly, but his long pause brought an *I'm out of here* look to her face. Diegert abruptly commanded her. "Dump your purse on the bed."

"What?"

"Dump it all out or I will."

She grabbed the bottom of her large bag and raised her long, slender arm over her head. The contents spilled onto the bed. All sorts of typical items were in the pile, but Diegert's eyebrows rose when he saw the strap-on dildo and three types of vibrators. He grabbed her wallet and extracted her driver's license. Crossing to the kitchen table, he placed it on the surface and took a picture with his phone. Handing it back to her and returning to the chair, he changed his tone, asking her, "Where around here could a guy go for some nightlife, Miss Shei Leun Wong?"

Returning her belongings to the bag, she replied, "A guy like you, looking for some free sex, I'd tell you to go to Luna-Sea on Rue Chea Remiur. They party hard there and hook up pretty easily."

Holding the dildo up in the air with the straps dangling around her wrist, she twirled the plastic cock and teased, "You sure you wouldn't like to try something a little different? My treat."

"No. You can take that and go."

She stood up, slinging the bag over her shoulder. They continued to look at each other with curious but suspicious eyes. Their mutual moment of infatuated mistrust was broken by the sound of sirens wailing from the southerly direction of Chateau Lambert. Shei Leun Wong spun on her heels and exited the tiny apartment.

He sat with his conflicted thoughts. Pulling off the hit was exciting, exhilarating, a primal rush. He was becoming more comfortable with it, which concerned him. He didn't want to lose his sense of self; he had to control his willingness to kill and not let it become an urge. What was his employer going to do, he wondered, now that he hadn't killed the girl? Had he passed or failed the test? His disconcerting thoughts gave him no peace.

After two hours of solitude in the safe house with no disturbance at his door, Diegert figured he could go hang out in a club for a while. Shei Leun's suggestion, Luna-Sea, was only fifteen minutes away, and the videos on his phone made him feel like he was holding the coolest party in town in the palm of his hand. A quick stop at an ATM put five hundred euros in his pocket. Twenty euros got him past the bouncer and to the coat check girl, who collected another twenty, even though he didn't check a coat. Entering the cavernous space of Luna-Sea, he was struck by the décor, which was a clash of new-age gauche and postindustrial distress. The pulsing beat of the electronic dance music permeated every space and penetrated every structure so that the music was not only heard but felt. Surveying the room, he looked beyond the gyrating bodies on the dance floor to see a group of East Indians gathered in a large booth in the far corner of the club. He also noticed a mixed group of young people hanging out in a smaller booth much closer to the dance floor.

Making his way to the bar, he had to wade through the crowd of dancers, some of whom were grinding their hips in tune with the beat, creating an erotic scene from which Diegert had trouble looking away. Without colliding into any of the randy couples, Diegert approached the bar and soon had the tender's attention. Gesturing to the unoccupied corner booth beyond the bar, Diegert said, "I'm going to take that booth. Please deliver a bottle of Grey Goose." Diegert's vodka request cost him two hundred fifty euros, but the order got the bartender to nod at the bouncer manning the posts and ropes. In the booth's minibar, Diegert found drink glasses, an ice bucket, and enough juice and soda mixers to keep the vodka interesting. After mixing his first drink, he looked up to see five young ladies lined up along the braided ropes like a murder of crows perching on a wire above recent roadkill. Diegert dispatched three of them with a wave of his hand. Pointing and then moving his fingers, he invited two of them into the booth.

The two girls' pretty faces degraded as they stepped from the inky haze of the club floor into the soft light of the booth. The one with short punky hair didn't say anything as she grabbed a glass and reached for the vodka.

Diegert quickly got his hand on the bottle so he could pour the pricey alcohol for her. Her eyes never left the glass as she swilled the drink without a mixer. The one with longer hair held out her glass saying, "Hey, I want some too."

Diegert held the bottle of vodka vertically. "Yeah, but you and your friend aren't staying." The long-haired girl looked at Diegert with desperate bloodshot eyes.

"What?"

"Get out."

Diegert nodded to the bouncer and watched as the big guy escorted them out of sight.

The night's big spender asked his waitress to tell the group crowded into the booth by the dance floor that the next round was on him. The news turned all heads Diegert's way, and he nodded and raised his glass.

Several of the women cast long glances at the dark-eyed, dark-haired man whose complexion was just a shade lighter than soft buckskin. His looks were intriguing and somewhat mysterious because he could pass for an Argentinian, Arab, or Italian. Women who liked dark, rugged men found him attractive, while others felt a sense of danger.

Diegert had mixed his vodka with orange juice, which made it easy for him to consume several quick drinks. Watching the dance floor, he was entertained by the thrusting hips and the back extensions of girls whose breasts were pressed outward and skyward as they undulated with their partners. He was mixing his next vodka with apple juice when he noticed a tall woman with a short skirt approaching the booth. Diegert nodded, and the bouncer unsnapped the rope, allowing her to pass.

She held a long-stemmed martini glass and lifted it toward Diegert. "I want to thank you for the drink. Everyone appreciated it, but I wanted to thank you personally." In the soft glow of the booth's lighting, Diegert was taken by the woman's beautiful Asian face. Her eyes were large, round, and brown and her cheeks dimpled when she revealed her perfect white teeth with a friendly smile.

"It looks like your martini is nearly empty. Sit down and let me fix you another."

Stepping into the booth, the beautiful lady sat next to Diegert, whose eyes couldn't help but notice the extra length of leg revealed as her skirt slid up when she sat down. The young lady offered her hand. "I'm Jung Hwa." Her hand was delicate but firm.

"I'm John Sullivan," Diegert said. "So what's in your martini?"

"Pineapple juice and cassis along with the vodka."

"I don't think I have any cassis, but I do have pineapple juice."

Gulping what was left in her glass and flashing an enthusiastic smile, Jung Hwa handed her glass to Diegert. "Do you live here in Paris, Mr. John Sullivan?"

"Please, just call me John, and no, I'm here on a business trip. How about you, are you in school?"

"Yes, I'm studying art at the Sorbonne. I'm from Seoul, my program will have me here for two more years."

Diegert handed her the drink. "Let me know if this tastes any different." Jung Hwa took a generous sip, and her eyelids widened as she swallowed her mouthful. Recovering from the surprise, she waved her hand in front of her mouth. "Whoa, it is very good."

"But it is much stronger than the one from the bar?" Diegert asked.

Jung Hwa nodded as she emptied the rest of her drink. Diegert refilled the glass again, going heavy on the Grey Goose.

"Is your business going well?"

"Yeah, today was especially good."

"What business are you in?"

"The stock market. I made a killing today."

"So now you're celebrating?" Jung Hwa raised her shallow glass and swallowed its contents in one gulp. As Diegert was mixing another, the music changed to a dance version of a popular song. Jung Hwa squealed with excitement. Diegert could see what she wanted.

"How about we get out on the dance floor?" he asked. Slurping down her refreshed drink, Jung Hwa grabbed his hand, leading him onto the crowded dance floor. As the floor filled up, Diegert could not deny the eroticism of the grinding hips that surrounded him. Jung Hwa faced away from Diegert as she backed into him, pressing her hips into his. Diegert picked up the rhythm and soon they both found the experience absolutely hypnotic. As the lyrics of the song faded away and the techno beat intensified, Jung Hwa turned to face him without reducing the contact at the hips. While they danced the coitus simularis, Jung Hwa leaned into Diegert's ear. "Get me out of here."

Out of the club, into the cab, and into her apartment in less than fifteen minutes. In that time Diegert had kissed the Korean beauty so enticingly that when the apartment door closed behind them, clothes were shed, and they recreated their carnal dance moves. In the bed, they found a passion neither of them had expected. Their libidos were driven by lust, and their bodies sought pleasure with a fervency neither had experienced before. Their intensity held up for nearly two hours until they fell asleep entwined in each other's limbs.

Diegert slept soundly until the sunlight streamed onto the bed, shining in his eyes. The sound of sizzling and a soft voice humming brought a smile to his face as he woke up. From the kitchen, the aroma of fresh coffee and eggs tantalized him out of bed. Poking his head into the small kitchenette, he got a smile from Jung Hwa, who wore a thick robe and had her hair tied in a bun on the top of her head. The glasses she wore gave her an intelligent look, which was, Diegert figured, probably well deserved.

"Good morning. Have you ever had gyeran mari?"

"Good morning to you too. No, I haven't. What is it?"

"It a Korean rolled omelet. You're going to love it. Do you want coffee?"

"No… I—I don't drink coffee."

She gave him the strange look he often received when he refused coffee. The caffeine dependent didn't trust the unaddicted and couldn't fathom why anyone would deny themselves the earth's most popular stimulant.

"Some orange juice, then?"

"Thanks," said Diegert as he poured himself a glass and looked over her shoulder at the rolled omelet cooking in the skillet.

"I like to make them for my guests. It's a little bit of Seoul right here in Paris."

As Jung Hwa lifted the finished gyeran mari from the pan to the cutting board, Diegert's gaze was drawn to the small TV across from him. The news broadcast grabbed his attention. On the screen, the police were lifting a dead body from the river. In the corner of the screen appeared a headshot of a young woman; it was Shei Leun Wong. Diegert nearly sprayed the kitchen with his mouthful of juice. He coughed loudly as he choked down the juice.

"Are you OK?" asked Jung Hwa.

Waving his hand and nodding his head, Diegert replied, "Yeah—yeah, I'm fine, but what's happening on the TV? I don't understand the French."

Jung Hwa had not been paying attention to the news but now focused for Diegert's sake.

"They're reporting that the body of a prostitute was pulled from the Seine this morning."

"Oh," said Diegert as his cheeks flushed. He didn't know how to respond, but Jung Hwa was looking at him curiously as she sliced the rolled omelet into pieces, revealing their concentric rings. The broadcast now displayed the anchorwoman speaking. Diegert concentrated on the television while Jung Hwa instinctively provided translation.

"They say there is some evidence that the woman pulled from the river may have been involved in a murder last night at the Chateau Lambert."

"Really?" said Diegert as a tingle of tension traversed his spine.

"Being a sex worker is so dangerous," observed Jung Hwa as she served Diegert a plate of hot, fresh slices of rolled egg with a filling of vegetables and cheese. Lost in thought, Diegert considered the unexpected news as he hungrily filled his mouth with the delicious gyeran mari.

He wondered if Wong had said something about him before being killed. Was whoever killed her now after him or was the employer simply accomplishing what he had failed to do?

"Whaddya think?"

The simple question confused Diegert as he continued looking at the TV's display of a well-dressed Gunther Mibuku. Did Jung Hwa know what he had done?

Realizing he was still engrossed in the TV, Jung Hwa clarified, "I don't mean about that. How about the gyeran mari?"

Diegert was embarrassed and relieved when he realized she was talking about her cooking and not his killing.

"This is the most delicious breakfast I've had in a very long time. I love the blend of the filling and the egg. The rolled-up slices make each bite full of flavor. I love it."

Diegert could hardly believe himself for being so effusive, but it refocused Jung Hwa away from the television.

"Well, thank you, I'm glad you like it."

They finished their breakfast together, and Jung Hwa told Diegert about her sister and two brothers in Seoul. She described to him the courses she was taking, and Diegert lied about his international business. Checking the time on his phone, Diegert said, "I've got a noon meeting, and then I catch a late flight back to the States, but I've really enjoyed myself, and if I could have your number, I'd love to see you again when I come back."

Jung Hwa hesitated and pushed her glasses up her nose before saying, "I will give you my number but no guarantee I will see you when you come back."

Recognizing the implications of their quickness to intimacy, Diegert replied, "Of course, I understand. There is no requirement here, but if you are available, I'd be happy to have dinner with you or tour an art gallery or anything else you'd like to do in Paris."

Jung Hwa's smile spread across her pretty face as her dimples tucked into her rosy cheeks, and she gave him her number.

12

Walking back to the safe house, Diegert received a message on his phone. His employer wanted another hit. The job was a Greek politician, Constantine Stavropoulos. The contract was worth fifty thousand dollars. The hit had to be public, preferably during a speech. The text on the phone directed Diegert to a secure website where the specifics on the job were laid out. In Athens, he would be put up in a safe house and supplied with a compact sniper rifle equipped with a remotely controlled automated sighting and firing system. He would be able to operate the weapon remotely carrying out the hit using his smartphone.

In the Gulfstream, on the flight to Greece, he discovered that Stavropoulos was giving two speeches in the next two days, then had no scheduled public appearances for the next four weeks. The first speech was in the atrium of a newly renovated hospital. The second was at a soccer stadium during a rally for the upcoming world cup bid. Greece wanted to host the soccer world cup tournament in four years. It seems they forgot all about the debt they still owed for the 2004 Olympics and the fact that the country was currently bankrupt.

Once he arrived in Greece, Diegert visited the hospital and checked out the atrium. It was a big space, but it was enclosed, and the vantage points to place the weapon were either too far away, requiring shooting through glass, or too close inside and would surely be observed. At the soccer stadium, a small stage was being constructed on the front steps. Across from the stadium and to the south was an apartment building whose roof proved to be an excellent vantage point. Thirty-six hours remained before the speech.

Diegert was very impressed by the rifle. It was a compact sniper design with a long barrel imbedded in a wooden stock. Since the rifle was designed to be operated remotely, the firing chamber made up the rearmost area of the unit. The triggering mechanism was pressure sensitive and operated by a servo. The sighting system fed digitally into Diegert's smartphone, from which he could control the weapon. The sighting and firing mechanisms were integrated, so when the rifle was in optimal firing position the trigger was engaged. Tiny movement sensitive gyroscopes detected and corrected subtle variances from the ideal firing position adjusting for wind or vibration. The feed to Diegert's smartphone allowed him to set the process in motion, but once it was engaged it couldn't be altered. On the secure website, there was a video game–style training program; Diegert used it to teach himself how to operate the system. After a few hours with the program, he was ready.

He wished he'd had such a system in Afghanistan. If the Army deployed this technology, a lot of American soldiers wouldn't be dead. Putting computers behind the rifles would not only have been safer but more effective.

The speech was scheduled for three p.m. Early that morning, Diegert was on the roof positioning the rifle. His employer was amazingly thorough, having included in the mission package everything he would need to pull off the positioning of the rifle. He used the digital sighting mechanism to aim at the point on the stage where his target would give the speech. He concealed the rifle in a foldout metal box that looked like an air conditioning unit. Only someone who knew the building well would be able to recognize that the box was a phony. Inside the box, he planted enough C-4 to destroy the rifle and all its components beyond recognition. He set up a pressure-sensitive wire mesh network on the gravel rooftop, fanning it out so that anyone who stepped on it would ignite the C-4 and destroy the weapon. After setting, concealing, and booby-trapping his weapon, he went and had a nice brunch at a café with a view of the Parthenon, up on the Acropolis.

At two p.m. a few early birds showed up, by two forty-five a crowd had formed, and by three p.m. Stavropoulos was late. No one was surprised or concerned except for Diegert. He wondered if Stavropoulos was even coming. *All the setup and training on the system, and if this guy doesn't show, I won't have another chance,* worried Diegert.

At three thirty Stavropoulos was introduced by the director of the local soccer federation as he walked onto the stage and started speaking. Having no idea how long his speech would last, Diegert wasted no time activating the system.

Diegert stood in the middle of the crowd and blended right in while he looked at his phone throughout the introduction. On his screen he saw the reticle squarely on the politician's chest. He engaged the system and instantly the rifle fired, hitting Stavropoulos. His chest imploded, and the bullet exited his back, ripping out his vertebral column. Lung tissue splattered the dignitaries behind him, and a quivering chunk of his heart fell onto the stage.

The panicked crowd stampeded. All video on his phone instantly disappeared, and his smartphone disconnected from the Internet. Diegert tried to ignite the C-4, but it wouldn't work. He left the crowd and returned to the safe house. The Web filled up with amateur videos of the hit, and Diegert stopped watching.

A few hours later during the police investigation of the shooting, they found the equipment on the apartment roof and triggered the C-4, destroying the weapon and themselves. Three officers were killed, and a building maintenance man was wounded. Diegert grew angry. Their deaths were unnecessary. He should've been able to detonate the C-4 remotely. Why was his employer disabling his phone? If he could have detonated the weapon, the police officers wouldn't have been killed.

His account now held a hundred and forty-five thousand dollars, but the unintended consequence of the police deaths weighed on Diegert's mind and forced him to recognize the violent risks he brought with him to an area of operation.

The disabled phone chirped back to life, displaying his next assignment, a hit on Mohammed Farooq Arindi, a financier of pirates in Mogadishu. The job was worth another fifty thousand.

Diegert replied beginning his message with: *Why was my phone disabled? I could have destroyed the weapon on the roof so no one else got hurt.*

Darkmass: *Your phone is obviously back to being operational, your concerns are tactical, not strategic.*

Next Chance: *What if I don't want to do this next job?*

Darkmass: *We'll turn you over to law enforcement.*

Pausing to consider the negative consequences of that, Diegert replied: *Where do I report for transport?*

The reply sent him to the commercial freight side of Athens International Airport, where he found the plane with the tail number NB7845. It was a large transport plane designed for freight—not people. His phone vibrated, and on the screen was the face of a man he had noticed when he'd first arrived. The instructions indicated he was to show the man the document now on the phone's screen.

The big, gray-bearded man said not a word to Diegert after inspecting the document. He walked him out to the plane, climbed up the back cargo ramp, and folded down a hard plastic seat from the wall.

"You'll sit here. Your parachute is right there."

The man slapped his hand on a large dull-green backpack that was affixed to the wall of the fuselage by some straps.

Adjacent to the seat was a door. "Pull the door latch. You'll have thirty seconds to jump before the door closes."

Diegert put on his best *no problem* face, but the bearded man's expression was doubtful.

"There's some printed instructions for the parachute in the outside pocket of the pack, and I'm sure you'll be instructed through your phone for everything else. Good luck to you." The man offered his hand. As Diegert shook it, he was informed, "This craft is airborne in twenty minutes."

His phone screen instructed him to lift the thin padding on the fold-down seat. There he found a large envelope with documents for his cover as a foreign aid relief worker. He was also instructed to inspect the contents of a duffel bag he found to the left of his seat. Inside he found a kit that included weapons, climbing gear, and tactical clothing. On the outside of the bag, three words were printed in black letters: "Duty, Honor, Mission."

In flight, he was instructed that on the ground he was to meet a man who would inform him of the target's vulnerability. When the job was done, this same man would drive him two hours away to a small airstrip, and he would be flown to Cairo. Arindi was the financier for the pirates of Mogadishu. He controlled the money by leading the negotiations for the ransoms, and Diegert's employer wanted him dead.

During the flight, Diegert familiarized himself with the parachute, since he had never used one before. His time in the Army included no airborne training. This being his first jump, he needed to learn what to do before leaving the plane. He remembered what his wrestling coach, Mr. Oliver, would say: *"Learn by doing."*

Two hours into the flight, Diegert found himself staring at the three words printed on the tactical bag: "Duty, Honor, Mission" Honor stuck in his mind, and he thought about his time in Afghanistan. On a night raid, his unit had invaded a family compound. Rousing everyone from bed, they'd gathered them outside in the courtyard. The tall, heavily bearded man of the house kept telling the interpreter that this was not being handled with honor. Lieutenant Prescott ordered that the house be torn apart to look for "evidence." Guns and money were found, but it wasn't what the lieutenant wanted. When he confronted the family man, the interpreter said the man was angry about what a dishonorable thing we were doing. Prescott hit the man across the face, knocking him down and shouting at him on the ground. The man went totally silent and argued no more. It was too dishonorable to argue and lose face in front of his family, so the guy shut down like an honorable man. The lieutenant ordered us to ransack the entire home. High moral standards of behavior, are you fucking kidding? This was war. You get honor for going to war and coming back, especially if it's in a coffin. But while you're there, while you're fighting, there was no honor in any of it. Honor was for the parades, balls, and barbeques back home, not the battlefield. Diegert had to ask himself, was there honor in what he was doing now? There sure weren't going to be any parades or barbeques. The thoughts annoyed him, and he turned the bag, so the words were no longer visible.

13

Crepusculous was the power behind the curtain, but the name on the front of the corporate curtain was Omnisphere, the world's largest private equity firm. The corporation was so massive that many of its holdings were publicly traded companies with their own stock market icons and board of directors. Brand names and companies that people use and interact with everyday fell under the broad umbrella of Omnisphere. Through its holdings, Omnisphere profited from energy, communications, agriculture, retail, insurance, financial services, entertainment, and health care. Through clandestine means, the huge firm also benefited from drug trafficking, arms sales, gambling, and money laundering. If there was a profit to be made, Omnisphere would develop a subsidiary to penetrate the market and gain advantage.

The face of Omnisphere was its CEO, Abaya Patel, an Indian-born, Harvard-educated businesswoman whom Klaus Panzer had personally picked to run the megacorporation for Crepusculous.

The board of Omnisphere was comprised of retired CEOs of the many companies that existed within the firm. It was an insular society that kept the business of Omnisphere powerful and private. Crepusculous, however, held the true power. Klaus Panzer and his three associates secretly and insidiously maintained control of all that Patel and the Board of Omnipshere were allowed to do. Panzer was a devout practitioner of the adage, "That which is unseen is the most powerful."

Abaya Patel received the meeting invitation from Klaus Panzer: *Thursday 2 p.m. Innsbruck,* as the summons that it was. In spite of her perch atop the world's largest corporate conglomerate, she felt like a naughty child remanded to the principal's office.

On Thursday at two p.m. Panzer anticipated her arrival at his home in Innsbruck, Austria. The mansion has thirty-five rooms on the shore of a private lake surrounded by a meadow at the base of a mountain. The building was divided into the residence and the business area. Panzer would receive Patel in his office, where he sat in the comfort of a leather chair at a massive oak desk. The wood-paneled walls featured the taxidermy conquests of his Alaskan hunting trips and African safaris. Through eyes of glass, the silent beasts peered with menace at the room's inhabitants. The fully maned African lion leaping from the wall above and behind the desk intimidated all but the strongest of hearts that sat across from Klaus Panzer.

Patel brought her admin assistant, her chief of counsel, and her COO with her. They waited patiently in the ornate foyer, which was furnished with a rich leather couch and a marble-top table with a massive bouquet of fresh flowers, and upon the walls hung the works of the German painters Hermann Anschütz-Kaempfe and Johann Jakob Dorner the Elder.

Seated on the edge of the couch, Patel recalled Panzer's manipulation of the Telexicon retirement fund problem four years ago. Telexicon was a holding of Omnisphere. Throughout the 2000s and up until 2012, the company was a major manufacturer of cell phones, the flip phone variety, with dedicated keypads and small screens. The phones seem quaint when compared to today's more versatile and powerful smartphones, but in their day, they were revolutionary and profitable.

As technology and the market changed, Telexicon was unable to respond, and the business languished. While losses mounted, Omnisphere stepped in to close the business. A review of the books revealed a tremendous debt obligation to retired workers of both Telexicon and its parent company, United Telephone. The retirees were entitled to payments and health care coverage equaling ten billion dollars per year. The fund had barely eight million dollars in assets. Corporate finance had been borrowing from the retirement fund to float the company against the losses. Omnisphere was going to feel this pain.

It was against this backdrop that Patel had first been summoned to the Panzer mansion. Abaya recalled how Panzer had greeted her with warmth and hospitality. His charming grace was disarming, and his confidence emanated more powerfully than his Clive Christian 1872 cologne. After making her comfortable, he asked her opinion of the Telexicon problem. He listened carefully as she described a plan to spread the pain across the broad business entities of the Omnisphere global portfolio, allowing the company to service the Telexicon debts.

Panzer, with his chiseled face, full sweep of gray hair, and penetrating ice-blue eyes, listened carefully and nodded agreeably throughout her monologue. She finished and waited for Panzer's response. The man cleared his throat, placed his elbows on the desktop, steepled his hands, then interlocked his fingers before thumping the leather desk blotter with his unifist. He informed Patel that he had a different perspective, which did not involve bailing out Telexicon. He instructed her to invoke the cellular financial model that Omnisphere had outlined in all corporate contracts. This clause allowed Omnisphere to sever any aspect of the conglomerate that was deemed to be no longer financially viable. Like a tree shedding deformed leaves or the human body sloughing off dead skin cells, Panzer was in favor of excreting the people of Telexicon and divorcing their debts from Omnisphere.

Patel protested, claiming they had a corporate responsibility to all the people whose lives were dependent on their retirement incomes. Panzer glanced away as he waved off the annoying gnat of a concern she had just expressed. He countered with a requirement that she was to fulfill his request, shed Telexicon, and report back to him in one week. His closing statement to her now reverberated in her mind. *"I can see this is going to be difficult for you but let me assure you the rewards will surpass the inconvenience."*

The dumping of Telexicon was a shit storm right from the start, and Patel was the face the media was given to hate. Panzer was right; the capability to leave the losses behind was built into the corporate agreements. It was legal, even though it impoverished thousands of retirees. Patel suffered the public's ire, the social media assault was brutal, and she was saddened by all the hurtful headlines to which her children were exposed.

The employees, retirees, and their families turned to her for help, and when she offered none, they turned on her like injured animals. These people had no chance to restart their careers and no safety net to keep them from drowning in debt. They had no lifeline, and their former employer didn't care. Following the "shed," Omnisphere posted one of their best financial years ever.

After facing the wrath of the public and the failed lawsuits brought on by opportunistic lawyers, Patel received a video from Klaus Panzer. The images displayed the most beautiful property in Europe, a villa on Lake Lucerne in Switzerland. The house was magnificent, the grounds immaculate, and the view spectacular. She sat transfixed by the serenity of the lake nestled within the surrounding Alps. She thought it was almost thoughtful of Panzer to send her this mini mind vacation after the hell she'd gone through for him. When the video ended, a deliveryman knocked on her office door and entered with a small tray in his hand. He stepped up to her and bowed, placing the tray within reach. On the tray was a small box upon which her name was embossed. She picked up the box, opened the hinged lid, and there lay a golden key. A card with the address of the lake house sat on a tiny velvet cushion. On the reverse side of the card, in scripted handwriting, it said, *Thank you and enjoy. K. Panzer.*

The house was hers. Had the rewards surpassed the troubles? Wasn't that why they paid the executives the big bucks, because they have to make the tough decisions? Business was business, and the objectivity of money didn't allow for the vagaries of the human condition. Those people would find a way, they always did, and the government bailouts would support them.

This rationalization played in Patel's head as she lifted the key from the cushion and hit replay on the video. Watching it a second time, she felt a surge of excitement to think this magnificent residence was now hers. Screw the guilt, savor the rewards. Patel booked the corporate jet to Switzerland for the next day. Panzer's seduction had corrupted her morals in a most delightful way. Patel relocated to Lake Lucerne and ran the business from the villa for the next six months, which was plenty of time for the Telexicon story to fade from the media's memory. Soon she was once again heralded as the world's most powerful executive, leading Omnisphere, the world's wealthiest company. She was the visible, public entity of corporate stewardship, assuring shareholders of profitability. Oh, how sweet was the success of corporate power.

Her palms were sweating as she wondered what Klaus Panzer would request of her this time.

After announcing her through the intercom, Panzer's administrative assistant, Marta, escorted Patel and her entourage into Panzer's office. She and her group stood quietly for a moment taking in all the animals. Panzer had grown accustomed to the pause his collection created in newcomers and sat quietly enjoying the head-swiveling effect of his trophies. After a moment, he rose from his seat. "Abaya, I'm so glad you were able to make it."

Panzer crossed in front of his desk to warmly shake her hand.

"Thank you, Klaus. Allow me to make introductions," Patel said as she turned to her people.

"Oh no, no, no, we don't have time for that. Marta, could you see to it that these fine folks are served refreshments and made comfortable in the foyer?" directed Panzer as he graciously extended his arm toward the door.

The three people, who considered Abaya Patel to be one of the most powerful people in the world, just had their perceptions adjusted by the person who was, in fact, the most powerful.

Patel's look of consternation was ignored by Panzer as he gestured for her to sit in a leather cushioned wooden chair under the head of a wildebeest. Craning her neck to inspect the ugly gray antelope, she took her place with some reluctance.

With feet on the floor and hips leaning on the front of his desk, Panzer began questioning her.

"Abaya, are you happy in your position?"

Offended by this direct and unexpected question, Patel answered quizzically, "Why, yes, I am."

"Good," said Panzer, "because we are about to embark on something truly remarkable."

Partel's confusion was now set in the wrinkle of her brow.

Panzer continued, "The financial sector of Omnisphere, at my direction, has developed a digital currency known as Digival."

"Yes, I am aware of it."

"Good. I want Digival to be in place and functioning even if, at first, it only has a very small penetration. I want it all set up so, when the economy is right and the dollar collapses, Digival will be the go-to currency for people concerned about the evaporation of their wealth."

"You're planning to profit from the financial ruin of the economy?" Patel said with a chuckle.

"Don't worry, you will too. With the system already in place and the public aware, a digital currency backed by the world's wealthiest corporation will be better than a government that is insolvent."

Realizing there was no jest in Panzer's proclamation, Patel said, "You really think you can change the world's monetary system?"

"I absolutely do, and you will help me. With banking, payroll, and payment systems already set up, we will make the transition during the time of crisis and recovery less disruptive."

"What crisis, and did you say payroll?"

"Yes, Omnisphere employees who choose to be paid in Digival will receive an automatic ten percent raise."

Patel looked at Panzer with a dropped jaw, which she quickly closed into a frown.

Panzer continued, "It will be a voluntary program, but with over five hundred thousand employees, I'm sure many will switch, and their success will bolster others. Digival will be seen as a haven for wealth, and people will be eager to transfer their finances rather than lose it all to a devalued dollar."

Patel now found herself snickering. "You really are going to pull this off."

"The world changes every day; we are just going to change the way money works for people. We launch Digival now, saturate the Web with information about how it's accepted at all the places people shop, and make transferring to Digival easy and worthwhile. We can offer a ten percent increase in the value of money transferred from dollars to Digival."

"You're making money out of thin air."

"We don't even have to print a thing, but you know as well as I that our vast holdings are more than enough to support this venture. Make no mistake about it; we will destroy the value of the dollar and replace it and all world currency with Digival."

"This is unprecedented."

"Thank you."

"That was not meant as a compliment; I'm concerned about all the fiduciary responsibilities we are taking on by trying to be the world's only currency."

"Abayya, I expect you will soon realize that the benefits of controlling the entirety of the world's money far outweigh the risks and responsibilities. We must think big. Consider all the inequities in the markets due to fluctuating currencies. How many times have we seen whole countries starving and struggling to survive because their money has inflated to worthlessness?"

"The US economy is the strongest in the world; you're not taking out some tin-pan despot!"

"Why must we bow to the United States, a country that is basically bankrupt and unable to pay its debts? It has no intention of paying what it owes. It arrogantly continues to borrow while dominating the planet with its mortgaged military."

"We draw a great deal of profit from the United States and have significant holding throughout the US," Patel said as she removed her glasses and, with a small cloth, polished the lenses.

"Of course, I know that, and we will continue to occupy the majority role in the US just like we have for the past two decades, but now we'll be supplying the currency. The old saying goes, 'Those who control the dollars control the men.' Please excuse the gender bias, but the new saying will be, 'Those who control the currency will control the world.'"

Patel, returning her glasses to the bridge of her nose, tilted her head forward, looking over them at Panzer, whom she considered brilliant, but this time she knew he was out of control.

The world's most powerful man hoped his words would get her to yield to his passion. Uncertain he had done so, Panzer made it plain. "Omnisphere will be the organization, Digival will be the mechanism, and you will be the competent, capable, trustworthy CEO orchestrating it all."

"And you will be back in the shadows calling the shots."

"I will remain discreet, but I have great faith that you will oversee the successful launch and eventual globalization of Digival."

"How is it that you are so certain the dollar will collapse?"

"The Crepusculous Board has a plan, which is being conducted on a need-to-know basis; therefore, I'm afraid I cannot tell you anything more."

"So I should just have faith that the four of you are doing the right thing?"

"Absolutely." Standing up and checking his Rolex, Panzer was ready to conclude the meeting. "I'll have finance get in touch with you, and I'm sure your associates are ready for your departure now."

Patel, realizing her audience with Panzer had just ended, stood and, after shaking his hand, headed toward the door. Her gaze caught the gleam of green eyes in the jet-black face of a snarling panther. The big black cat's sinewy body slunk around the leg of an overstuffed wingback chair. Gasping with a start, she reflexively pulled her hand to her mouth as a slight screech escaped. Turning, she saw a devilish grin on Panzer's face, who was so pleased to have frightened her with the unexpected placement of the rare and deadly panther. Patel, annoyed at being the source of his amusement, straightened herself as she exited the room.

14

After four more hours of flying, Diegert's plane made a gradual descent and his phone alerted him to prepare for the drop. He secured the duffel bag in front of him and the parachute on his back. Dressed in tactical clothing, he put on the helmet and stepped to the door. He thought about the fact that thirty seconds after the door opened was all he had to make his jump.

He pulled up on the latch, the door popped open, and the force of the slipstream sucked him out of the airplane. He tumbled and rolled while falling ten thousand feet above the most poorly governed country in Africa. The darkness and the rush of the wind disoriented him, but he was able to stabilize himself by extending his arms and legs. It was a strain against the force of gravity, but the extra surface area slowed his fall and stopped his rolling. With his right hand, he grabbed the release and pulled the cord. The chute unfolded and yanked him forty feet up in the air, or at least that's how it felt. He grabbed the lines above him, stabilizing his movements as he began descending at a gradual pace.

From his skyborne position, he saw a very dark earth below. In fact, he could see nothing below him at all. It was disorienting, because the lack of any distinguishing characteristics in any visual plane left him with only his internal balance system for an indication of which way was up.

As he struggled with his lack of orientation, a cold, wet mist plastered his face. Droplets of water condensed on his warm skin and clung to his hair and clothes. He was passing through a cloud.

When he emerged from under the bank of suspended vapor, his sense of orientation to the world returned.

Although he still had eight thousand feet to fall, he could now see lights below, and every minute he was able to see more and more distinguishing features of the earth's surface.

Soon the shoreline was clear, and the intermittent lights of Mogadishu twinkled, evidence of an urban population. Certainly nothing compared to the city lights of an American or European city, but it was his target from the sky. As he floated past Mogadishu, Diegert realized he would land in the desert northwest of the city.

Darkness distorted Diegert's sense of both speed and distance. He hit the rocky ground hard with both feet, and a gusty surface wind filled his chute and yanked him farther north. He struggled to pull the parachute down, but instead it dragged him through the scrub brush and thickets that dotted the sand and rock surface of this little piece of Africa.

While being dragged, Diegert undid the buckles of the parachute pack, and the wind ripped off the cloth attachment, sending him tumbling into a patch of thorny bushes. Watching his chute blow across the scrubland, Diegert was grateful he still had his duffel bag. He changed out of his tactical suit and put on his khaki relief worker costume. Following his compass, he hiked into town.

Diegert had never seen a place more chaotic and dangerous than Mogadishu. All the men and boys were armed, and his white skin attracted unsettling curiosity. Even the stray dogs were threatening. This city, which had endured decades of warfare and civil strife, was on the rebound—at least parts of it. Coastal areas of the southern section of the city were benefitting from foreign investment, with several new hotels being built by the beaches. The north, though, was under the control of al-Shabaab, an Islamic organization that was at odds with the Somalian federal government and used terrorism to advance its agenda. The northern part of Mogadishu hadn't changed much in the past twenty years, and Diegert's mission took him deep into an area known as Shibis, where conflict and tension hung in the air along with the stench of rotting garbage.

Although it was past ten p.m., he was to meet his contact in the dusty bar of the Hotel Curuba. This establishment catered more to the locals than international travelers, so Diegert's light-mocha skin, often the darkest in the room in Minnesota, looked as pale as the dingy white tablecloth in front of him. He was seriously questioning the wisdom of his contact in selecting this bar as their meeting place.

The contact's name was Charles, or at least that was his English name. Charles approached Diegert cautiously but quickly sat down and informed him that Arindi lived in the old Hotel Duprie, which, on the outside, looked dilapidated and uninhabited but inside was well appointed and comfortable. The structure had an enclosed inner courtyard, and every morning Arindi spent fifteen to thirty minutes quietly secluded in a private retreat enclosed by large palm fronds and tropical ferns. This is where he would be most vulnerable. Charles gave Diegert the address where he would meet him for extraction when the job was done. Their business concluded, Charles took a quick exit, leaving Diegert to the uncomfortable stares of the well-armed men chewing khat in the Hotel Curuba. Within minutes he realized it was time to leave.

The Hotel Duprie was heavily guarded in spite of its decrepit appearance. At night, though, so many of the men in Mogadishu were spent from chewing khat, that as guards they were worthless.

Diegert climbed the farthest outside wall of the four-story building, using the foldout grappling hook and strong paracord from his kit. On top of the roof, he changed into his tactical suit, ate a beef burrito MRE, and prepared to lay low for the night. The desert night was clear and surprisingly cold. Diegert put on a black tactical jacket and a dark knit hat. As he lay on an eight-foot slab of concrete set within the stone-covered rooftop, he could hear the barking of a distant dog, the crying of a hungry baby, and frequent bursts of automatic gunfire from guys he figured had more bullets than brains. In the short time he had been in this strained urban part of Africa, he had seen more abject poverty than he ever imagined existed. It made his American life, with its solid roof, public school, and clean running water seem like more than one should expect to be granted. To the west he could see the illuminated concrete skeletons of coastal hotels under construction. They represented a glimmer of hope for the future and a reminder that many would continue to be ignored in this tropically attractive yet tragic place. He never really slept but rested with his MK 23 pistol in his hand in case others sought to take in the depressing view from atop the Hotel Duprie.

In the morning, with his pistol holstered on his right and the Ojibwa knife on his left hip, Diegert crept to a position where he could see down into the courtyard. Arindi had women and children living with him. They talked and played on the balconies facing into the courtyard as the day began. Suddenly, the children were pulled back into rooms and the women cleared the balconies. Arindi emerged on the ground floor and strode around the courtyard, stretching his arms and legs. He followed a little path into the grotto of large green plants. Diegert seized his opportunity.

Dropping a rope into the courtyard, Diegert descended to the ground floor. Withdrawing his silenced pistol, he walked quickly down the little path. Inside the grotto Arindi had a water fountain making a peaceful bubbling sound. Where Diegert expected to find the financier of thieves sitting like a cross-legged Buddha, he found only empty space. From the right a tremendous force cross-chopped Diegert's forearm, knocking his pistol to the ground. Diegert was struck in the face with a powerful punch. Dazed and off balance, he was kneed in the gut, doubling him over. Arindi was strong and hit hard. Diegert anticipated the next strike and blocked it with his right arm. Using his left hand, Diegert grabbed Arindi's throat and squeezed with all his might. Diegert wanted to disable him, but he also wanted to keep him from calling for help. Grasping the antler handle, he drew his knife. Arindi grabbed Diegert's right arm with his left hand, and the struggle became a stalemate. Unable to fully ventilate, Arindi surprised Diegert at how powerful he remained. Diegert kneed him in the groin, and although the pain shone in his eyes, the African hung on to Diegert's arm. Diegert drove him back through the plants until he collided with the wall. Diegert smacked Arindi's head repeatedly against the concrete wall until the African's grip on the assassin's arm slackened. Yanking his right arm free, Diegert plunged the knife into Arindi's chest, forcing the inscribed blade up and dissecting the aorta from the heart. Blood poured out of the African financier's chest as he slumped forward into Diegert's arms. Arindi looked at Diegert as he was laid down, but the expression was so bewildering that the assassin had no idea of the dying man's final thoughts. Diegert made a quick video of the corpse and sent it to his employer.

Covered in blood, he went over to the water fountain to wash his hands and arms as well as rinse some of the blood off his sleeves. The water turned dull crimson as it mixed with the blood in the recirculating fountain. Diegert had picked up his pistol, put on his dark-brown facial distortion mask, and adjusted his dark knit hat when a piercing shriek blasted down from the balcony. He instinctively turned to the sound, seeing two women at the rail of the second floor overlook screaming and pointing.

Turning his face away, he quickly walked out the front door of the old hotel. Two lazy guards were surprised when this man in black walked out of the building they were supposedly protecting. The mask made his face look weird, confusing the two guards. Diegert shot the first one in the forehead. The second tried to raise his AK but failed when Diegert shot him in the chest and then in the face. Rounding the corner of the building, he moved briskly down the street. He grabbed a large white sheet off a laundry line, wrapping it around him in Mogadishu fashion.

At the address Charles had given him, Diegert found the door open. He knocked and stepped down the hall, expecting Charles to greet him. At the end of the hall, he turned the corner to see Charles's body seated in a chair with his severed head on the floor.

The hallway darkened as a figure blocked the light. Diegert didn't hesitate, firing two rounds down the hallway, which dropped a body at the door. The hallway lit up with automatic gunfire as Diegert backed into the opposite room hoping to find another door. Charles's wife and two children were huddled in the room. She looked at him with dread and simply pointed at the window. It had no glass but was a large square hole in the wall covered by a curtain. He climbed out the window, knowing the next men to enter that room would be getting the same directions. He ran down the alley, tucking in behind a large rain barrel. Peering down the alley, he saw three men exit the window. One turned and went in the opposite direction. The other two came his way. Placing a fresh magazine in his pistol, he racked the slide as he pulled back against the wall. He could see their long shadows preceding them as the morning sun shone from behind. When the head of the shadow crossed the plane of the barrel, Diegert rose up and fired into the face of the first man. The second was surprised, but he had been carrying his AK-47 at the ready and immediately pulled the trigger. The shots whizzed past Diegert, ricocheting off the barrel and pockmarking the walls. Squatting behind the barrel, Diegert fired his pistol low, shattering the Somali man's legs. As the thin, dark man crumpled to the ground, Diegert rose up and killed his attacker with a lethal shot.

With both men down and the whole neighborhood awake, he sprinted out the alley and onto the street. He had no idea where he was except that the ocean was to the east.

Everyone on the street was an informant, and Diegert knew he needed a safe place to hole up. He just kept moving, knowing that very shortly the whole town would be looking for him. Fortunately, the northern part of "The World's Most Dangerous City" had a lot of dilapidated buildings where a hiding place could be found. The trick was that each bombed-out building was fully occupied by the desperate residents of this city of despair.

The façade of the building Diegert finally found said only "OTEL" in sandblasted letters. He climbed to the second floor and found an unoccupied room. The sparse furnishings included an old couch and nothing else. He took some cord from a utility pouch and tied it to the door, running it around a bare water pipe in the corner of the room. He positioned himself behind the couch, removed his mask and the sheet he'd been wearing, and waited to see if his location had gone unnoticed.

Several hours passed, and Diegert's hopes to escape in the darkness grew. As he formulated a plan to exit the city at night, there was a delicate knock on the door. He pulled the string, opening the door and revealing a small boy with a bottle of water to sell. The boy was small and undernourished. Diegert could see he had recently skinned one of his knobby knees. He was dressed in baggy gym shorts and a T-shirt that read, "Denver Broncos, Super Bowl Champions." When the boy smiled, his lips revealed a pair of buckteeth and a lack of oral hygiene. Diegert smiled, though, to see the friendly little water merchant whose bright eyes expressed his hopeful anticipation of making a sale. As the boy stepped inside, a metal canister was tossed in. The explosion ripped through the room, tearing the door off its hinges and vaporizing the poor little boy. Automatic gunfire followed the explosion, and the room became a maze of flying bullets. The couch offered minimal protection as it was being torn to shreds.

Men entered the room, and Diegert took two of them down. He had to fight, or they would overwhelm him. Rolling across the floor, he grabbed one of the AKs. He fired out the doorway, driving back the attackers. From the window, he looked outside to see a Somali man on the back of a pickup truck with a mounted machine gun, known in Mogadishu as a "technical." The driver of the armed vehicle pointed to the window, shouting at the other man to fire his weapon. The man with the gun fired a series of staccato rounds through the open window and into the surrounding walls. Diegert ducked down as splinters of wood and chunks of plaster flew through the room. Suddenly, the rounds from the truck ceased, and gunfire again filled the doorway. Diegert returned fire at the room's entrance, looked out the window, and realized the gun on the truck had jammed. He quickly shot the man who struggled with the incapacitated weapon. Diegert leapt out the window onto a heap of garbage. The truck's driver struggled to get a pistol out of his pants pocket. Diegert struck the man in the face with the butt of the AK, grabbed him by his flimsy shirt, and dragged him out of the truck, tossing him to the ground. In the dusty road, the driver managed to extract his pistol, but not before Diegert perforated his chest with a spate of bullets. Off the dead man's belt, Diegert unpinned a grenade and tossed it into the second-floor room. Jumping into the technical, he sped down the street as flames and smoke exploded out the second-floor window.

15

Diegert drove the pickup truck, dodging donkeys, goats, merchant stalls, old men, and young kids. The lack of signage forced navigation by landmarks, Diegert using the ones that oriented him to the sea. Soon he was at a northern seaport in an area known as Abdiaziz. Decades ago, this port had welcomed Europeans coming to enjoy the fabulous beaches, tropical temperatures, and the beauty of the Indian Ocean. Today the port was home only to vessels that had been captured by pirates and brought there to be held for ransom.

Diegert drove along the packed sand track that ran parallel to the waterfront, then brought his vehicle to a stop. Doing a quick self-assessment, he wiped blood from a gash on his forehead, his ears ringing, and from a wound on his forearm, he extracted a small piece of white shrapnel. Inspecting the curious object drew the buck-toothed smile of the small water merchant across his mind as he realized he held in his fingers one of the little boy's front teeth. Diegert's stomach turned as he tossed the tooth out the window.

He was surprised at the variety of boats secured to the aging docks: cabin cruisers, fishing vessels, and sailboats with their masts removed. The boats and the entrances to the docks were occupied by thin Somali men with large weapons. Their hard stares made Diegert anxious, especially when they leaned toward one another, exchanging questioning gestures. As a white man driving a technical, he knew any interaction with these AK-47-wielding land pirates would be fatal.

Diegert continued along the waterfront until he came upon a sailing yacht with its mast still in place, beach headed away from the other boats. Two Somalis guarded the vessel. One was asleep on the sand. The other was grooving to the music in his earbuds. Diegert exited the truck and used his silenced pistol to allow the sleeping guard to enjoy permanent slumber. He stepped onto the yacht. The second guard was on the deck of the stern, dancing and singing as if the whole ocean was his audience. Diegert stood behind him, raised his pistol, and quietly used a bullet to end the distracted guard's career as an entertainer. The body landed with a splash.

Diegert stood still for a moment, relieved that he hadn't drawn attention to himself. Returning to the pickup truck, he tied the steering wheel with a rope and placed a rock on the gas pedal. The truck accelerated off the end of an ancient concrete break wall and plunged into the channel passage. Diegert quickly returned to the yacht. He pulled up the mooring lines and the sand anchors, started the engine, and quietly backed the vessel away from the beach. He knew there was a risk he would encounter pirates as soon as he left the port, but the alternative on land was no better. This mission's original extraction plan had gone to shit. He reasoned, however, that if any pirates attempted to take the yacht back, they were going to find out what it meant to defend a vessel by all means possible.

The power of the engine delivered him away from the port. His first priority being escape, he now realized he should check his fuel supply. Throttling the engine back, he went below for the first time. In the dining area next to the galley kitchen sat a gray-haired, weather-beaten old man. Diegert flinched when he saw someone else on board. The man's hands were bound and leashed to the table. A rag, tied around his head, gagged his mouth.

The old man's eyes went wide with surprise, and his startled look actually calmed Diegert, who could see the old guy was sizing him up. At six foot two and 190 pounds,

Diegert was lean, strong, and very fit. His black tactical outfit, with vest and boots, was dirty and sweat-stained. The old man's gaze lingered at the splotches of dried blood on his pants. Diegert needed a shave, but his dark stubble only made him appear all the more imposing.

He untied the rag. The grizzled guy made a series of awkward faces as he tried to bring comfort back to his lips. Diegert looked at him squarely. "Is this your vessel?"

"Aye," the old man said, looking at his replacement captor. "What now?"

"Now I go check the fuel."

The old man shouted after him, "The gauge is on the far right, near the anchor chains."

Returning from the engine room, Diegert told him, "There's less than half a tank."

"It'll be enough if we start using the wind." The old man lifted his tethered hands, yanking on the leash that held him to the table.

Diegert looked at him wearily. "What's your name?"

"Barnard Pinsdale, this vessel is the *Sue Ellen*. She's named after a beautiful girl I knew when I was young. I've been captive for five days. The fools think I'm rich, and they're hoping for money. What are you doing in Somalia?"

"Never mind."

Diegert knew he could not sail the boat himself, and this man didn't seem like a threat, yet he was hesitant to free him and allow him to take charge of the vessel. He went up on the top deck and looked out. The shore was receding, and all around was vast distance. The great expanse made him uncomfortable, and he realized he would need the old man's help.

Diegert freed the man from the tether and untied his hands. The old man rubbed his wrists as he slid out of the galley booth. He rose on wobbly legs, and Diegert could see the wiry man had a paunchy belly, but his forearms were taut bands of muscle under deeply tanned skin. The old man extended his weathered hand.

"You can call me Barney."

The two shook hands, but Diegert didn't offer his name. Barney held on longer than Diegert expected, but it had probably been awhile since the old man had been touched without violence. Barney shut the engine off and directed Diegert to drop the anchor.

"What? We've got to get out of here. We're not just going to sit here and let them come after us."

"Listen, darkness is falling; we'll keep our lights off. The winds are a doldrum; we can't sail. In the morning, we'll catch the warming winds and soon be far away from here. Besides, I haven't been in my bed for five nights. Now come over here and let me show you how to release the anchor winch."

The two men remained separate through the night with Diegert on deck and Barney stretched out on his bunk below.

As the sun rose, Barney directed Diegert on how to control the sails and handle the sheets, and soon the yacht was on a true course. With good wind and calm waters, the two passengers rode in silence as the boat delivered them away from a place they were happy to leave behind.

16

As the day passed, they traveled nearly a hundred nautical miles.

Barney commented to Diegert, "We're making good progress. The winds are being kind to us, and you sure are a quiet fella."

Diegert looked at him, smirked, and said nothing.

"So why won't you tell me what you were doing in Somalia?"

"I was doing hunger relief work."

"With which agency?"

"Ahh...the International Association for Hunger Relief," replied the younger man while continuing to look out at sea.

"Never heard of 'em."

Turning to face Barney, Diegert addressed his inquisitor. "We're a new agency, and I was doing the lead work of establishing relationships and securing facilities for our operations."

"How'd that go?"

"Not well. The Somalis are very short on trust and have long memories for disappointment."

"You sound like a do-gooder, you just aren't dressed like one. Speaking of hunger relief, let's eat."

Diegert's face lit up with the mention of a meal.

"When the Skinnys were here, they fed me uncooked pasta and raw canned meat."

"Well, what do we have now?"

"Now I'm going to cook it."

Barney stepped down into the galley. Diegert sat on the stairs. Barney got out the pot and pulled out a bag of egg noodles and a can of ALPO "Country Stew" dog food. The can had a picture of a handsome yellow lab, and Barney set it next to the noodles. He handed Diegert a large cooking pot. "Go fill this half full with water."

"From the ocean?"

"No, why don't you go pump some from the well?"

Diegert rose and returned with the pot half full of seawater.

Once the water was boiling, Barney put in the noodles.

"The Skinnys didn't like pasta. Of course, they never figured out you had to cook it. They tried it raw, and that's how they fed it to me."

"You never told them about cooking it?"

"I wasn't going to be their Julia Child. It's the small victories that help you survive being a captive."

"Who's Julia Child?"

Turning away in disgust, Barney checked the boiling noodles and used a can opener on the dog food.

"What's with that?" asked Diegert.

"This is our meat."

"That's dog food."

"Yeah, the Skinnys couldn't read; they took one look at the picture and thought it was dog meat."

The old man was laughing as he recalled the Somalis' reaction to the canned food.

"In fact, that's what they called me. They'd say, *"Hey, Dog Meat."*

Chuckling again, Barney drained the boiling water, mixed the contents of the can with the noodles, and returned the pot to low heat to simmer.

Diegert was incredulous as he watched the meal being prepared.

"Who's Julia Child? Come on! You don't even know the greatest chef to ever have a TV show. Why don't you Google her?"

Diegert pulled out his smartphone.

"I don't have a connection."

"Of course you don't. Your generation doesn't know shit. You think intelligence is being able to manipulate technology. You know how to look stuff up, but you can't remember a thing. You've traded knowledge in your head for gigabytes in your hand, and when your technology fails, you're left with a brain that ain't worth shit."

Diegert wasn't listening; he was torn between the rumbling in his stomach and the realization that the only relief of hunger was Barney's canine cuisine.

"I cook, you clean." Barney handed Diegert a plate of warm, tender noodles in a rich, beefy gravy with generous portions of cubed meat and finely chopped vegetables. With a shake of Parmesan, it actually tasted good, and Diegert eagerly emptied his plate and looked up for seconds.

"One serving is all you get. There is no more."

Barney finished his meal and pulled out an old disc player. He put in a CD, pressed a button, and a symphony of music came forth from the speakers. He leaned back, closed his eyes, and waved his hand with his index finger pointed as if he were conducting the musicians. Diegert listened to the classical music and felt like he was at the movies with no movie. Even though Barney was enraptured, Diegert asked, "What kind of music is this?"

Barney, pulled from his reverie, said, "You don't recognize this?"

"No, I never listen to this kind of music."

With a critical scowl, Barney informed Diegert, "This music is the most beautiful and complex in the world. All modern music owes a debt of gratitude to this work."

"Oh, come on, all music?"

"Yes, the work of Mozart revolutionized the way music was written, played, and appreciated, such that any musician who does not recognize his contributions to the art form has no sense of historical significance."

The symphony hit a high note just as Barney concluded his statement. The musical accompaniment to the diatribe spewed forth by Barney forced Diegert to feel the impact of his words with a silencing effect. He struggled to say only, "OK."

As Diegert literally licked his plate, he watched Barney close his eyes and return to conducting Mozart's Symphony no. 1 in E-flat Major. Diegert wondered if he would one day like this music when he was old. His mind wandered to another question, though, and he interrupted Barney again: "Hey, what happened to your dog?"

Opening only one eye, Barney replied, "I've never had a dog on board the *Sue Ellen.*"

"You mean, you meant to eat the dog food?"

"It's way cheaper."

Diegert couldn't hide his disgust as he gathered the dirty dishes and went below.

"Use seawater for washing. Don't waste any fresh."

Barney sat on the deck as the sun, augmented by Mozart's symphony, slowly set.

After cleaning the kitchen, Diegert came back on deck.

"Night watch," said the old man. "We've got wind tonight, so we'll each take a six-hour shift, during which it is your responsibility to maintain course and report any equipment problems or severe weather changes. I'll go first, so you go below and get some sleep."

Diegert went belowdecks and found two berths. One had obviously been used by Barney, the other had become a repository for junk.

Diegert moved the boxes of canned dog food as well as various towels and tarps covering the old mattress upon which he was going to sleep. Once he was lying on the mattress, he found it very uneven and uncomfortable. Getting out of the bed, he pulled up the mattress, uncovering a case. It wasn't his business to know what was in the case, but the latches gave way with a soft snap. Lifting the lid, he could see black foam formed into the outline of a rifle stock. Other areas of the foam were specifically cut out for the barrel, ammunition magazine, and a high-powered scope. Encased in foam on the top of the lid were two pistols with sound suppressors as well as more mags of ammo. Diegert looked at the arsenal and thought again about Barney Pinsdale and the Somali pirates. Could this set of weapons have belonged to the Somalis, or was Barney something more than just a wandering sailor? He closed the lid facing the same storage difficulty that led to it being stored under his mattress. There was nowhere else to put it. He set the case on the floor and piled the tarps, towels, and boxes of food on top of it. He stretched out on the old mattress and put his head on the dirty pillow, and even though he had made this perplexing discovery, he was so fatigued that he instantly fell asleep.

The *Sue Ellen* had made its way into the commercial shipping lanes, which were the best routes through the ocean. The ships sought efficiency in their transit, and corridors through the ocean could become busy and dangerous places for smaller vessels, especially at night. Barney had the *Sue Ellen* outfitted with solar-charged lights on the bow, stern, and atop the main mast so that she could be illuminated all night long. This was an appropriate precaution, but it also presented a risk. Pirates traveled without lights and finding a lit vessel at night was easier than searching through the day. All day while they sailed, Barney had known they were still in dangerous waters but had hoped for the best. In addition to the wind and the weather, Barney was keeping his ears alert for the sound of any approaching outboard engines.

After six hours, Barney's watch had passed without incident. Below in the cabin, he woke Diegert and waited up top to review the change of the watch. Diegert found it hard to wake up; he could've easily slept longer. At the top of the stairs, he was impressed with how dark the night was. He could see by the light from the boat's illumination, but otherwise the ocean was a very black place on this moonless night.

"The winds are light without much variation, but we're still making progress under sail. Keep the tiller within the range I showed you, and we'll stay on course. Not many stars out tonight, so just hold the line."

"Right."

"One last thing, lad, keep an ear out for sounds of motor engines. If you hear the running of an outboard engine, I want you to wake me."

"Why, what is it?"

"We're still in pirate waters. They cruise around in skiffs. You can hear them before you can see them. These devils are smart, though; they've learned to muffle the engines very well. If you hear something, wake me up."

Sitting alone on the deck in the dark, Diegert looked suspiciously into the blackness, imagining approaching pirates. Over time, this gave way to thoughts about his family. His father and brother didn't garner much reflection. He knew they were in the middle of deer season, hunting every day and spending every night at the Moose Jaw, drinking too much beer and talking too much bullshit. His father never took him deer hunting. Excluding him was the highest form of rejection in northern Minnesota.

His mother would be working long, hard hours at the Triple Crown Diner. Taking orders, serving meals, and cleaning tables, she had to do it all, and she only knew one speed, full bore and wide open. She worked herself so hard so that she didn't have time to think about a different life. She's the one who would be missing him. She would be thinking of him, and it hurt that he hadn't talked with her in such a long time.

Diegert had never met his grandmother, but he knew she'd been raped by a white guy, and that's how his mother was half Ojibwa. Denise was born but not accepted by the Ojibwa as a true native. As she grew up and went to school, the white kids called her half-breed and treated her like shit. After high school, short, fat, bald Tom Diegert asked the tall statuesque but socially crippled beauty to marry him, and she did. Her own mother, David's grandmother, had committed suicide years before, so she was alone at the Justice of the Peace ceremony. She moved into Tom's dump of a house, and within a few weeks, she had it cleaned up, painted, and looking pretty good, even though the small two-story house lacked an efficient furnace and any real furniture.

Physically, she was out of his league. From time to time, he would have to take the joking insults that flew around the Moose Jaw. The guys called him "chief" and asked if his "squaw" was good in bed. He would drink away the embarrassment and go home to fuck her with anger. Eventually, she got pregnant and Jake was born to grow up looking just like his dad.

She would like being out on this boat. She had never seen the ocean, but every vacation he had spent with her was a camping trip. Just the two of them, hiking or canoeing to a remote, beautiful place in Minnesota's Boundary Waters. They would set up camp, and only after she had done the work of making their site homey would she sit down and relax. She would say, *"It's a real vacation when it's cheaper to be away than it is to stay at home."* Spending time with her in the wilderness, he'd developed an appreciation for independence. He learned a lot from his mother, and although not all the lessons were good, he found in her a person he knew loved him and took pride in his accomplishments.

What would she think of what he was doing now? Killing people and running away. Grief rose up in him and made him feel as dark and lonely as the ocean was without light and seemingly without end. He thought about those he had killed, both the targeted and circumstantial. He wanted to shed the tears he felt were forming behind his eyes, but they wouldn't flow. He couldn't find a way to release the guilt for his violent acts, and therefore he retained the pain in his soul. It was a long, dark, lonely night, and Diegert began to fear that the night and his life were becoming indistinguishable. An assassin lived a sad and singular life.

Six hours later, Diegert's watch ended without incident and with a beautiful sunrise.

Barney's disheveled hair and sleepy face appeared in the stairwell.

"Well, we survived another night," Diegert said, greeting his shipmate.

"Survival—your generation doesn't know shit about it," Barney replied as he continued up the stairs onto the deck.

In a mocking voice, the old man began, "Oh my God, I survived college, or I don't think I will survive the holidays. What bullshit. You people mistake effort and a moment without complete comfort as something to endure. You think it's a great virtue to have succeeded where there was very little chance of failure and absolutely no threat to your life."

Diegert caught Barney's wrinkled stare and looked away from the old man's scorn.

"Come out here," Barney said, sweeping his arm out over the ocean. "No grocery store, no police, no hospital…no fuckin' Internet, and then you can talk about survival."

Diegert looked at the exasperated old man and waited to see if he was finished. He gazed across the empty horizon, then brought his eyes back to Barney's, saying, "Yeah… Like I said, we made it through the night. What's for breakfast, Milk-Bones?"

Barney pulled from his pocket a foil-wrapped Wild Berry granola bar and tossed it to Diegert.

"Eat your fruit. The Skinnys stole all my oatmeal and sold it to some guy to feed his donkey."

With breakfast over, Barney set a large plastic bucket on the deck. From behind the door of the cabin, he pulled a toilet seat and placed it on the bucket. He dropped his pants and sat down.

Diegert's expression couldn't hide his surprise.

"I've seen you piss off the stern, but this is where you shit." Barney leaned to the side and tapped the toilet seat, "And this is a luxury. I expect you to appreciate it."

Before long, a whiff of the wind told Diegert the old man was done and it was his turn.

Barney informed him, "Make sure you clean it when you're done."

"I gotta clean your shit?"

"I'm the captain. This is my home. I'm very comfortable out here. Clean the rags too."

"Rags? You mean there's no toilet paper?"

"No."

A short time later, the bucket was clean, the toilet seat was on its door hook, and two rags were drying in the wind.

17

And so it went for several days. Diegert withstood Barney's criticism of his generation and ate dog food while the old man taught him about life at sea and how to sail. Diegert fleshed out his lie about the relief agency he worked for, but he felt that Barney was not convinced. As the days passed and they crossed great stretches of ocean, Diegert found himself humming to Mozart and developing a bit of trust in the old man. On an evening following a particularly tasty dinner of ALPO "Prime Beef Cuts," Diegert decided to share the truth with him.

"I'm not a relief worker."

"Well, that's a relief, because I've been wait'n for a helicopter to drop a crate of food and old clothes on us."

Diegert's eyes turned to the old man as he fought the urge to curl his lips into a smile.

"So now you're gonna tell me what you really are, besides a liar."

"The truth is as fluid as this ocean," Diegert said, gesturing with a wave of his hand over the gunwale.

"Just like the wind and the water are taking us northwest," said Barney, "the truth is the only thing that's going to get you through this journey."

Diegert looked at the old man, realizing that the isolation of the ocean and having to rely on each other allowed him to relieve himself of his secrets.

"I was a soldier in the Army, but it didn't work out, and I was dishonorably discharged. Then I got a job as a bouncer at a bar in Austin, but that didn't go so well either, and... I ended up killing two guys."

"Murder or self-defense?"

"Definitely self-defense. I had to escape, so I went on the darknet and found a job as an assassin."

"Dare I ask, what is the darknet?"

"It's an underground network on the Internet. It uses software originally developed by the US Navy called Tor to keep information private and anonymous. I loaded the Tor software on my phone, got on the darknet, and replied to a posting looking for someone to do a two-part job. One hit in Miami and the other in France. A clean job in Miami got you a free flight to Paris on a private jet. No airport security on either end. It was just what I needed, and I was relieved when I got an immediate response."

"Wait a minute, you decided to become an assassin after killing two guys in self-defense?"

"Look, it was self-defense, but the guys were mobsters and there was no going to the police. I had to get out of Austin, or I would've been killed. I completed the job in Miami and hopped on the plane to Paris. From there it was a job in Athens and on to Mogadishu."

"Hold on a second, you were all alone on the flight from Miami, no one to explain anything or brief you regarding the next mission?"

"Well, there was a flight attendant. Her name was Amber, and she was gorgeous. She provided food and drinks and was very happy to talk with me. She asked the right questions and didn't question any of my answers. As the flight continued, she told me she would like to have sex with me and that the cabin at the back of the plane would be an ideal place for us to be together. We went into the cabin, with its huge bed, and she started undressing, and so did I. She stepped over to me completely naked. I wrapped my arms around her and hugged her and we had sex." Diegert grinned as he quietly dwelled on the memory.

"Whoa, whoa, whoa...you can't stop there. You're talking to guy who hasn't been with a woman for months and months."

"Months? Come on, you look like a guy who hasn't been with a woman for years and years."

Barney's face hardened as they looked at each other. Diegert realized he'd crossed a line, but he didn't care. "Oh, wait, I wasn't thinking about women who get paid."

"It's true that female companionship has become a commodity in my life, but it has only been a matter of months, not years, since my last transaction."

"Whatever... Amber was beautiful. Sometimes you fuck the girl, other times you get laid. Amber was an erotic artist. She had me feeling pleasure like I had never felt before. She had the right pace, fabulous rhythm, and she performed pleasurable acts in ways I will never forget. The sex was incredible, and when it was over, she lay down next to me and hugged me. She kissed my neck, and I began to sob. She said 'shh' in my ear, and I started crying like a baby. She said, 'There, there, just let it out, don't be embarrassed, just let yourself cry.' I cried uncontrollably for a long time. All the killing, all the running, all the looking over my shoulder every minute just built up until I couldn't take it anymore. Being up that high with such a beautiful woman on a clean, soft bed, I just had to let it out. She was so soft and warm; I was able to find peace like I hadn't for weeks. She never asked me to explain what I was feeling; she just used her body to comfort me, and in the state I was in, it was better than the sex. I fell asleep and had the deepest rest I'd had for weeks. When I woke up, she was still there. She told me we would be landing soon and that she hoped I would always be able to find peace when I needed it. I thanked her for giving me what I needed when I needed it. She slipped on a robe and left the cabin."

Barney blinked his eyes several times before turning and looking up at the sky. "I don't know if that is the sexiest or saddest story I've ever heard."

"Let's keep it private. It was a very personal thing, and it taught me a lot about coping with this life."

"Whaddya you mean?"

"Killing for a living. It takes an emotional toll for which you must atone, or you'll go crazy. Other guys just bottle it up and try to be tough, but they will emotionally implode. They drink too much and become very sanctimonious and judgmental. I've seen it in the Army. When you kill someone, you hurt inside. You know it's wrong on many levels, but you justify it; even if the circumstances require it, it's wrong and it hurts. If you let that out and express the grief, you can process it and move on. Letting it out allows me to continue."

"You sound like a priest trying to sell the confessional."

"I've never been in a confessional."

"Maybe you'll get the chance someday. But crying is what helps you?"

"It's the coping mechanism I discovered with Amber at thirty thousand feet."

"Look, that was quite a bedtime story. I'm gonna let you take first watch, and I'll see you in six hours."

18

Barney went below to sleep and Diegert stood on the deck looking out into the inky blackness. Diegert kept himself from falling asleep by pacing around the deck. The pacing also kept the chill of the night from penetrating his cotton T-shirt. After two hours Diegert heard the low rumble of an engine. He looked out to sea in spite of the futility of searching the darkness. The sound was growing closer, but he had no idea from which direction. He stepped down into the cabin to wake Barney. He gently shook the old man's shoulder. "I hear an engine."

The old man's eyes opened with an expression of dread. "Let me speak with them."

"What? Let's kill the fuckers before they even get on the boat."

"They're already on the boat."

At that moment Diegert heard footsteps along the gunwales, and then men were shouting in Somali as they descended into the cabin. Armed with AK-47s, they poked the barrels into the chests of the two sailors, forcing them up on to the deck. The pirates went about the business of taking over the boat as if it were so very routine. Diegert was ready to snap. None of these skinny guys looked like they could withstand even one body blow, let alone the kind of strike combinations he would deliver. It was as if they expected no resistance.

"Just remain calm. They may not take anything or find us very interesting."

"These guys are pussies. Let's kick ass."

"Oh no, you don't. You start a fight with them, and they will simply scuttle the whole boat, leaving us without even a life raft."

"Bullshit."

The Somalis shouted for them to stop talking. There were three pirates on board and three more in the skiff. The small size of their open-hulled, rundown old boat surprised Diegert. It wasn't more than ten feet long, and Diegert wouldn't have wanted to cross a Minnesota lake in that thing, let alone the Indian Ocean.

One of the pirates went belowdecks and searched for valuables. The other two stayed above and kept their AK-47s in their hands. The pirate belowdecks let out a loud ululation and rejoiced for whatever he had found. The pirate guarding Barney shouted down to him, and when the other pirate shouted back, he couldn't stop himself and went down below. The single pirate on deck was also distracted by what was going on below. Diegert seized the moment. He elbowed the pirate in the chest, bashed him in the mouth, grabbed the back of his head, and drove his face into a cleat on the mast, splitting his cranium on the rigid piece of metal.

Barney motioned for Diegert to stop, but the younger man stripped the AK off the dying pirate and descended into the cabin. The two pirates belowdecks were so amazed with the case of guns they'd found that, when they turned to see who was coming, Diegert struck the first one with a buttstock to the face. The second received a hand blade strike to the larynx. Both were dazed, and Diegert wrapped the strap of the AK-47 around the first guy's neck and backhauled him over his shoulder. The force of the maneuver broke the pirate's neck, and Diegert knew it when he heard the vertebrae snap. The second guy was coughing and struggling to breathe. Diegert noticed a knife on the man's belt. He grabbed the man's knife, slashed his throat, and plunged the blade into his chest. The pirate crumpled to the floor as blood bubbled out of his neck.

Three down, three to go. Diegert took the AK-47s and ascended the stairs. He tossed one to Barney and proceeded to the stern where the pirate's skiff was tethered to the *Sue Ellen*. The men in the skiff were confused by the commotion on board. Diegert took full advantage of their lack of communication and their expectation that sailors wouldn't fight back to open fire with the AK. The volley of bullets cut down two while striking the legs of the third.

With the dull illumination of the stern safety light, Diegert could see the third man was wounded, having fallen onto his back in the boat. Diegert's weapon had a flashlight taped to it. Turning it on, he could see the remaining pirate better. The guy was young, maybe fifteen or sixteen, yet he had a rifle and was pointing it in Diegert's direction. The defender of the *Sue Ellen* hesitated to see if the boy made any gesture of surrender. When the wounded pirate leveled his barrel at Diegert, he sealed his fate. With a rapid burst, the young sea robber's life ended with bullets to the chest and head.

From the moment the second pirate went down into the cabin until the last shot was fired, barely two minutes had passed, and six lives had ended. Diegert's adrenaline was on full blast, and he was still on point, making sure there were no other threats.

"Relax," said Barney. "They're all dead and we're OK."

Diegert stepped back for a better look at the skiff where he saw no evidence of life. Barney looked down into the cabin. It was a bloody mess with the two bodies heaped upon one another. He sat down on the bridge with slumped shoulders. Diegert came up along the portside and stepped into the cabin entrance to stand next to Barney.

Neither man knew how to begin the conversation. Diegert thought some statement of gratitude from Barney might be in order, or at least an "ataboy." He knew Barney had wanted to handle it differently, but this outcome allowed them to continue their trip without interruption. Barney stood quietly as his breathing returned to normal.

"Well, lad, you certainly know how to handle yourself. I have never seen a man use violence with such precision and speed. Maybe I'm just getting old, but I could barely see what was happening, let alone assist."

"It's how I've been trained."

"Well, apparently you haven't been trained to follow orders. I'm angry that you disobeyed me," said Barney, stepping onto the deck to look Diegert in the eye. "I'm the captain and I run this ship. If I tell you to do something, or not to do something, I expect your compliance."

Diegert let out a long sigh and chose his words carefully. "I will obey your orders. I'm sorry to have disrespected your authority."

Barney looked at Diegert, quite taken aback by such a humble reply. "We've got a mess to clean up, and we may still face consequences, so let's get busy before the sun rises. I'll keep the sails set so we can ride these winds as fast as possible."

Diegert dragged the bodies up from the cabin and laid them on the deck. He also moved the pirate from the base of the mast so all three were lined up together. Barney boarded the skiff and found fuel, weapons, and ammo, as well as grenades, food in the form of dried fish and coffee, fresh water, and a battery-powered drill with a huge bit on it. In the pocket of one of the men, Barney found a satellite phone. He and Diegert transferred the items to the *Sue Ellen*.

"We have to perforate both the chest and the abdomen of each man so the bodies will sink," Diegert said. "I have the knife that one of them was wearing. I'll do the job and jettison the bodies." Diegert went to work. He stripped them naked, viewing the tattoos and scars on each man. These bodies had not had easy lives but were now committed to the sea and on their way to the bottom of the Indian Ocean. All the clothing, worn out and tattered, was placed in a bag and sealed so it had no air. It was then tied to the outboard engine, which Barney and Diegert, both standing in the skiff, removed and sank.

"What about the boat itself?"

Barney hoisted the heavy drill. "We'll scuttle it. That's what this is for. If a vessel gives them trouble, they drill holes below the waterline and soon the boat is a relic on the ocean floor. So we'll put holes in the vessel of these devils and send it to the bottom along with everything else we've sunk."

Diegert took the drill from the old man, saying, "I'll do it, you climb back on board."

Wearing a life vest and tethered to the *Sue Ellen,* Diegert started in the stern and put several holes through the hull of the skiff. Soon the whole boat was underwater, and Barney cut the rope. The craft made a slow descent, fading out of sight.

As Diegert watched it sink, the image of the last pirate to die played across his mind, a boy who should've been in high school. Then the face of the little boy blown up in Mogadishu appeared in the placid water, haunting Diegert with his toothy smile.

Diegert hauled himself up the tether and back on board the yacht. As the sun rose, the only remaining signs of the night's events were the bloodstains. Barney and Diegert spent the morning quietly cleaning the bloody splotches off every part of the *Sue Ellen.*

19

Breakfast was more granola bars, and Barney supplemented his with Somali dried fish. They both appreciated the coffee, hoping the caffeine would supplant the lack of sleep. With their course set, Barney picked up the satellite phone. "This phone is GPS equipped, so they could be tracked as well as being able to communicate while on the ocean. I have no idea if they communicated what was happening out here. When I found it in his pocket it was on, but who knows if a call had been placed."

"Check the record on the phone?"

Barney had that look of technology ignorance that defines people of different generations.

"Let's have a look." Diegert took the phone from Barney. "We used these phones in Afghanistan."

Pressing the keypad, Diegert brought up the phone's call history. "Look, they placed a call shortly before midnight, and that was the last one."

"Midnight would make it just before they came aboard. So their cohorts on land know they encountered a vessel. Hopefully they didn't get our name."

"So what if they did? They couldn't catch up to us."

"No, but they could task another skiff to come looking or they could use an aircraft."

"Aircraft?"

"Yes, all that money they get for ransoms buys old airplanes so they can patrol the skies and direct their skiffs more efficiently."

"I can't believe they are that sophisticated."

"Why not? The ransoms corporations pay to get their cargo ships released are in the tens of millions. That kind of business attracts a lot of very smart criminals; please don't be so naïve. You must realize your violent actions may not be the end of our troubles."

"Throw it in the ocean so they can't track us with the phone."

"The phone has been off since I found it."

"You can turn the phone off, but the GPS will still connect with the satellite. Bottom line, the phone can be tracked."

"Very well, then." Barney snapped open the phone, pulled out the battery, and tossed the device overboard. "Now we are in a race to the Red Sea."

Barney got out a map and showed Diegert where they were and where he felt they would be safe. "It'll be about two days of sailing to round the Horn of Africa and enter the Gulf of Aden. Pirates operate in the gulf, but the US Navy has a very big presence. I think we'll be safe. To sail across the gulf will take another day, and then we'll enter the Red Sea."

Diegert reviewed what was described on the map and nodded with understanding.

"We've got a good wind coming up. Let's unfurl the jib and really capture its strength."

When the jib sail was fully engaged, the *Sue Ellen* flew across the ocean faster than Diegert had yet experienced.

When duties returned to refinement and adjustment of the sails, Barney asked, "So you told me about leaving America because of killing two men, and last night you killed six. When was the first time you killed a man?"

"The first thing I ever killed was a frog. My dad was a hunter. He was always hunting, with deer season being the most important. My older brother, Jake, and he would go on hunting trips all the time. When I was seven or eight, I begged him to take me hunting. He got out a BB gun and we went frogging. We waded into ponds and waited for their big-eyed heads to surface. My dad shot the first two, right between the eyes. They just floated there dead for him to scoop up in a net. He handed me the gun and reminded me to only shoot big ones."

"Sounds like a good old American bonding experience."

"Yeah, we spied one that was big enough, and I sighted the gun on the head and fired the tiny metal BB, hitting the frog but not killing it. The frog started flopping around, splashing in a circle. My dad was quick with the net and scooped up the frog, which entangled itself in the net."

"We waded ashore, and I could tell he wasn't happy. He stepped over to a big stone in the woods and said to me, 'Now you have to finish him.' I cocked the BB gun. He said, 'Not with a BB.' I looked up at him confused about what he meant. He said, 'Whack his head on the stone.' He handed me the net. I untangled the frog and could see that I had hit him on the side of the head near his circular ear, debilitating but not fatal. I held the frog by the legs and looked at my dad, who made a powerful downward thrust with his fist."

Diegert demonstrated by forcefully slapping the back of one hand into the other.

"The stone had a jagged edge. I raised the frog over my head and brought him down as hard as I could. When the frog struck the rock it started screaming." Diegert paused. "You'd be surprised at how frogs can scream. The sound was shrill, and the pitch turned my stomach. I started crying, and my dad told me, 'He's suffering, boy, you've got to finish him.' Through my tears, I struck the frog on the rock again and again and again until his screaming stopped, and his body went limp."

Diegert's face was sallow, his head and shoulders slumped, and he couldn't meet Barney's eyes.

"I dropped the frog and turned away from my dad, choking back my tears. I swallowed the pain and wiped my tears on my sleeve. 'Quit cryin' like a girl,' my dad said, 'we gotta clean these frogs.' I picked up the frogs, and he showed me how to clean them, cutting off their legs and stripping the skins. We ate them that night, and my dad never took me hunting again."

"Were you disappointed about that?" asked Barney.

"Yeah, but I learned what I was capable of and how I would react."

"Whaddya mean?"

"I mean, I was capable of killing, but it hurt. I could do it, but I'd feel it," Diegert said forlornly.

"But the feeling didn't stop you."

"I wanted to go hunting because I wanted to be with my dad. Killing frogs wasn't really what I was after. I figured the killing would be fine. He and Jake killed animals all the time. I was unprepared, though, for my emotional reaction to the struggle and suffering of something that's trying to hold on to its life."

"The fight for survival," spilled almost absentmindedly from Barney.

"Absolutely, the desperation and despair that even a frog experiences all because you chose to kill it. It's tough, but if you deal with your emotions, you can get through it and continue."

Diegert looked at Barney, who held his gaze while pressing him with his next question.

"What about the first man?"

"The first time I ever killed men was those two guys in Austin."

Barney's eyebrows rose as he glanced at Diegert.

"I was being held hostage by the Russian mafia, and my captors were going to rape me. I snapped, fought back, got a gun from one of them, and shot them both."

Barney, caught in thought, paused to form his next question. "Why were you being held hostage?"

"Because they used me to make it seem like I'd killed a guy three days earlier. They were holding me so they could eventually turn me in."

"And they figured as long as they're holding you, they might as well man-rape you."

"Yeah, so I wasn't having any of that shit. Once you start fighting with guys like that, though, it's to the death. The one guy already had four assassinations to his credit."

"The situation sounds somewhat like the pirates. Disarming men and using their weapons to kill them."

Diegert reacted with a slight chuckle. "I guess so."

Barney kept his gaze on Diegert, who stared down at the deck of the boat.

"So you began killing in self-defense, and you've progressed since then."

"I'm not sure I'd call it progress, but I have…diversified. I've also learned the value of a good clean head shot."

20

In the afternoon quiet, Diegert was concentrating while sailing the *Sue Ellen*. He paused for a moment, feeling a shift in the wind.

"Hey, did you feel that?"

Smiling, Barney replied, "Good for you, a shift from the east, and it's now coming offshore. Trim the sheets and I'll bring the boom around."

Diegert pulled on the main sail's sheets while Barney used the tiller to change the boat's angle. They ducked as the boom passed overhead to the portside of the vessel.

"We're secure," said the ship's captain.

As they sat on deck working the sails and enjoying the speed of the boat Diegert asked, "Who was Sue Ellen?"

"Sue Ellen? We all have a Sue Ellen," began Barney. "The girl you fell in love with but only you knew. Or maybe some others knew, but she didn't, and if she did, she never let you know she knew."

"Was this a real girl?"

"She's as real as love and as thrilling as lust. She's the delight of attraction and the disappointment of unrequited advances. She's the reason your heart took flight and the reason your heart is broken."

Barney's semi-poetic words struck Diegert as maudlin. "I don't have a Sue Ellen."

"If you don't, I worry about ya and I feel sorry for ya, but I can't say I admire ya."

"So you named your boat after a disappointing girl who broke your heart?"

"No, I named her after youth, beauty, hope, and the heart-pounding excitement of loving someone special."

Diegert held his gaze upon Barney as if he were looking at an oddity in the zoo. "Weird."

"I certainly hope you don't grow old without having a Sue Ellen in your life."

The sudden realization that he might one day be as alone and lonely as Barney hit Diegert hard. Nevertheless, he replied with, "Whatever."

Diegert felt hesitant, but he was compelled to ask Barney something more. "I have another question for you."

Barney eyed the younger man from under his bushy gray brows.

"Tell me about the guns in the case?"

Barney looked out over the ocean and gazed across the expanse of the sky. "They're not mine."

"Then whose are they?"

"I can't tell you."

"Why not?"

"I have been entrusted with them, but they are deadly. They bring a curse upon this vessel and its occupants. I hate the contents of that case, and it's all I can do not to throw them overboard."

Diegert sat quietly with the uneasy feeling of having intruded, while at the same time being even more curious about why the weapons were even on the *Sue Ellen.*

"I prefer not to talk about it again. Now go tighten the halyards and keep her on course." Barney descended the stairs into the cabin below.

Diegert had learned a lot about sailing in his time at sea with Barney. Still, he was a bit surprised the old man just left him to skipper the boat under the current strong winds. Necessity enhanced learning, and Diegert didn't want to slow the boat, so he worked the sails to keep the pressure on the windward side. The course Barney had set brought them closer to shore, and off the portside Diegert could gauge progress as landmarks on shore passed by. If the guns in the case were a curse, Diegert took comfort in the fact that the dolphins off the starboard side were a blessing. A school of eight dolphins raced alongside the *Sue Ellen*. Their speed and power was awe-inspiring and their interest in the boat and desire to stay by her side thrilled Diegert. Just having these beautiful creatures nearby took away the boredom and loneliness that was such a difficult part of life at sea.

Having alienated the only other human on board, Diegert appreciated the harmonious relationships represented by the school. Even if it were only in his mind, he felt a kinship with these high-speed mammals. He wondered what it would be like to live your life in such a huge expanse of water and need nothing but your body in order to thrive. Humans always needed stuff to live. Even if you adhered to a strict code of poverty, you couldn't survive in any environment with nothing but your body. He also wondered if the dolphins were curious about life outside the water or contemplate what life must be like sailing on a boat. All this thought was suddenly brought to an end when Diegert looked off the starboard gunwale and the school of dolphins was gone. Just as unexpectedly as they'd appeared, the group of fast-moving gray bodies had disappeared. He checked back again and again, but they were gone. The fleeting kinship left him feeling lonely again.

Barney resurfaced, but Diegert didn't tell him about the dolphins.

"You've really learned to handle her well. We're making good progress, skipper."

Barney's compliment got a big smile out of Diegert and went a long way toward reestablishing their camaraderie. "It's OK that we're so close to shore?"

"Yes, the waters are deep. Plus, the hot air rising off the land draws in the cool air from the ocean, producing these powerful winds that are ushering us up the coast."

"I didn't realize that, but it makes sense."

Barney stretched out the map to show Diegert that they were only about fifty miles from rounding the Horn of Africa at Cape Guardafui They would soon be in the Gulf of Aden as they continued making progress on the powerful offshore winds.

21

After rounding the Horn of Africa, the strong westerly winds guided the *Sue Ellen* across the Gulf of Aden and into the smaller Gulf of Tadjoura, where she made port at the city of Djibouti. Going ashore for the first time in so many days was a refreshing experience for both men. Being able to pace more than a few feet awakened muscles and joints to ranges of motion not possible on the boat. The central market was a crowded and busy place, but it gave the two mariners an opportunity to buy fresh fruit and meat. Barney was negotiating for a leg of goat while Diegert was inspecting mangoes. The stalls were full of produce, some of it delicious looking and enticing while other vendors' wares were rotting on the stands. A very friendly vendor stepped out from behind his stand to shake Diegert's hand. The two did not share a common language, but their smiles spoke for them. The friendly man brought Diegert over to his juice bar. The vendor's stall had a counter at the front, and the man had several electric blenders on his work area in the back. Hanging from the ceiling were nets filled with fruit.

A very pretty dark-skinned young lady indicated that she would make a juice drink with whatever fruits he chose. This woman had a dazzling smile and perfectly straight white teeth. Diegert enjoyed the twinkle in her eyes that glimmered each time she smiled. He couldn't understand a word she said, even though she spoke French as well as her native language.

Diegert just kept smiling.

The young lady eventually selected the fruits for him, cut them up, and blended them into a thick, juicy beverage. Even before his first sip, the tropical aroma of the blended juices tantalized Diegert's nostrils. When he sipped the drink, it was exquisite both in flavor and texture. His enjoyment of the drink was obvious to its creator, and she touched him on his forearm, communicating that she understood his pleasure. Diegert finished the entire drink, paid the pretty lady way too much, and happily kept looking back at her as he walked on through the market.

Barney had gotten some grains that could be made into porridge on the boat and had also filled their fuel cans. He had negotiated for the leg of goat to be cooked and he would pick it up later. Diegert had purchased two-dozen eggs and a bag of flatbread. The two shoppers rejoined at one of the nightclubs that served lunch during the afternoon. Over their meal of hummus, sprouts, and goat meat wraps Barney laid out his plan to stay in port one night and sail into the Red Sea tomorrow. That plan was fine with Diegert, who was curious to see if Saturday nights in Djibouti were anything like those in the States. After finishing their food, they drank a couple more beers and observed all the activity of the market from their café seats.

"I had a juice drink from the vendor just down there by the corner. It was great, and the girl at the shop was real friendly."

"When you've got money to spend, everyone here is friendly."

"I know, but I recommend their juice drinks."

"I'm going to go get our leg of goat, and I will meet you at the dock so we can take our stuff to the boat. You can stay on the boat tonight if you want, but I'm going to stay in a room here in town."

"Really?"

"That berth I sleep on may look comfortable, but tonight I'm going to sleep in a big bed with clean sheets on a solid floor."

"OK, I'll be on the boat."

When they returned from stowing their provisions, it was six p.m. The sun set fast in the tropics. When darkness fell, the markets closed, tarps were drawn, and some stalls even chained guard dogs in front of their businesses. The hustle and bustle of the vendors and shoppers was gone, but the volume of sound increased as the clubs started playing French and American rock music. Cars, trucks, and SUVs started pulling into places previously occupied by donkey carts. French and American military personnel from Camp Lemonnier flooded the strip of nightclubs to mix, mingle, party, and, for a lot of the guys, pay to get laid. Diegert recognized the camaraderie of the guys as they swaggered into the bars and were as loud and boisterous as they wanted to be. Having worked on base all week, it was time to cut loose.

In addition to the gaggles of partiers, there was also the familiar MP jeeps. The Military Police had the assignment of ensuring that, although the peace may be disturbed, it was not destroyed. Mickey's seemed to be the bar of choice for the first arrivals.

Diegert thought back to times when he and his squad mates got to go on leave from Fort Hood. They would drive to Austin and help the city fulfill its request to "Keep Austin Weird." They would dance with girls and get rejected. They would get in fights and get arrested by the police who would call the MPs and turn them over. What fun to be young, off duty, and out with friends with a handful of dollars to drink. Even though these guys were Navy, Diegert was drawn to hang out with them and have some fun. His hair was kind of long, and he wasn't clean shaven, but that shouldn't matter. He hoped he would be welcomed since he was American and a long way from home.

Barney had rented a room from one of the cheaper hotels away from the waterfront. A view of the water was nothing special to him, and he was more concerned with the quiet for his night's sleep. Of course, Barney was lonely too—lonely for female companionship, and for a price, any guy could pay a woman to spend the night with him. Barney took a center barstool at Mickey's and started drinking whiskey fast and hard. Soon several Ethiopian women were vying for his attention and using the simple English they knew along with their smiles and plunging necklines to seduce him into making a selection. Barney was the happy king of his own pathetic harem.

When Diegert walked in, he caught sight of Barney and his competing concubines. He shook his head, stepped to the far end of the bar, and ordered a beer. When the bottle was served, the young man was soon also surrounded by willing women who wanted to be his for a cheap price. Diegert did not engage them and instead walked over to observe the game being played on the pool table. The Navy men controlled the table as their regular turf. They were drinking beer and were largely ignored by the ladies of the night. Diegert stood leaning against a chest-high counter with his beer in hand. After performing several impressive shots, one of the sailors stood next to Diegert.

"Nice shooting," Diegert said.

"Thanks. What are you doing here? I didn't think there was a cruise ship in port."

"I'm not on a cruise."

"Well, what brought you here? We don't see many American tourists."

Diegert offered his hand. "Gary Nelson, I'm on a sailing vessel heading for the Mediterranean, but I used to be in the Army."

"Don't say that too loud." Taking Diegert's hand, the Navy man introduced himself. "I'm Andrew Clark, but people call me Clarky. My buddies and I are stationed at Camp Lemonnier."

Clarky shouted out, drawing the attention of his friend's. "Hey, fellas, we got ourselves a real live Army man here. I know he's not green and carrying a bayonet rifle over his head." At that crack, several of the guys raised pool cues over their heads, posing like the classic plastic toy. Everyone chuckled. Clarky continued, "But let's show this fellow American some good old Djibouti hospitality, even if he did choose the caveman's branch of service." Clarky lifted his beer and everybody banged their bottles together. Diegert was in with the group for the evening, and although it felt good, he worried that he would regret making friends.

Barney's whiskey was taking over his brain. He was firmly planted on the barstool, or he might very well have been on the floor. The ladies around him were realizing that they would be able to get money from him with no sex at all.

Diegert and Clarky teamed up to play pool, and Clarky told him that his squad mates were all aeromechanics who kept F/A-18s and Predator drones flying. It was steady regular work with lots of it to do. They all lived in container barracks, no windows, one room, three guys. The structures were air conditioned, otherwise they were literal ovens in the desert sun. Each time Diegert went over to the bar, he checked on Barney.

"Hey, man, I think you've had enough."

"You think I've had enuff... I'm the one who'll decide when I've had enuff. Scroow you!"

"OK, but just watch your money; you've got a lot of pretty little vultures circling."

"This isn't the first portside bar I've been in. I know what those ladies want."

"Just keep your money in your pocket."

"Just mind your own fucking business."

Having grown up with his father, Diegert recognized an angry drunk. He knew it was the right time to make an exit.

Over at the pool table, they faced their opponents, Omar and Moe. Omar Pascal was a special agent with the Naval Criminal Investigative Service, and he observed Diegert with unusual interest. He was in Djibouti completing training for the Foreign Area Officer Program. His ability to speak both French and Arabic, in addition to his racial background, provided the Navy with a highly qualified special agent who assisted in the interdicting of piracy.

Omar stepped over to Diegert. "How ya doing? I'm Omar Pascal."

Shaking the hand that was offered, Diegert introduced himself. "Gary Nelson, and Clarky says he's gonna run the table."

"We'll see about that."

Clarky only sunk one ball, allowing Omar to put his cue to work. The dark man quietly and efficiently sunk four balls before missing the ten in the side pocket. Diegert was lucky to knock in three before turning the table over to Omar's partner, Moe.

Commenting on Omar's shooting, Diegert said, "You shoot pretty well. Are you a mechanic like Clarky?"

"No, I work with computers. What division of the Army were you in?"

"1st Cavalry out of Fort Hood."

"Oh, really? Maybe that's why you look so familiar. I think I've seen your face before, but I couldn't place the name Nelson."

"Oh yeah," is all Diegert said as a cold chill ran down the back of his neck.

"I did my undergrad at UT. Did you ever get down to Austin for South by Southwest?"

"Yeah, we'd go to the fest. Austin's a cool place."

Diegert eyed Omar wearily as they watched Moe take his next shot. After he sunk two and missed the third, Clarky was back on the table. With three balls left before the eight ball, the slightly inebriated Navy man had difficulty deciding which ball to focus on. When he finally took his shot, three balls and the eight ball remained for Diegert.

"Damn it!" shouted Clarky.

Omar had only the eleven and the eight ball left. He placed the eleven securely in the far right corner. The eight ball lay against the bumper, but Omar had a suitable angle from the cue ball's position. Using simple geometry, and a steady straight cue, Omar sunk the eight ball in the far left corner to conclude the match.

"Nice game," said Diegert. "You got winner?"

"Nah, I'm done. Moe's gonna find somebody else."

Omar walked away from the pool table, heading toward a window seat.

As he walked away, Diegert watched him tapping on his phone.

"Hey, Clarky," said Diegert. "Where does Omar work?"

"Omar? He's with NCIS. He's doing some foreign regional training thing. He got hot on the table, didn't he?"

"He certainly can shoot." Diegert turned slowly to observe Omar from below his raised eyebrow.

Diegert could see that Omar was engrossed in his smartphone. Getting two fresh beers, Diegert walked over to where the NCIS officer was sitting. As he approached,

Diegert could see Omar's phone screen. Upon the screen Diegert saw a picture of his face underlined by his real name on an Austin Police Department website.

"Hey, Omar."

The dark man nearly fumbled his phone to the floor when he heard Diegert's voice.

"Sorry to scare you, but I just gotcha a beer." Diegert handed the cold bottle to the man who had hurriedly stuffed his phone in his pocket.

"Ah, thanks, but I don't drink."

"Oh, I didn't think that was allowed in the Navy."

"Maybe not the Navy of the past."

Feeling the rising awkwardness, Diegert said, "Well, you shot a great game, and I just wanted to get you a…something."

"Thanks, but I bet you can get Clarky to drink that beer."

As they both looked at their goofy friend, who was trying to balance a pool cue on a single finger, Diegert said, "Definitely."

Extending his hand, Omar said, "Look, I'm gonna get going. It was nice to meet you Dav… Gary."

Diegert looked at the man through narrowed eyelids, saying, "You take care," as he relaxed the tension in his grip on the Navy man's hand.

Omar moved to the entrance of the bar and went outside. Diegert watched the entrance, and within five minutes his concern was warranted; in came the MPs with Omar right behind them. Diegert set down his beer and stepped over to Barney. He grabbed his arm and pinched him hard. Barney yelped and looked at Diegert like he was crazy. "Listen very carefully, my cover is blown, MPs are coming to arrest me, I'm leaving now. Don't say anything to them about the boat. Get back to it, and we are outta here."

Diegert stepped past him and ducked through the back kitchen to leave the bar.

The noise, the crowd, and the music all made moving and seeing through the bar very difficult. The MPs were taking directions from Omar, but by the time they got to the pool table, Diegert was gone and Clarky was confused, until Omar showed him the wanted notice posted on the Austin PD's website. As the MPs looked around, Barney was attempting to leave by the front door. His harem of competitors was down to just two women. One of the women pulled the hair of the other from behind while taking her out at the knee, knocking her to the floor. Screams erupted, and the woman on the floor kicked out, knocking down both her competitor and Barney. The two women began to fight on the floor, punching, scratching, and pulling hair. The commotion impeded the MPs. Barney fell hard on the floor and struggled to get to his feet with the assistance of friendly patrons. He brushed himself off, thanked his helpers, and staggered to the door.

The two Ethiopian women were tossed out by the bar's bouncers and continued their argument as they strode down the street. Clarky and Omar were at the door of the bar, and they pointed Barney out to the MPs as he exited. The MPs, two male, one female, stepped over to Barney. The leading male officer said, "Excuse me, sir, but could we ask you a few questions?"

Barney continued walking, and Omar stepped next to him. "Sir, would you please stop walking?" With Omar standing next to him and the MPs nearby, Barney couldn't avoid acknowledging them. He certainly was drunk, but he was going to play it up for all it was worth.

"What...what... Whaddya want?"

"Sir, we just have a few questions for you," Omar said.

"What questions? What do I have to do with you?"

"Sir, back in the bar you were seen speaking with a young man. Do you recall that?"

"I recall speaking to some young ladies, which I enjoyed, but I'm not interested in young men. I'm not that way."

"Sir, you don't recall speaking with a male in the bar?"

"Do you mean the bartender? He was male."

"No, sir, this male was white."

Barney put his hand to his chin, stroking his stubble. "I don't think I talked to any white guys, but I'm not prejudiced, you know."

"Yes, sir. Are you attached to a vessel here in port?"

"I was...but the ship left without me, and now I'm looking for a new one."

"Sir, do you have a place to stay?"

"An old sea scallop like me is always able to find a shell for the night."

"Sir, if we would like to talk with you again, is there an address where we could find you?"

"I appreciate you calling me 'sir,' but I do not have an address. If you want to talk, I will be at Mickey's. I'm not in the Army, and I haven't done anything wrong, so good night and good-bye."

The three MPs and Omar watched as Barney staggered into the shantytown of local residences. A place no member of the US military would ever walk, especially at night and drunk. When he was out of sight, the MPs went back to their jeep.

"Thanks guys, I appreciate the backup," said Omar, who then looked at his phone again at the list of crimes for which Diegert was accused.

* * * *

After exiting the kitchen at the back of Mickey's, Diegert walked down the alley and toward the waterfront.

He wanted to go straight out to the *Sue Ellen*, but he also wanted to assist Barney if things went bad. He went to the rowboat they'd used to come ashore. He found an old tarp covering a nearby collection of lobster traps. He dragged the tarp over to the rowboat, which had three benches in its interior. The oarlocks and oars were at the middle bench. Diegert climbed in and tucked himself into the space behind the last bench and the stern wall of the boat. He covered himself with the tarp, held on to his pistol, and lay quietly, waiting and hoping that Barney would recognize the rowboat and use it to get out to the *Sue Ellen*.

Eventually, closing time came, and those who were not spending the night with a prostitute made their way back to the base, with the MPs dutifully following the sailors' vehicles back to Camp Lemonnier.

22

Looking at his watch, Barney could see it was past closing time and it was safe to make his move out to the *Sue Ellen*. For the past two hours, he'd wandered the slums of Djibouti and had slowly begun to sober up. He'd also got angrier at how Diegert's problems had ruined his plans for a comfortable sleep in a bed for which he had already paid. He returned to the spot where the line of bars, the waterfront, and the entrance to the slums converged. Looking through the darkness, he recognized the rowboat they'd used to come ashore. He lifted the bow of the boat and began pushing it out into the water. From the back end of the boat, the old man heard his name. "Hey, Barney…Barney, it's me under the tarp."

Barney stopped pushing.

"Diegert?"

"Yeah."

"Stay there. We'll be offshore in a second."

Barney heard a voice behind him on the shore. "Excuse me, sir… Sir, I'd like to speak to you." Turning around, Barney faced Omar Pascal, who seemed intent on continuing his investigation. "Sir, I'm sorry to approach you like this so late at night, but I saw you in the bar tonight speaking with a young man who it turns out is a fugitive and is wanted for murder."

"Murder? I guess there's all kinds of criminals here in Djibouti."

"I saw the two of you arguing at one point, and I just want to make sure you're safe."

"Well, that's mighty kind of you, but I don't recall talking to a young man. I remember the ladies, though."

"I saw you drank an awful lot, and so I was worried you might be vulnerable."

"As you can see, I'm fine." Continuing to push the boat, Barney stumbled and nearly fell into the bow. Awkwardly righting himself, he said again "I'm fine, really, I'm fine."

Omar stepped forward while Barney stumbled, offering, "How about I row you out to your boat and make sure you get there safely?"

"No... No, that's not necessary. I'll be fine."

Diegert stepped out from under the tarp pointing his pistol at Omar.

Barney shouted, "What are you doing?"

An agitated Diegert quickly stepped forward. "Shut up. He's NCIS. I can't let him go."

Diegert grabbed the agent, pointed the pistol at his head, and frisked him for a weapon. Omar was unarmed

"Get in the boat."

Diegert forced Omar to row the boat. When they reached the *Sue Ellen,* the rowboat was brought next to the ladder so Barney could climb out.

"Attach the dinghy's line to the mooring," Diegert commanded Omar.

Omar did as directed, while an ashen pallor took the color from his skin.

"Now climb up."

On board, Diegert took Omar belowdecks, tied his hands behind his back, secured him to a bolt eye in the wall, and gagged him with a thick piece of cloth. Barney untethered the boat, started the engine, and began motoring out of the port.

From Djibouti, the Red Sea was north by northeast. Its gateway was a strait known as Bab-el-Mandeb. Under the cover of darkness and with the motor running at full speed, the *Sue Ellen* was quickly in the open waters of the Gulf of Tadjoura. As they left port, Diegert removed the battery from Omar's smartphone, snapped the SIM card in half, and dropped them in the water.

"What now?" asked Barney.

"A few miles out, I'll take care of him."

"Will that resolve the problem?"

"Did you ever mention the *Sue Ellen* to the MPs?"

"No, I told them I had been left behind by a merchant vessel and was hoping to get on another."

"Good. Then here's the situation. I was sighted in Djibouti by US servicemen. My presence was never confirmed by the MPs or corroborated by other reliable sightings. I was never seen again. Coincidentally, the NCIS agent who reported seeing me has gone missing. If you were the investigator, you would certainly put those two things together and then you would find nothing to support your hunch. The last known position of his smartphone will be the Djibouti port, where he spent the night partying."

"It's not much to go on."

"It sure isn't, so poor Mr. Pascal is going to the bottom of the ocean so we get away scot free."

"You really think he must die?"

"If we let him live, he presents an uncontrollable risk. He's a lawman, and everything he represents will work against us."

"I leave it to you, then."

Diegert went belowdecks and untied Omar from the bolt eye. He pushed him up the stairs. On deck, Omar saw that they were far out to sea. It was a dark dawn, and no land was in sight. Barney never even looked at the man as Diegert directed him to the stern of the boat. With the gag still tied, Omar's attempts at speech came out as pitiful moans. Tears spilled over his lower lids, and their streams were absorbed by his gag. Diegert was in kill mode as he forced Omar to face the ocean off the stern deck. He kicked him in the back of the leg so the man fell to his knees like a good Catholic about to receive communion.

Even though they were miles from shore, Diegert rotated the suppressor on to the end of his pistol. He placed the barrel on the occipital of the NCIS agent's head and pulled the trigger. Omar's suffering was over and Diegert stripped the clothing off his body. He thoroughly perforated the abdomen and thorax so that Omar's body would remain on the bottom of the ocean. Using buckets of seawater, he rinsed the deck clean. Omar's clothing was placed in the boat's burn can, doused with petrol, and ignited. When the clothing was reduced to ash, the contents of the burn can were dumped in the ocean, leaving a black trail in the wake of the *Sue Ellen* as the sun rose with spectacular beauty over the Gulf of Tadjoura.

23

The Red Sea began after The Strait of Bab al-Mandab. The sea was long but not very wide. Sailing south to north was preferable, because the winds were more favorable. Barney had traversed this body of water before, and although it was deep in the center of the sea, there were shallow shelves off both coasts. The *Sue Ellen* didn't draw too deeply, so Barney was confident of their safe passage.

Djibouti demonstrated the worldwide reach of the Internet. Even on the other side of the earth, Diegert's identity and crimes were just a Google search away. The reach of modern technology had led to Omar's death. Killing a US serviceman disturbed Diegert and Barney both, but leaving Omar alive would've certainly brought a search and their eventual capture. Diegert realized that if he were to remain free, it would cost other people their lives—not only by continuing his work as an assassin but killing others would surely be necessary to keep from being captured. *Fuck it,* he thought, *no one but Barney knows I killed Omar. There is no evidence and no one to accuse me.*

The stable winds and good weather allowed the *Sue Ellen* to traverse the Red Sea in two weeks' time. Diegert and Barney ate well and relaxed between watches. They passed by the tremendous luxury yachts of the Saudi Royal Family. They saw beautiful sunsets bathing the water in a deep-crimson glow, the phenomenon that gave the sea its name. When they arrived at the northern end, they passed through the Suez Canal and entered the Mediterranean. The history of this body of water was ancient, and on its shores the most dominant civilizations on earth had found their birth. After clearing the canal and setting a northeasterly course, Diegert asked, "Where are we headed now?"

"Greece."

"What part of Greece?"

"We're headed to the northwestern port city of Alexandroupoli. I have some business there, and you'll be safe."

After sailing past the isle of Crete, the Mediterranean becomes the Aegean Sea. An extensive archipelago delineated the Aegean from other waters of the Mediterranean, and sailors had to navigate carefully to avoid running aground on the many islands and shoals. Barney Pinsdale was very familiar with the region and slowed the pace, paying close attention to guiding the *Sue Ellen.* Diegert felt like he was back at day one. The movement through this region required a lot more adjusting of the sails, according to Barney's directions. As they continued north, passing the islands of Naxos, Lesvos, Chios, and Limnos, they would soon drop anchor at the port of Alexandroupoli.

Barney slowed the pace and kept the boat out on the open water. The winds were calm, the air was balmy, and a bright half-moon hung in the sky, casting shadows across the deck.

Following their evening meal, Barney played a Brahms violin concerto in D major, which put them both into a contemplative mood. Barney took advantage of the tranquility, saying, "Son, there's something I have to tell you."

Diegert looked at him with surprise, because, although Barnard Pinsdale was a very kind sea captain, he had never called Diegert "son" before.

"This whole trip may have seemed to you as a chance encounter, but I was in fact in Mogadishu to pick you up."

Diegert turned his head, wrinkling his brow as he intensified his gaze at Barney.

"Do you believe fate or chance has more to do with determining the events of your life? Do you think all that has happened to you was simply a series of random events?"

Diegert could detect the rhetorical nature of these questions, and he folded his arms across his chest and remained silent.

"The contact you made on the darknet, his name is Aaron Blevinsky, and he's the operations manager for Crepusculous, a secretive and very powerful organization. Your actions in Paris and Athens, as well as your adaptability, perseverance, and improvisation in Mogadishu, impressed those who are watching."

"Wait a minute. I found you with a gag in your mouth chained to the galley table."

"An unfortunate occupational hazard when you sail into a port full of pirates. You can now imagine how glad I was to see you."

"This doesn't make sense."

"Was I not the only sailing vessel in the port with its mast still intact?"

"Yeah."

"Was it not fortunate that the two men guarding my dear boat were nowhere near as committed as the thugs on the docks?"

"True, they did go down awfully easy."

"I arrived a little early and underestimated the pirate's perceived value of the *Sue Ellen*. I thought they were only interested in large commercial vessels now. I can assure you, however, that I wouldn't have been in those waters were I not assigned to your extraction."

Diegert was getting angry; he didn't like the idea of being a pawn in someone else's game.

"Who's behind all of this? Who are the people watching me?"

Barney raised his hands in order to calm him. "Please let me continue, and it will all make sense. Did I not listen to your stories without interruption?"

Diegert rolled his eyes and looked away before returning his attention back to Barney.

"Once contact was made on the darknet, it allowed Blevinsky to directly influence your actions. The jobs in Miami, Paris, Athens, and Mogadishu were all sanctions that were authorized and orchestrated by the Board of Crepusculous."

Barney stopped talking and let the last word sink in. Diegert sat quietly feeling both angry and naïve. Shouldn't he have realized these were all connected? Of course the hits carried out for the employer were connected but being observed and selected without notification was both flattering and disconcerting.

"What is Crepusculous? It sounds disgusting."

"Crepusculous means 'in the shadows.' It also refers to twilight at the beginning or end of the day. I can't tell you who they are, but as an aggregate, they are the most powerful people in the world."

"The world?"

"Yes, they possess tremendous wealth and control global corporations; they are a select few who cooperatively influence governments, markets, and the worldwide economy. We like to think that no one is above the law, but that is not true. The Board of Crepusculous follows its own code and conducts its business as it sees fit to preserve the world order as it deems appropriate. Their influence infiltrates all aspects of government on every continent, and the most important thing to them is power. They stay in power by being unknown."

"And I'm one of their hit men."

"You have been a contract agent for them, but they also train and maintain their own squads of special service operators. You've been selected to undergo training at their facility in Romania."

"Romania?"

"Yes, we'll dock at Alexandroupoli in the morning. You will be met by a vehicle that will take you across Bulgaria into Romania and on to a Crepusculous training facility."

"Do I have a choice in this?"

"Of course you have a choice. You can choose not to go with them, and you'll be a free man in Alexandroupoli, Greece. You'll no longer be a passenger on the *Sue Ellen*. You'll have to avoid apprehension on your own, because you're a wanted man all over the world."

With his chin in his hand, Diegert shifted his gaze away from Barney.

"I can't be certain, but the instructors in the facility could use you as a training target."

"What?"

"Capturing or killing you would be the type of mission that would put the skills of developing operators to the test."

"Do they have it in for me?"

"Not at all, but your rejection of their interest would change the nature of the relationship. Hunting you down and taking you out would be a challenging mission and would assure that what I'm telling you is not broadcast."

"Will you tell them to kill me?"

Barney's wan smile revealed his recollection of Diegert's lethality. "Not at all. I won't be asked to make any suggestions. The instructors plan the training, and they won't speak to me about it at all. I'm just telling you this because of things from the past."

"So I really don't have a choice," Diegert said with his gaze fixed across the deck of the boat.

"Your choice to be independent will result in capture, conviction, incarceration, and probable execution. Or you can join a program designed to support and enhance the lethal capabilities you've already demonstrated." Without turning his head, Diegert shifted his eyes to meet Barney's. "You've told me that you plan to make your living by killing people," Barney continued. "Since I have seen what you can do, I believe you will find Crepusculous to be an ideal place for you to practice your chosen career."

"I'll become one of the horses in a stable of assassins."

"You, my friend, will be a stallion. Besides, don't they owe you some money?"

Recalling he was owed for the Mogadishu job, Diegert nodded.

Raising another question he had been holding on to for some time, Diegert asked, "Whose guns are those in the case?"

"They belong to you."

Diegert looked at him quizzically.

"I mean they belong to you now," Barney said.

"Well, I suppose I should thank you, but to whom did they belong before now?"

"You're not the first assassin to be a passenger on the *Sue Ellen*. I have worked for Crepusculous for many years as a courier of operators. A free-moving ocean vessel is an ideal insertion and extraction vehicle to deliver and retrieve operators to and from missions. That case of weapons belonged to a previous operator, Shamus McGee. A fun-loving and funny Irishman who, like you, had a killer's instinct. He and I traveled extensively; he learned to sail, like you, and he became conflicted about what he was doing and found the big open space of the ocean a good place to contemplate the role he was playing. One night, we went ashore in Tunis, and as we were heading back to the boat, we were ambushed. I was hit with a Taser and drugged. When I came to, I was back on the *Sue Ellen.*"

"And you think it was Crepusculous? There could have been many people who wanted an accomplished corporate assassin dead."

"Aye, you're correct, but there was a note stuck in the cabin door. It said Shamus had been killed and I was to set sail before morning or the *Sue Ellen* would suffer a drone strike. Only Crepusculous has the capacity to strike with their own drones."

"What have they got on you that keeps you working for them?"

"We all have our secrets, which others can exploit. It's best you not let anyone know yours. You can grow close to someone when you're together out at sea. I used to think of Shamus as the son I never had, but I've learned not to grow close to you guys anymore."

Diegert looked to the floor of the deck.

Barney continued, "Shamus's weapons will serve you well. He'd like to know they went to the right person, even though you and he are very different."

"How so?"

"Shamus would've let Omar Pascal live, and he would have set those pirates adrift. He was a good Irishman, he loved his Guinness, and he was a hell of lot funnier than you. You seem more suited to this life. I don't think Shamus ever found a way to absolve himself like you have."

Diegert lifted his gaze and held the old man's stare as Barney delivered the next statement.

"I think you have a very dark future in this dirty business. You seem to be free of remorse."

The quiet of the half-moon night enveloped them, and Barney suggested that Diegert go below and get some rest before they switched the watch. Staying up on deck, the old man thought of why he still worked for Crepusculous. His own attempt at being an assassin had failed miserably, but not without criminal guilt. His skills at sailing provided a reliable option for the movement of assets. Barney, a man who loved the sea, had found a way to make his living sailing the waters of the world. He'd learned to accept the compromises that allowed him to be the constant captain of the *Sue Ellen*.

24

On the dock the next morning in Alexandroupoli, Diegert stood at the side of the *Sue Ellen* with his MK 23 in his pocket and the case of weapons clutched in one hand. He shook Barney's hand, saying, "I hope to voyage with you again one day."

Barney took Diegert's hand, firmly replying, "It would be an honor to have you as a passenger again, no matter what the circumstances."

The two men smiled, and Diegert turned and walked off the dock and into the parking lot of the marina.

As he crossed the dock's gangplank, two big guys dressed in black with their pants tucked inside their tactical boots were standing next to a vehicle that looked like an Eastern European version of the Hummer. Diegert eyeballed them, anticipating their indication that he was to ride with them. The two guys ignored him completely. As he walked, Diegert kept looking back at them, convinced that they would soon recognize him. "Ahem...Mr. Diegert?" said a voice that startled the assassin and made him step back to look at the person now in front of him. "Are you David Diegert?"

"Yes, I am."

"I am here to give you a ride to Videle, Romania."

"Okay."

"The truck is over here." The young man walked over to a Derways Plutus dual-cab pickup truck. The guy looked to be maybe twenty-one, with long, dark curly hair and an unkempt, scruffy beard in need of a shave. He was wearing loose oversized khaki cargo pants right out of the nineties and a T-shirt with Super Mario brandishing a shotgun and an assault rifle. He had a cigarette in his hand, from which he took a long drag as they approached the truck. "You can put your stuff in the back."

When they were both seated in the truck, Diegert drew his pistol and grabbed the guy by the collar, pulling him across the cab. The guy looked at the pistol inches from his face and didn't say a word, although his lips were quivering and he was breathing in shallow, ragged gasps.

"Tell me about Crepusculous," said Diegert.

"I don't have a disease...I don't what you're talking about."

"What's your name?"

"Oh, I'm sorry, I should've told you before. I am Beduna Lucianus. My uncle owns a cab company in Bucharest. Usually I just give people rides around the city. We use this truck to move stuff, refrigerators, washers, stuff like that. Please, you put the gun away now?"

"I will decide when the gun goes away."

Diegert loosened his grip on the young man's shirt. His obvious fear and complete lack of any defensive actions told Diegert this kid was just as he appeared, a slacker cab driver. They both sat back in the seats of the truck, but Diegert held the gun on Beduna.

"All I know is my uncle tells me to drive down here and pick you up. Why you cannot take a train or a bus, I do not know, but now you're getting a cab ride all the way to Videle, over seven hours of driving. You tell me what is so special?"

"Where's your GPS?"

Holding out his smartphone, Beduna replied, "On my phone."

"Let me see it." Diegert scrolled through the GPS route and saw it was indeed the most direct route between the two places. Placing the phone in the center console cup holder,

Diegert said, "Do not vary from this route. We only stop to piss, eat, and get gas. Understood?"

"*Da.*"

Placing the pistol in the plastic map pocket of the truck's passenger door, Diegert instructed the young man, "Let's go."

Two miles into the trip, Beduna pulled a cigarette from his pack. Diegert reacted immediately. "No smoking."

"What?"

"I said no smoking—I do not want you smoking cigarettes while you're driving."

"But I smoke all the time."

Grabbing the cigarette from his hand and the pack from where it lay on the console, Diegert lowered his window and threw them out. Beduna slammed on the brakes.

"That pack was practically full. I'm going to get it."

Diegert picked up his pistol and pressed it into Beduna's ribs.

"You're not smoking in this truck today, and if you don't have cigarettes you'll not be distracted. Now get your foot off the brake and continue driving."

"FUCK," shouted Beduna.

Leaning forward and getting right in the angry man's face, Diegert said, "There'll be no fucking swearing either, now drive."

Fifteen minutes passed, during which Diegert said nothing and Beduna grew more angry and agitated. The Romanian driver turned on the radio, which loudly blared heavy death metal. The guitars screeched, the drums boomed, and the vocals were relentless, incoherent screams. Diegert let it go for two minutes, after which he turned the radio off and pulled the control knob from the panel. Beduna looked at him with even more anger when he realized Diegert had disabled the radio and placed the knob in his vest pocket.

"I hate that shit."

"I thought you said no swearing?"

"I said no fucking swearing from you."

One hour later, which was quiet and peaceful for Diegert and aggravating and annoying for the nicotine-deprived driver, they approached the border. Diegert checked their position on the GPS. The Greece-Bulgarian border was just a kilometer ahead, and the first city on the other side was Svilengrad.

"When we cross the border, let's find a place to stop in Svilengrad."

"Da."

The place they stopped had gas pumps out front and a convenience store just steps away. Beduna filled the truck with gas while Diegert used the restroom and bought a bottle of water. Beduna paid for the gas and got a large coffee and a pack of cigarettes. Diegert, standing outside the store, stretched his stiff back. Beduna came out, saying, "Look, I will smoke only when we are not driving. You can hold the pack while we drive."

"Okay, but give me the keys so I can move the truck and let other people use the gas pump."

Beduna, with a cigarette already in his mouth, handed Diegert the keys and gleefully lit his smoke. The nicotine hitting his nerve endings must have felt really good, because it took him a few seconds to realize that Diegert had pulled the truck onto the road and was driving away. The dumbfounded Beduna fashioned a belief that Diegert must be doing something and then coming back. A full five minutes passed before it sunk in that he had been abandoned.

Diegert smiled, having rid himself of the annoying, drug-dependent wastrel. He had the GPS on the phone and a full tank of gas, and the kid knew nothing about Crepusculous and couldn't provide him with any useful intelligence, so the whole trip would be better without him.

25

The drive across Bulgaria took Diegert four hours through rural countryside and small villages. After crossing into Romania, another hour and a half brought him to Videle. Videle had a few stores, a pub, a petrol station that also served as a mechanics shop, and several areas of mixed housing. "Mixed" meaning some of the places looked nice with lots of European charm, while others looked like impoverished hovels. The address Diegert was looking for was a couple more hilly kilometers outside of Videle. The building was a three-story gray structure with peeling paint and green slime water stains running down from the flat roof. It looked to be abandoned and in disrepair. It certainly was out of place in the forested land that surrounded it. Diegert checked the GPS; the phone indicated he was in the right spot. He thought to himself, *I've come all this way for this? It must be better than it appears.*

Diegert turned off the road onto the gravel drive and stopped at the gate. He opened the side window and looked at the camera with an exaggerated smile. The gate opened, and he drove to a small parking lot next to the building's entrance. Two burly guys dressed in black combat fatigues and boots came out of the building and approached. Both men had sidearms on their hips. The first one said, "Welcome, please follow me." Diegert motioned to the back of the truck. The second man stepped to the truck and lifted the case out of the back. The three of them entered the building.

Once inside, things were different. The place was clean, well lit, Spartan in its interior design, but solid and functional. Diegert was escorted to a counter behind which stood a man who appeared to be in his midfifties. He was of medium height and looked to weigh about two hundred pounds with at least forty of those protruding out of his abdomen. He was bald on top with a crescent of gray above his ears and around the back of his head.

"Hello, I'm Aaron Blevinsky, I'm the director of this facility, and I'll be your host during your stay. We refer to this facility as the Headquarters, and it includes both learning centers and living quarters for individuals undergoing training. Today we'll complete the intake process, get you situated in your quarters, and introduce you to your training officer. Where's your driver?"

"He's in Bulgaria."

"What happened to him?"

"I last saw him smoking cigarettes in Svilengrad. He's OK, here's the key."

Diegert placed the truck key on the counter, and Blevinsky looked at him quizzically, expecting more to the story. Diegert said nothing more about his ride to Videle.

"Is there a bunch of paperwork for me to fill out?"

"No, we have your data in the system, but you will need this."

Blevinsky handed Diegert a magnetic swipe card with his picture already on it. He then snapped open the long case and looked at the rifle and two handguns.

"Personal weapons are not allowed in the living quarters. All personal weapons are registered and held at the armory. Do you have any other weapons?"

"No other guns, but I do have a knife."

Blevinsky motioned with his hand. "All sharpened blades are to be registered."

Diegert placed his bag on the counter. Unzipping the bag, he stuck his hand in, searching for the knife. As he felt inside the bag, he was unable to locate the knife his mother had given him. He started pulling everything out of the bag, making a mess of all his stuff. With the bag practically empty, it became obvious to everyone that Diegert didn't have a knife.

"Damn, I'm sorry, but I must have lost it." Diegert thought that Beduna had taken it, but that kid was never near the bag. No one else had touched the bag, and he never used the knife during the whole trip. Could he have left it on the boat? God, what a careless idiot, how could he lose something so special? He struggled to recall the Ojibwa inscription: *The blade is both a tool and a weapon let it work for you and defend you. Great,* he thought, *you can remember that, but you lost the fucking knife.*

"If you do not have a weapon to register, then I'll introduce you to your instructor."

Blevinsky and Diegert walked down a hallway with doors spaced every thirty feet. They turned a corner, and the hallway was half glass, so Diegert could see about a dozen men practicing hand-to-hand combat in a padded room. After traversing the hallway, they turned down another and stopped at a door. Blevinsky knocked. The name "Fatima Hussain" was engraved on a plastic nameplate. The door opened to reveal a Pakistani woman with jet-black hair and eyes. She was taller than Blevinsky, and Diegert figured she was not yet thirty. She looked strong and fit. Wearing the same black combat pants, boots, and black T-shirt that everyone wore, her clothes, especially the T-shirt, did not conceal her feminine form. With her terse look and her hair pulled back into a tight bun, she revealed no softness; instead, she seemed sinister, potent, and deadly.

"David Diegert, I would like to introduce you to your training officer, Fatima Hussain."

Diegert extended his hand but said nothing; she shook his hand with an assured sense of strength and said nothing as well. Blevinsky said, "Fatima, will you please show Mr.

Diegert to his quarters and the mess hall? Dinner begins in an hour."

"Of course," replied the strong, confident woman.

As Blevinsky left, Fatima turned to Diegert, saying, "Give me a minute to finish what's on my computer."

She closed the door, and Diegert stood in the hall. As the time dragged, Diegert recalled the caption of a cartoon on the single restroom in the diner where his mother worked: *The length of a minute depends on which side of the door you're on.* Diegert's watch revealed that a "minute" for Fatima Hussain was more than eighteen minutes long. When the door opened, she stepped out, closed it behind her, and began striding away. Diegert stepped quickly to catch up and maintained a fast clip to keep pace with her. She turned down halls and climbed stairs, turned down several more halls and climbed more stairs, until all Diegert knew was that he was on the third floor. At Room 365, she stopped, swiped the lock with her card, opened the door, and walked in. Diegert followed her in to find quarters designed for single occupancy. The room was sparsely furnished but adequately appointed. Bed, dresser, closet, desk with a chair, and a computer, as well as his own bathroom.

"See you in the mess hall in thirty-five minutes."

"But where is the mess hall?"

"Follow the signs."

"I didn't see any signs."

Fatima took a step closer to him, intensifying her words. "Then let's see how good you are at reconnaissance. Follow the smell and make sure you're wearing the right clothes."

She exited his room. Diegert stepped to the door, watching her depart, imagining her hips under those dark pants.

Diegert changed into his black uniform, which was all there was in the closet. He left his room and used the time to walk around, familiarizing himself with the facility. He found the armory and indoor shooting range, the garage, the fitness center, the pool, and the locker room, which led to the outdoor training facilities. He was slightly concerned that the food may be bad, since the medical center was located next to the cafeteria. Diegert got in line, got a tray full of food, and sat down by himself at a table in the mess hall. The dining room had a dozen large, round tables, and there were about twenty-five people eating. The majority were men, who looked fit and strong. The few women in the room looked matronly and clerical. After sampling a few bites and finding the food to be pretty good, he enjoyed his meal. Fatima set a small plastic box down on the table and sat next to him.

"I can see you were able to find your way."

"Oh, yeah... I've been around. In the Army: Afghanistan. I've also been to Miami, Paris, Athens, Somalia."

"Don't forget Djibouti," interrupted Fatima. "I know all about you, where you're from, what you've done, and what I don't know I will learn in your training sessions."

She opened her box and took a small bite of a spinach salad.

"When do I get to learn about you?" asked Diegert.

"You don't. I'm the teacher. You're the student. I'm the expert. You're the newbie. You do what I say, when I say, and in the manner in which I instruct you. Thinking about and talking about who I am is a waste of time neither of us can afford. When you're finished eating, report to the outside training area."

Fatima ate the rest of her salad without discussion. Diegert did the same, but not thinking about Fatima was going to take a level of self-discipline he doubted he possessed.

Diegert returned to the locker room, which led outside. He noticed the lockers were large and wide. They were fronted by pressed metal screening through which Diegert could see heavy jumpsuits, boots, wet weather jackets, climbing gear, and helmets. He got the impression the outside training occurred regardless of the weather and probably involved heights. Outside, he found Fatima. "I sure hope finding the exit isn't your best quality."

"I was just looking around."

"Come on, I want to show you some areas you won't find on your own."

They walked down a trail and covered about a quarter mile before she turned onto another trail and continued a half mile deeper into the woods. Diegert observed that she had a pistol in an integrated holster sewn into her pants. The carrying mechanism allowed the weapon to remain concealed, yet it was firmly held in place by strong webbing and could be conveniently deployed through the extra-large pocket slit that ran parallel with her seam. That she was carrying a weapon was not surprising, but it was unsettling since he didn't have one.

When they arrived at the corner of a chain-link fence that ran through the woods, Fatima opened the sliding gate with her swipe card. They stepped inside and the gate closed. They walked a bit farther, and there was a second fence. This one was higher and topped by rolls of razor wire. Again, Fatima swiped the card and opened the gate.

Within the woods, several structures appeared of different sizes and shapes. It looked like a ghost town or, more accurately, a movie set for a post apocalypse sci-fi adventure. Some buildings were just façades, supported only by scaffolding. Others were fully framed with skeletal interiors. Still others looked like the abandoned apartments one would expect to find in a war zone. Fatima continued the silent tour, showing Diegert an area with dozens of concrete blocks five feet high by five feet wide. The blocks were bullet pocked and worse. They had suffered many gun battles, and the dark-crimson splotches were evidence of the human toll taken in this training area. Finally, Fatima brought him to a swamp that was filled with high reeds and murky water. Through the swamp was a series of narrow bridges that were the only means of traversing this treacherous area. Fatima led Diegert across a bridge until they reached a dry stand of pines.

"Is this the end of the tour? Can we go to the souvenir shop now?"

"Not funny," replied the humorless dark-haired lady. "Your training here is serious business. You will demonstrate a number of skills and abilities and accomplish several difficult missions, and when you survive all of that, you and other trainees will be placed in herc to compete in a tournament."

"A tournament? You never showed me the tennis or shuffleboard courts."

Without a hint of a smile, Fatima narrowed her eyes. "This is a tournament to the death. As your trainer, I want you to win that tournament and show the boys that I'm better than them. The only way that happens is through you. I read all the dossiers of potential trainees, and yours was the only one that impressed me. I fought to be your trainer. Don't let me down or show me I chose poorly. I want you to win, and I will help you do that."

"So we're a team?"

"No, you are my trainee, and you must win. Do not cloud your mind. You must win in here or we both fail. There is no team in the tournament."

"I take it you've won this tournament before?"

"All instructors here are tournament winners."

"Then when do we begin training?"

"No training is allowed in here, and technically I shouldn't have shown you this place. So your first test is to keep this tour secret—tell no one you were here. Let's go."

Returning to the compound, Diegert entered the men's locker room. Inside were two guys who had just finished a practice session. They were dressed in tactical suits that were like nothing Diegert had seen before. The suits were a woven material that seemed to move easily as the guys were stowing their equipment. The outfits were formfitting without baggy or bulky parts. They had built-in harnesses for attaching climbing lines. The chest and back armor plates were flexible and appeared to be made of composite foam that hardens on impact. The suits made the guys look invincible, and Diegert hoped he might get fitted for one soon. The guy with the beard said, "Hey, new guy, what are you doing down here?"

The guy was taller than Diegert, perhaps six foot four, and spoke with a Russian accent. He weighed at least two hundred pounds, and sizing him up gave Diegert reason to pause.

"I was just touring around, trying to get the lay of the land."

"Oh, I'm Alexi Strakov, and this is Curt Jaeger."

The other guy didn't have a beard but was practically the same size as Strakov. Diegert could see that these two would be a formidable team, and he hoped he would be on their side. They both shook hands with him, and Strakov said, "You really shouldn't be down here without your trainer."

"My trainer is the one who was taking me on the tour."

"I don't see your trainer," remarked Strakov as he pulled off his outer shell, revealing the padded under portion of his suit.

"Well, she's not going to come in here."

"SHE!" exclaimed the big bearded guy. Both men began laughing.

"Where did you go wrong to get the girl as your trainer?" asked Strakov.

"Blevinsky must not think much of you if he assigned you to her," said Jaeger, who had also removed the composite foam piece of the tactical suit.

"Hey, maybe you get to fuck her."

Jaeger chuckled at the Russian's comment, saying, "I never got to fuck my trainer."

Laughing, Strakov said, "Maybe you're just the perfect guy to take orders from that bitch."

Diegert felt angry and embarrassed, but he didn't reply to the joke except to turn and leave the locker room.

"What's wrong with the new guy?" asked Strakov. "Was it something I said?"

26

What a fucking idiot I am, thought Diegert. He hadn't given the fact that he was being trained by a woman a moment of consideration. Training with her already put him on the wrong team from the rest of the guys. *I have to change this.* On the way back to his quarters, he stopped at Blevinsky's office and knocked on the door. "Can I speak with you, sir?"

Blevinsky was engrossed in his computer. Without moving his head, he raised an eyebrow and directed his pupils at Diegert. Returning his gaze to the computer screen, he said, "What can I do for you?"

"I was curious about the process by which trainees are assigned to instructors."

"Are you really interested in the process or are you concerned that you have a female trainer?"

"Umm... Yeah, I was wondering why I have the girl trainer."

Blevinsky took his hands off the keyboard, leaned back in his chair, and looked at Diegert.

"What's the matter, did someone make fun of you or are you just having a chauvinist moment? Fatima Hussain is one of the toughest, most resourceful operators I have ever seen. Whatever deficit she has in strength, and it ain't much, she more than makes up for in intelligence, cunning, and perseverance. Her willingness to risk her own safety in order to accomplish missions is far greater than any man in this facility."

Blevinsky paused to let that assessment sink in before continuing. "No one rises to the position of trainer without fully earning it. As an instructor on my staff, she has proven herself, and for you to question her is absolutely insulting and will not be tolerated. Do I make myself clear?"

"Yes, sir."

"You should tell Strakov and Jaeger to go fuck themselves," said the tired and agitated man. "I want you to know that I will be right here when your training is done, and you want to thank me for assigning you to Fatima Hussain."

Diegert swallowed hard but didn't respond.

"Hey, another thing," said Blevinsky. "That girl you failed to kill in Paris. You actually did me a favor. I got rid of her for less than half of what I was gonna pay you."

"I won't kill women."

"Yeah, right. Mr. Gender Restriction. Yet here you are bitching about your trainer being a woman. Fuckin' get out of here and figure yourself out."

Back in his room, Diegert tried to figure himself out. Killing bad men, criminals, those who knew they were playing dangerous games but took the risk anyway, he could justify that. But killing women just didn't fit. Blevinsky could assign him whatever he wanted, but if he wanted him to shoot a woman, Diegert decided he just wouldn't do it.

It was still early, only nine p.m., but the clean, comfortable bed beckoned to Diegert, who was looking forward to a good night's sleep. He got himself ready and climbed into bed. He thought about his family, his father and his brother and especially his mother. It had been such a long time since he'd spoken with them, and it seemed as though it would be a long time before he spoke with them again. As he thought about them, he realized missing his father and brother was an emotionally hollow experience. They certainly weren't thinking of him. Missing his mother hurt, though; he knew that without him she was all alone in her own family.

The thought of her living with Jake and Tom on the dirt road in Broward Minnesota made David feel very far away.

He longed to go for a walk with her as she found beauty all around her in the natural world. She had a calming, reassuring effect upon him which he missed very much. Even a strong, young, powerful man like him still needed his Mother's love. With a disconcerted sense of uncertainty Diegert fell into a fitful sleep.

After too short a time, the door to Diegert's room opened and someone quietly stepped in. "Don't be alarmed," said the pretty voice of a woman. "It's me, Fatima."

Diegert opened his bleary eyes and saw her silhouette outlined by the light of the door. "It's time to begin your training."

"What?" asked Diegert as he struggled to wake up.

Raising her voice and slamming the door behind her, Fatima shouted, "Get up. It's time to start your training."

Fatima hit the light switch, blinding Diegert with the fluorescent glare of the overhead rectangles. Disoriented and confused, Diegert remained under the blankets. Fatima grew furious. She forcefully extended her arm, snapping a collapsible baton to its full length. Diegert was alarmed by the loud, metallic snap, but he was shocked by the strike across his thighs as Fatima shouted, "Get out of bed now. Stand up and get ready for training."

Diegert complied and stood next to the bed, wearing only his boxer shorts. He eyed her with derision and contempt. Fatima stepped right up to him, placing the end of the baton under his chin and lifting his face away from her eyes and into the blinding brightness of the ceiling fixtures.

"Don't you look at me with such contempt. I'm your superior, not only in rank but in ability. We are not some weak-willed government agency. You will survive this training or die. There is no other option."

Pointing to the closet with her baton, she instructed him, "Put on the outfit marked 'Street Clothes.' Diegert dressed in front of her, and she directed him to the desk chair. She handed him a dossier, saying, "Find this man and get him to give you two hundred euros."

She handed him a Jericho 941 9 mm pistol and suppressor. That she would equip him with an Israeli firearm was surprising, but then again, the gun is only a tool. "You have twenty-four hours to complete the mission."

"What, no push-ups or pull-ups?"

"If you need to increase the strength of your body, do it on your own time, but I don't want to see you back in that bed."

Fatima left the room much more abruptly than she had entered.

27

Diegert noted the time, 11:05 p.m., as he opened the dossier on Sebastor Sbrebetskov. The man was a midlevel mobster of the Bucharest underworld in an organization headed by the notorious Michka Barovitz. It turned out Sbrebetskov's appetites were bigger than his abilities, and he was in debt to Barovitz for a large sum of money. Furthermore, Barovitz was not entirely happy about the sideline businesses Sbrebetskov was running in Bucharest. Sbrebetskov was extorting protection money from local merchants, and the speculation was that he planned to establish himself independent of Barovitz. The risk he was taking was significant; either he would become his own boss or a corpse.

Barovitz's criminal empire extended throughout Romania and beyond. He was at the top of a self-made criminal pyramid, which he preserved with bribery and force. It was reported that he views Sbrebetskov as an interesting plaything, which he controlled through puppet strings. Diegert's mission was to find Sbrebetskov and convince the mobster to give him two hundred euros. He would begin at a pub called the Loyal Dog just over the Ialomita River in Bucharest where Sbrebetskov typically hung out at night.

Diegert signed out a Saab from the motor pool and drove into the night. The bridge over the Ialomita was closed to vehicle traffic for repairs, however foot traffic was allowed. Diegert parked and crossed the bridge. The pub faced the river fifty meters from the bridge. Diegert took a stool at the bar and ordered a beer. Soon he was talking with an older man sitting next to him. Diegert steered the conversation to Sbrebetskov. The old man said, "Everyone knows that man is in debt to Barovitz, and I believe he has a price on his head."

"You mean, they want him dead?"

"I think the price is more reflective of the debt he carries."

"Is this the kind of debt that can be repaid or is there something more Barovitz holds over him?"

"Barovitz surely has much to hold over him, but Sbrebetskov wants to have his own organization. Right now, he only has two men. He would need a lot more to challenge Barovitz. Even the men he has are actually being paid by Barovitz. He's on thin ice."

"Tell me more about Barovitz."

"Ah, the Scorpion. He's ruthless, and his rise to power has been paved by executing the competition."

"Sounds tough."

"Well, he's older now, more refined, but as a young man, he removed his rivals with a revolver. He was called the Scorpion because he also used poison. He would give those who didn't follow his rules the option of drinking poison or being shot."

"Unfortunate choices."

"He would also offer the choice to business people who didn't want to pay protection money."

"Is he still around town?"

"No, he has a villa on an island in the Aegean. He conducts his business through associates. He doesn't have to twist arms himself anymore. What Sbrebetskov needs is a settlement."

"What do you mean?"

"I mean, he needs Barovitz to offer him a deal that will allow him to save his hide and save face. Partial payment on his current debt and a percentage of future business, that sort of thing. Sbrebetskov isn't foolish enough to pass up a settlement from Barovitz, but he hasn't been offered one yet."

The old man pointed to an empty booth in the back corner of the bar.

"That's Sbrebetskov's booth over there. It's the last place in town where he has any clout. I imagine he'll be here later, but I will not."

The man swilled the last of his beer and offered his hand to Diegert, saying, "An old man needs his rest, while a young man seeks excitement. Good night, stranger."

Looking down at the coaster under his beer, Diegert noticed it had a scorpion insignia. Wiping the coaster dry, he ordered another beer and a shot of Romana Sambuca Black Liquore to be served over at the empty booth in the corner. Diegert sat there for twenty minutes before Sbrebetskov and two men arrived. The two thugs preceded Sbrebetskov to the table.

"Hey, get out of that seat," the first one, who had a flattop buzz cut, managed to say.

"This booth is ours. You must leave," offered the second guy, who sported a dark goatee, sounding almost polite in comparison.

Diegert raised his silenced Jericho just above the tabletop and placed the red laser on the forehead of the more belligerent thug. Speaking directly to Sbrebetskov, who stood behind the two men, Diegert said, "I'm here to talk to you. Tell your men to wait at the bar or climb into a grave."

Sbrebetskov, not wanting a public spectacle, gestured to the bar. "Have a seat and a beer."

Sbrebetskov was a big man, very heavy, with a large sloping abdomen. He was dressed in a tailored suit because he wouldn't fit well off the rack. His full head of dark hair was only beginning to show the gray, which would likely be the color of all his hair should he live long enough. He slid his bulk into the booth and made himself appear comfortable. The waiter brought him his beer in a tall glass with an embossed Ursus logo. Diegert wasted no time. "I'm here to offer you a settlement."

Sbrebetskov's eyes widened.

"Ten percent of your debt buys you six months to come up with the balance."

Sbrebetskov's look of surprise caused Diegert to go on.

"Barovitz believes in you, and he's taking the long view that you will do well for him in spite of your current setback."

"How do I know you represent Barovitz?"

Diegert placed the coaster with the scorpion on the table and then set the shot glass with the dark-black liquid on the coaster. Placing his pistol on the table, Diegert folded his arms in front of him.

"Ten percent of your current debt, and I will leave you to celebrate your good fortune this evening."

Sbrebetskov pulled out a roll of cash and counted it. "A thousand euros, this is all I have tonight."

He handed the money to Diegert. Returning his gun to its holster and putting the cash in his pocket, Diegert stood up.

"I will be back tomorrow night for the rest."

Diegert picked up the shot glass of dark fluid and poured it on the floor, saying, "We wouldn't want an accident." He stashed the scorpion coaster in his coat pocket.

Stepping outside the pub, Diegert walked along the river and started to cross the bridge. He counted out two hundred euros, placed it in his jacket pocket, and put the rest in the pocket of his pants. Glancing back, he noticed the two thugs exiting the pub and pointing at him as he ascended the bridge. Over its span of the river, the bridge rose to a height of fifteen meters above the water. The thugs sprinted after him, and as he reached the peak of the bridge, he slowed his pace, and the thugs closed the gap.

As they approached, guns drawn, one shouted, "Hey, stop right there!"

Diegert halted, grasped the handle of his Jericho 9 mm, and withdrew it as he spun to face his attackers. His first shot pierced the frontal bone of the flattop thug just above the right eye. As the man's body began to drop forward, Diegert kicked him into the second thug. The force of his comrade's body knocked over the man with the goatee. Diegert fired, striking the guy's right arm, causing him to drop his gun. Diegert grabbed the shattered forearm, and with ligament-tearing force pulled it behind the guy's back. The thug swung wildly with his left and cracked Diegert on the cheekbone. The blow stunned Diegert, who dropped his pistol and stumbled backward. The thug stood up and punched Diegert repeatedly in the ribs. With the wind knocked out of him, Diegert fell to the deck of the bridge. The thug reached for his fallen pistol, and when he turned back Diegert delivered a kick to the guy's right knee. Falling on the damaged knee, the man with the goatee held on to his pistol. Diegert reached behind him, grabbed his gun, and both men pointed at one another. Diegert flipped on his laser sight, dazzling the thug's vision as the muffled spurt of the bullet permanently ended the henchman's struggle to survive.

Diegert rose to his feet. Quickly assessing his situation, he heaved the two bodies into the river, with every tug of his muscles on his rib cage causing intense pain. He pocketed the pistols while descending the bridge to his car and drove back to Headquarters.

* * * *

Diegert had cleaned himself up when Fatima came to his room at 2:33 a.m. "Here's your two hundred euros," said Diegert, extending the cash.

"Is he dead?"

"No, but his two thugs are. I thought we had a gentleman's agreement, but it seems I overestimated Sbrebetskov's commitment to a pact made in honor."

Folding the money and placing it in her pocket, Fatima stepped to the door, turned, and looked over her shoulder just soon enough to catch Diegert checking out her ass.

"I'll see you at 0700 for tomorrow's training brief. I hope your dreams are satisfying."

His dreams were not satisfying; sadness and grief had built up inside him. All the deaths—Paris, Athens, Mogadishu, the pirates on the *Sue Ellen,* Omar Pascal, and now the two thugs—were exerting their psychological effect. Barney, whom he considered a friend, was now out of his life. He needed to express the grief and release the sadness, but when he tried to, he just couldn't. He relaxed in the privacy of his little room, and with his face pressed to the pillow, he opened himself to his painful feelings, but tears wouldn't come. He thought of the hurt and the pain, the violence and the loss, but the expression of those emotions needed something more to come to the surface. He needed to cleanse his soul and perform penance for his actions. He was frustrated at not being able to purge these feelings. Tossing and turning, he eventually fell asleep but awoke to his five thirty a.m. alarm feeling lousy.

28

Arthur Cambridge was a successful real-estate developer in England. His company, Cambridge Holdings, owned property worth over eight hundred million pounds. The apartment and office buildings produced rental income in excess of five million pounds a month. His father, Sinclair Cambridge, had developed the business with the assistance of Dean Kellerman, a member of the Board of Crepusculous.

Through wise investments and reinvestments, Cambridge Holdings grew until it was a self-sustaining real-estate entity. Kellerman remained an investor but didn't take part in the operations of the business. Arthur learned the business while completing his studies at Oxford, and Sinclair gave him a prominent position in the company upon his graduation. So it was no surprise that upon the elder man's death, his personal estate worth over twenty-five million pounds was turned over to his only son, who was now president of Cambridge Holdings. With such a large volume of money now at his disposal, Arthur had to invest it quickly or lose most of it to taxes.

He and his investment assistants looked at the Eastern European market for a suitable place to purchase large housing stock at very low prices. With their past success, they were certain they could keep the properties occupied as they did in England, the Netherlands, and France. The twenty-five million pounds bought forty buildings in Romania. Each building had one to two hundred apartments per unit. The income potential from rent was enormous, and Cambridge Holdings was poised to become a force in the Romanian real-estate business.

Government regulations in Romania were significantly less complex than British bureaucracy. The lawyers of Cambridge Holdings completed the necessary paperwork, putting Arthur Cambridge in business in the Balkans within a month of inheriting his father's wealth.

Cambridge visited the country and toured several of the buildings he had purchased. He realized the numerous structures were in various states of repair. Some were in good shape with charming features, while others needed to be condemned and would take a substantial investment to restore. Like a bushel of apples, there were some bad ones. Cambridge directed his business planners to take a complete inventory of the entire purchase and put together a restoration plan for him to review. Upon his return to England, Cambridge prepared to celebrate Christmas with his family on their thirty-acre country estate.

The e-mail arrived in the inbox of Nigel Flannery, director of finance for Cambridge Holdings. The document laid out in extensive detail the payment expectations of Michka Barovitz. The payments were required for protection, and fees were listed for every building the company had just purchased in Romania. Nigel thought for a moment but couldn't recall any contracts with security companies for any of the buildings. Security was handled through keyed doorways and neighborhood watch efforts. Spending extra money on security was not a practice of Cambridge Holdings, except for special residents who purchased such services. In the contracts written to purchase the assets in Romania, no security fees were included or required. What also struck the Oxford-educated financier was the use of the word "protection" rather than "security."

Corruption and bribery were part of the history of the Balkans, and Nigel had read about such circumstances in the news and in spy novels, but he certainly never expected the fine company of Cambridge Holdings to be faced with thugs demanding bribes. The thought was so repugnant that he hesitated to bring it to Arthur Cambridge's attention, especially during the Christmas holidays. Barovitz's note, though, demanded a reply and stated that lack of protection payments may result in criminal activity affecting the properties. Nigel gave it some thought and realized he would have to reply to this e-mail in an unequivocal manner.

December 22
Dear Mr. Barovitz,

Regarding your e-mail of December 21, I am afraid we will not be fulfilling your demand for payment. Cambridge Holdings has made the purchase of the Romanian properties without establishing building security contracts. Building security is handled through lock-and-key mechanisms as well as good relations with local law enforcement. Your demand for "protection" payments strikes me as nothing more than extortion, and we simply will not be held hostage to such requests. I request that you never contact our company again, and furthermore a copy of this notice and your request for extortion payments will be forwarded to the local police in the areas where our buildings are located. I trust this will conclude our correspondence and that you understand that your draconian ways of doing business will no longer be tolerated or indulged by Cambridge Holdings.
Sincerely,
Nigel Flannery, Director of Finance, Cambridge Holdings

Nigel sent the e-mail to Barovitz. He also forwarded copies of the e-mail and the request for payments from

Barovitz to the police headquarters of every district in which they held buildings. Feeling as though he had thoroughly addressed the issue, Mr. Flannery turned his attention to other business.

29

David Diegert moved through the line of the cafeteria collecting his breakfast. As he slid his tray on the metal counter, he looked into the soft hazel eyes and gentle smile of Elena Balan. Elena was a charming young woman with wispy blond hair pulled back into a ponytail. Diegert hadn't seen her in the cafeteria before and was captivated by her plain but pretty face and her smooth, soft skin.

He looked at her without expression until her smile faded and she asked him, "What do you want?" Diegert pondered how he could tell her that he desperately wanted to hug her and hold her in a private place and share with her the passion that was erupting inside him. She looked at him quizzically and repeated, "What do you want?"

Diegert snapped out of it and replied, "Eggs, please, and some sausage." Elena spooned his request onto a plate and slid it under the glass guard. Her smile returned, but she looked at him rather strangely as he stepped down the line. Out in the eating area, Fatima, dressed in the black uniform of the day, directed him to sit at a table with her. "I want to brief you on today's training assignment while you eat."

With only the two of them at the table, Fatima asked, "So how is it that you got the two hundred euros last night, but Sbrebetskov is alive and his two body guards are dead?"

Diegert was not paying attention to her question as he poked and picked at his meal.

"Hey, I asked you a question," the dark-haired trainer snapped.

"What?"

"I asked how is it that Sbrebetskov is alive and his two body guards are dead?"

"You asked me to get him to give me two hundred euros, you didn't assign me to kill him. I convinced him to give me the money, and then his dudes tried to jump me and get it back. My ribs are killing me, by the way."

"Do you need to go to medical?"

"Thanks, but there's nothing they can do for injured ribs."

Diegert dug into his eggs and took a big swallow of orange juice.

"Very well. Our training today isn't so physical as intellectual. I'll develop your skills as a hacker."

"Computers?"

"Of course. We may be assassins, but our ability to infiltrate, acquire, and sabotage information is our greatest asset, and that's what's going to give you longevity in this business."

"Is hacking part of the tournament?"

Fatima looked over her shoulder, returned her gaze to Diegert, and lowered her voice. "Never mind the tournament. You have many other tests to pass before you concern yourself with that."

Folding his toast over his last sausage link and consuming his impromptu sandwich, he asked, "Are you going to make me a lethal geek?"

"I will first try to make you a competent code breaker. Report to Room 278 at 0800."

Leaning forward and locking eyes with him, she said, "Don't be so obvious staring at my ass when I get up and walk away."

Diegert forced himself to look down at his empty plate until she'd left the room.

When she was gone, he took his plate and went for seconds. There was no one in line, and Elena stepped up to serve him. From the other side of the glass guard, he handed her his plate, and she asked, "More of the same?"

"Yeah, thanks." He smiled wanly at her and tried to convey a friendly nonverbal message. It might have worked, because she smiled back at him, but he didn't know if that was special or just the way she interacted with everybody. He read her name tag as she filled his plate and handed it back to him.

Diegert didn't know what to say, so he said, "Your name is so pretty. What does it mean?"

Her smile lit up. "Thank you. Elena means…bright, shiny…like sunlight on water."

"Wow, that's beautiful! My name's David…David Diegert."

Diegert set his tray on the metal counter and looked at her and then started to feel awkward and unsure what to say next. Elena seemed to feel the same and asked, "What does David mean?"

Diegert had never considered the meaning of his name and had no idea how to answer. He pretended to ponder for a moment and then said, "I'm afraid I don't know."

This made the awkwardness all the more palpable, and he picked up his tray and said, "I gotta go. Thanks for the seconds."

She just smiled sadly and waved her hand. He walked out into the eating area feeling like a jerk.

* * * *

Room 278 had no windows and a lot of computers. Its fluorescent lighting, numerous workstations, and powerful air conditioning made it a cold and serious place. Fatima was already there, wearing a thick zip-up hoodie—black, of course.

"It's just you and me in here?" asked Diegert.

"For now, but in my opinion, this is one of the most underutilized facilities on the campus."

"Campus? Now I really feel like I'm back in school."

"You are in school, only this time if you fail you die."

"Wow," said Diegert sarcastically.

"Information is our most crucial commodity. That's been obvious for decades. All information is now in a digital form. That's convenient, it allows for large-scale storage and retrieval, and it lends itself to easy analysis. None of this is news. Information, though, is vulnerable to being observed, copied, altered, stolen, or destroyed. When a system can be breeched using remote electronics, then the infiltration happens from a room like this."

"Keyboard spies of the future."

"Right, no one is in actual danger. But when critical data can only be accessed by direct infiltration, then we come into play. The danger is something we're already trained to deal with, but you're of no value if you get in the building but can't get into the data."

"Alright, the keyboard is mightier than the AK-47."

"Definitely. Everyone around here has their big guns and can't wait to use them. But with the right information, you can disable an enemy just as effectively as shooting him." Fatima smiled at Diegert, and it appeared to him that she was just as happy to hack as shoot someone.

"The first thing you have to understand is code. All computer information is coded, and the code allows the information to be specific and unique as well as portable, compressible, and in many ways permanent. Think of how government spy agencies collect all that data and sift through it looking for terrorists. It's through manipulating code that they can identify what they are looking for from all the rest of the tons and tons of data they collect. Using code, you can put yourself on the other side of the firewall and see what's going on in the network. Here, let me show you."

Fatima took her smartphone from her pocket, activated an app, and scrolled through some screens. "I have a program that allows me to bypass the firewall on the Headquarters network."

"Are you supposed to have that?"

"I have it. Once inside, I can access things like personnel files, after-action reports, construction plans, even Internet browsing history. Care to know what some of the guys were entertaining themselves with last night?"

Diegert met her mischievous gaze with a curious look. Fatima proceeded to tap on the screen of her smartphone. "Here's someone who was on Hulu watching *Mission Impossible III*, as if we don't get enough of that around here. Someone else was watching *The Outlaw Josey Wales,* a Clint Eastwood movie from 1976! Here's Bassmaster.com, where someone was watching The Greatest Places for Bass in South Carolina. I guess someone is planning a fishing trip. Gunsandammo.com with the search "Decibel Reduction without Loss of Velocity," the best sound suppressors being made today. Now that's someone doing their homework."

"Can you tell who?"

Smiling again, Fatima replied, "I was wondering when you would ask that. Every log on to the Internet requires an IP address. This piece of code identifies which computer is using the Internet. You may not always know who's using the computer, but you do know what computer is using the Internet. We may have to make some assumptions or gather evidence about who is actually using a computer, but there are ways of doing that with user IDs and passwords. People think that a user ID and password makes their access secure. It does, but it also is their personal identifier. So our subject interested in silencers is, no surprise, Carl Lindstrom, the Headquarters armorer."

The two snoopers looked at each other, shrugged their shoulders at the innocuousness of it, and moved on. "Now here's an interesting Internet address: Gayboy.com. Not that we're concerned with that, but the video that was watched was "Suck it Long and Strong." This was being watched on the computer registered to..."

Fatima held her finger over the screen, not yet scrolling the information into view as Diegert's anticipation built. "See, this is why I want you to learn about data and be able to manipulate code. You can see how powerful this capability is and how much can be learned by knowing how to access information."

"Alright... Alright. Who is the gay boy?"

Fatima touched her finger to the screen and scrolled up the name assigned to the IP address: Alexi Strakov.

"No," gasped Diegert.

"Come on, now, we aren't supposed to care about that anymore."

"No way..." continued Diegert incredulously.

Fatima left Diegert in Room 278 with some basic coding exercises that would allow him to learn rudimentary elements of code design and the interface process. The exercises required Diegert to write some simple programs to get the computer to do some calculations and store the data in specifically identified files. The tutorials provided step-by-step instructions, allowing students to progress as they succeeded. Fatima didn't think the work was very complicated, but given the number of assignments he had, she anticipated Diegert would be at it all day.

30

Barovitz was not amused by the e-mail from Nigel Flannery.

"Fucking British pricks! They have no respect for how business is done here. They think we'll just do things the British way. Well, bollocks to them."

Barovitz had risen to his current position of power and prominence through strength of will and persistence. Of course, for him to be so successful meant that others were intimidated and threatened into paying him regularly and consistently from the proceeds of their labor. A mobster like Barovitz extorted money from all businesses in the country and kept law enforcement officers on his payroll. His business required him to create no product or service; he only had to siphon payments from those who did actually contribute to the economy. The Balkans had functioned in this way for so long that Michka Barovitz actually had earned the respect of many for his rise to power and his ability to stay in power for so long. His business was the envy of many, and young boys were told to dream of growing up and being Barovitz.

In consultation with his most loyal and ruthless assistants, Barovitz made a plan to show the wealthy bastards that you didn't just buy your way into Romania without respecting the business culture. They met for an hour, and Barovitz felt satisfied that their plan would bring the Brits into line and give them a new appreciation for Balkan business practices.

* * * *

Diegert found the code difficult to follow, and he was frustrated by the complexity of the number and letter patterns. In the Army, he'd used programs all the time but never had to write one. His smartphone had all sorts of apps, but he didn't have to create them. He patiently tried to accomplish the first simple task but was stymied each time a new pattern had to be mastered. Even though he was good at math, he was failing at coding. The tutorial required progress before opening the next challenge, and Diegert was getting angry at not being able to move forward.

In the afternoon, he had abandoned his first unfinished trial and opened a different tutorial, which presented him with a file to be opened without knowing the password. Diegert spent two angry hours trying to open the file, and he cursed at his inability to do what was asked. The tutorial informed him he had one last chance and it would close in fifteen minutes if he remained unsuccessful. A quarter hour later, Diegert was swearing out loud at the computer and angry at his failure to learn the password.

The next tutorial provided a lesson on establishing a firewall against a virus. Diegert found the whole concept of digital defense mystifying. The program instructed him to create a digital barrier that would thwart the program's virus. Try as he might, each code combination he created failed to prevent the virus from corrupting the files he was to protect. The trial was the most frustrating of all, because each time he failed, he had to reread the instructions he didn't understand in the first place. He felt he was put in a no-win situation, with insufficient instruction to be able to do the things expected of him. He imagined getting through the tournament would be easier than this.

By the end of the day, he had accomplished nothing. It was dinnertime, and he was hungry. He was relieved Fatima hadn't come back to check on him, although he figured she was probably keeping track of him remotely. It was stupid that she thought he would just be able to learn all this stuff on his own. From the printer station, Diegert took out a piece of paper, folded it, and put it in his pocket as he left the room.

The cafeteria was serving spaghetti and meatballs, and there were a lot of guys who were much more physically fatigued from their day of training waiting in line ahead of Diegert. While he waited, his phone buzzed. The text was from Fatima: *Pretty lousy work on the coding. I thought you were smart.*

When Diegert came through the service line, Elena smiled to see him and gave him an extra meatball. Her beautiful smile made him feel a bit better about his lousy day. While he ate his dinner, he took out the piece of paper and wrote:

Please visit me, Room 365
David

He watched the exit of the service line until no one had come out for five minutes. He then went back for more to eat. Elena smiled when he entered, and as he approached, she said, "Beloved."

"Excuse me?"

"Beloved," repeated Elena. "Your name means 'Beloved.'"

"Oh," said Diegert.

"David is a name of Hebrew origin that has been adopted by almost every culture in the world, and it means 'The Beloved One.' So you are Beloved."

Reaching her hand under the glass guard, she said, "You want seconds?"

"Yes, please."

Elena placed the food on his plate, again giving him an extra meatball. She slid the plate under the glass guard, and

Diegert slid his paper note to her side of the guard, saying only, "Thank you."

After eating his fill, he placed his dirty dishes in the cleaning area and went back to his room. He figured Elena was off duty in the next hour, and if she was going to come, he wanted to be there.

In his room, he sat alone on his bed where thoughts of his violent acts plagued him. He saw the bullet strikes and the blood splatters in vivid color. He felt the thud of the falling bodies and the terror of the frightened mothers caught in the crossfire, risking themselves to protect their children. He recalled the fading light in the eyes of his victims whose final gaze was upon the face of their killer. The emotions he felt left him sad and dejected. They preoccupied him as if the garbage can were full and had to be emptied before one more piece of trash could be put in it. Yet he couldn't breach that container and get it to tip over and dump its noxious contents.

These dreadful feelings were juxtaposed by the attraction he felt for Elena. She was kind and friendly. Her smile so genuine, he melted when she looked at him with her bright eyes. Her service uniform hid the outline of her body, but Diegert imagined she was femininely curvaceous, and he was eager to find out. Being emotionally and sexually attracted to this young woman gave Diegert a jolt of life, making him feel energized and excited. His conflicted state, though, clouded his thinking and occupied his mind.

It was while he was jumbled in turmoil that a knock on his door reverberated through the room. He opened the door and looked into the warm eyes and sweet smile of Elena. She stood at the threshold with her smile masking her apprehension. She knew she was breaking a protocol she had been trained to obey.

"Thanks for coming," said a grateful and anxious David Diegert. "Please come in."

He stepped aside so she could enter the room and closed the door behind her.

"First, thanks so much for coming to see me."

"Thank you for inviting me."

"I've thought about you a lot since we first met, and I was hoping we'd be able to become friends."

"Friends or lovers?"

Diegert was taken aback by her forward question, but it was exactly what was on his mind.

"Lovers, I hope."

He looked into her kind, gentle eyes and was captivated by the soft feminine features of her caring expression. He held out his hand, and she took it. He slowly pulled her into him and hugged her lovely body. He was embarrassed but unable to stop as the first tears crested his eyelids and rolled down his cheeks.

They moved onto the bed, and lying side by side, he burst into tears, crying bitterly, angrily, and forcefully, letting all the pain, sadness, anger, and grief come out of his body, his soul. She brushed his hair, stroked his neck, and quietly said, "Shhh...let it all out, sweet David the Beloved."

Diegert poured it out for twenty minutes, during which he relived the tragedies of the deaths he had created. When the memory of Omar's death came up, he was especially tortured. The serviceman was a brother in arms and just trying to do the right thing. Diegert deeply regretted killing him and was now facing the emotions of his wicked act. The exit from his heart was punishing. Elena held him tight as he suffered the disemboweling sensation of exorcising his guilt. Having saturated the pillow as well as the shoulder of her blouse, he was exhausted. She had never seen a man cry like this, and it struck her as deeply intimate. This man entrusted her to see him at his weakest moment, with his most painful emotions on unshielded display. She was awestruck.

He lay quietly with her, opening himself to make certain the trash can was empty, and he was able to be himself again. As he lay there with her, he had to admit to himself that this need for emotional catharsis was part of him. He was grateful for the comfort this lovely woman shared with him, and now he had no idea how to discuss this with her. He hoped she wouldn't ask for an explanation. He went for the simplest phrase: "Thank you."

She caressed his hair and face, saying, "I'm glad I could be here for you."

Diegert looked into her eyes and saw her desire. He moved forward, bringing his lips to hers. She pressed forward as well, and the pressure of their mouths ignited their sense of pleasure. Diegert pulled her closer in his arms. Elena slid her leg between his, allowing their hips to exert an erotic pressure. Elena opened her mouth, and their tongues intertwined, dancing in a flurry of exquisite pleasure. Diegert's hands ran down her body, feeling the sweep of her rib cage into her narrow waist and then the sensual curve of her hips. Diegert rolled her to the side, sliding his hand up until he caressed her clothed breast.

Elena moaned as Diegert gently squeezed her sensitive chest and started unbuttoning her blouse. Elena's excitement exploded, and she broke from Diegert to strip off her clothes. Diegert used the moment to do the same, and then the lovers were back on the bed, naked and enthralled with the sensation of skin on skin.

Elena's breasts had never been exposed to the sun and looked like soft alabaster with rosy nipples. Diegert hungrily took one of her sensitive buds into his mouth, and

Elena responded with an erotic moan and intense thrusts of her hips. Diegert's shaft was fully engorged, and Elena pressed herself against the stiff member. She broke Diegert's nipple kiss and slid down his body so she could take his erection into her moist mouth. Diegert looked to the ceiling and gave himself over to the pleasure she was providing. She stroked his shaft with her lips, altering her actions according to his pleasurable responses.

Diegert enjoyed her sensual pleasures, but he wanted to share the climax. He guided her to straddle him and inserted himself into her. The lovers found their rhythm, thrusting their hips in time with their mounting desire. Their timing was just right as Diegert reached the peak of pleasure a moment before Elena's body exploded into a transcendent orgasm that lasted longer than any Diegert had ever witnessed. She crashed down on top of him, pressing her body against his.

They lay quietly, comfortable in their mutual silence. Diegert heard the swipe of plastic through the door's electronic lock. The latch popped open with a loud snap, and the room filled with the bright light of the hallway, causing both of them to shield their faces.

Entering the room, Fatima was shocked to see two bodies entwined on the bed. She stopped abruptly and gasped at the sight before her. Diegert got up, stepped past Fatima, and closed the door. Elena swung her legs to the floor and struggled to get dressed. Diegert stepped into his boxers while Fatima caught her breath and formed her next statement.

"This is not supposed to happen."

"Calm down, I don't have to explain this to you."

"As a matter of fact, you do."

"You can mind your own fucking business."

"When you're fucking a Headquarters employee, that is my business."

"We're adults who don't need your approval."

"One of your points can't be argued, but on the other, you're clearly wrong."

Returning next to her on the bed and grabbing her hand, Diegert told Elena, "You're the kindest, most gentle woman I've ever met, and I'm so grateful for the time you spent with me."

Fatima blurted out, "Shut the fuck up." Turning to Elena, she said, "Get out of here right now before I call security."

Elena glanced at Diegert with a quiet smile, stood up, faced Fatima with eyes like daggers, and walked out. Diegert sat on the bed looking at the floor.

Fatima sighed, saying, "This is over. You are not to fraternize with Headquarters employees. I'll see you at 0700."

31

To be a member of the choir of Westminster Abbey you not only had to be a boy between the ages of eight and fourteen with the gift of voice, but you also had to be fully committed to the schedule of daily performances and enroll in the abbey's choir school. The school was specifically designed to allow the boys to complete their educations while fulfilling the performance requirements of the choir. The choir's schedule included daily participation in services at the abbey as well as state and international performances.

Andrew Cambridge was eleven years old and one of the principal voices in the choir. His parents, Arthur and Elizabeth, were so very proud of his participation, and their generous sponsorship allowed the choir to stay at some of the finest hotels in the world when they traveled to perform. Andrew thought all the songs were kind of old fashioned, but he was so accustomed to being with his friends in the choir that the very uniqueness of his privileged but demanding life didn't even occur to him. Even at the age of eleven, he enjoyed the fantasy of Christmas. He and his family made the most of the story of Father Christmas and his chimney-sliding habit of bringing gifts on Christmas morning.

The choir of Westminster Abbey performed at the classic midnight mass as well as the morning services, but in between, Andrew Cambridge and the other boys were allowed to go home and have Christmas morning with their families. Andrew was so very excited about the holiday that the butterflies in his stomach flapped all day.

Midnight Mass was a tremendous affair, attended by the royal family and a thousand other parishioners. The cathedral, dressed in lights and decorations for the holiday, had a magical feel for this special season. Andrew's parents, as well as his older sister, Victoria, were all in attendance at midnight Mass, so Andrew was a little surprised when a dark-suited man approached him after the performance and informed him he would be providing Andrew transport to the Cambridge estate. But Andrew's excitement wasn't diminished by the fact that he was riding separately to the family's home in the country. As a member of the choir, he was always being driven to one place or another. The car certainly looked right, a big black Rolls-Royce. The man opened the rear door, Andrew climbed in, and the man followed. The car immediately drove off the grounds of the abbey and turned in the direction of the estate.

Andrew asked, "Was Victoria with my parents?"

"I'm sure she is," replied the man in the seat beside him.

"She is becoming such a bother to Mum and Dad. She's doing the teenage thing really badly, rejecting everything Mum and Dad want her to do. I wouldn't be surprised if she just pissed on midnight Mass and stayed home."

The man remained silent but smiled weakly and looked out the window. Andrew looked out the window as well, and it looked like they were getting on the freeway, which was certainly not the route to the estate. When Andrew turned to question their route, he was startled to see the man had a small mask over his nose and mouth. He looked to the driver, and the window between them was closed tight. The man held a small spray bottle. Andrew put his hands up to defend himself, but the vapors found their way into his lungs. Within a minute, he was unconscious, and the man opened the moonroof to aerate the cabin. The driver continued on to the airport, where Andrew was loaded on a private plane and flown to Bucharest, Romania.

When he received notice that the abduction had succeeded, Michka Barovitz sent an e-mail to both Arthur Cambridge and Nigel Flannery.

Gentlemen,
Apparently, you have some lessons to learn about doing
business in the Balkans. I will instruct you to make the
payments I outlined in my earlier e-mail or your son will
suffer the consequences for nonpayment. Hopefully he will
learn early to abide by the cultural practices of different
regions of the world. When payment in full has been made
and a consistent payment history has been established, your
son's tour of the Balkans will conclude, and he will be
returned. Until then, his location and well-being will be at
my direction. I wish you a Happy Christmas.
Michka Barovitz

When they got the e-mail, it concluded the two hours of worry about the disappearance of Andrew, but it extended an already long night.

Elizabeth Cambridge was hysterical. She cried inconsolably, hyperventilating to the point of fainting. Arthur felt powerless yet was resigned to resolve this with dignity. Nigel Flannery was at the family estate. He explained to Arthur the earlier correspondence with Barovitz and was so very apologetic, though he could never have imagined that this would be the consequence for refusing to be extorted. News of the boy's kidnapping spread quickly, and the British online tabloids feasted on the story, speculating on all sorts of dreadful possibilities and probable suspects.

When Dean Kellerman heard the news, he was taken by the plight of his friend and business associate. Being a parishioner of the abbey and a member of the same exclusive golf club as Arthur, he felt compelled to offer his assistance. Unlike so many people, who offered to do whatever they could even when there was nothing they could actually do, Dean Kellerman's wealth and position were substantially greater than the rest of London's elite. As a member of the Board of Crepusculous, he played on the world stage and belonged to the small group of the world's most influential people. In spite of his lofty position, he could feel the pain and sorrow his friend's family was going through. It certainly wasn't pity he was offering, and he was aware of Cambridge Holdings's new properties in Romania. With that knowledge, he speculated the problem emanated from the Balkans, although no such information had left the mouths of either Arthur or Nigel.

When Kellerman's name appeared on Arthur's phone, he wisely took the call. "Hello, Dean."

"Arthur, my dear chap, this is a dreadful situation. Let me save us some time and share a speculation with you."

"Thank you for calling. I appreciate your concern."

"Right, my good man. I'm curious to know if this has anything to do with your recent acquisition of properties in Romania?"

Arthur's shocked response was audible through the phone. "Why…yes."

"I was afraid so. Dreadful buggers, those Balkan businessmen. Extortion is such a part of the culture that they don't even perceive it as wrong. Did they say which country he's being held in?"

"I believe Romania, but the message said he will be on a tour of the Balkans."

"OK, here it is. I have assets in the Balkans that are trained to deal with situations like this. They are Special Forces types who work for me as mercenaries when I need them. I'll deploy them to find and retrieve your son, but I will ask that you do not tell the police, the press, or your family of this arrangement. I do hope you can appreciate the sensitivity of training and maintaining such resources?"

"Yes, of course, I will tell no one."

At that instant, Arthur turned and looked at Nigel, who was hearing only half the conversation.

Kellerman broke back in. "Arthur, you certainly can inform your good man Nigel, but no one else. I'll call you on this number with news as things develop in the theater. Keep up your spirits and Happy Christmas."

"Yes…thank you, sir."

Kellerman hung up the phone and called Blevinsky. He informed him of the situation and tasked him with locating the boy and assembling a team to retrieve him. Fortunately, Barovitz operated with such brazen impunity in Bucharest and kidnapped whomever he wanted, that his locations were known in the underground community. Blevinsky put together a reconnaissance plan tasking three operators to infiltrate and investigate Barovitz's most likely locations. He informed Fatima of the situation and told her he wanted Diegert to be one of those operators.

32

It's Christmas time, and this fucking place doesn't even have a Christmas tree, thought Diegert as he ate his breakfast. Fatima appeared, and as usual didn't eat any cafeteria food. "Why don't you eat anything?" asked Diegert.

"Because I choose not to poison my body with the junk they serve."

"What have you got? A hot plate, bean sprouts, and a teapot in your room?"

"Never mind, I'm here to task you with a mission."

"You got rid of her, didn't you?"

"What?"

"Elena, the girl in the service line, you got her fired, didn't you?"

"That's right, she doesn't work here anymore, and her husband's not too happy about it. It's going to make it a lot harder for them to feed their two children. But I suppose you never thought about that?"

Diegert drew a long breath as he looked down at his plate. Turning his gaze to Fatima, he said, "You didn't have to get her fired."

"Employees are not to fraternize with trainees and vice versa. It was her or you. So you're lucky you're still here."

"Yeah, lucky me."

Fatima sprang up, grabbing Diegert's right hand in a wristlock and twisting it behind his back. She picked up his fork and placed it against his neck. "I have told you this is serious shit, and I'm not going to fuck around with you. If I kill you right now, no one will care and I'll suffer no consequences, you understand?"

She pressed the fork until blood ran down from the four tines. She kept going deeper until Diegert spat out an answer. "Yes, I understand."

She took her hand off the fork, leaving it embedded in his flesh, released the armlock, and stepped back. The cafeteria grew talkative again after the passing of the dramatic moment. Diegert reached up and extracted the fork.

Fatima instructed him, "Meet me in Room 240 after you're done poisoning yourself."

The bleeding wouldn't stop. Diegert had to go to medical, where an antibiotic ointment was applied, and the wound was covered by a large bandage. The medic said it was a good thing he came, because impalements usually got infected, especially when egg and saliva penetrated the skin.

Room 240 was behind a windowless door. When Diegert stepped inside, he noticed all the walls were padded and there were no windows at all. The floor was also padded. Fatima stood across the room dressed in her black combat uniform and tactical boots. Her dark hair fell below her shoulders in lustrous waves. She looked at him and giggled. "You look like you're trying to hide a hickey."

Diegert didn't reply, but his furrowed brow told her he did not find her amusing. With a playful, seductive smile, she bounced over to him and asked, "Do you know why I brought you here?"

Diegert was disarmed. He had never seen Fatima show her sexy side, and it was very sexy indeed. She approached him looking into his eyes with hers wide and her smile broad and appealing. "I brought you here because I can't stand it any longer. You really turn me on."

"I do?"

"Yes, of course. You may have misinterpreted the way I've been treating you, but it's because I want you so bad," Fatima said as she reached out and stroked his dark hair.

"Bullshit! This is total bullshit."

"You don't believe me? Why wouldn't you believe that I'm hot for you? You don't find me attractive?"

"You just stabbed me with a fork, and now this?"

"You didn't answer my question. Do you find me attractive?"

"No... No. I mean, yes, you're very attractive. But what about all the other shit you've been doing to me?"

Stepping close to him and placing her hand on his chest, she said, "I have to keep up appearances around here, you know." She turned from him and walked a few paces, moping sadly. Looking back over her shoulder, she said, "I was really jealous of that other girl. The one you had in your room."

"And you certainly fixed it so you won't have to worry about her anymore."

"I thought, doesn't he see how much I want him, how sexy I think he is, and how much I want to be with him? So I brought you here, to the most private room in the whole place, so we could...share some passion." Standing with her feet in a wide stance and her hips turned and tilted, Fatima pulled her T-shirt over her head, revealing her black sports bra.

Diegert was amazed, and this woman was hot, even though it was so unexpected. If she wanted to have sex, he was more than willing to take pleasure from her body.

"Why don't you come over here and I'll give you a real hickey to hide."

"I don't believe this. You're fucking around with me so you can get me in more trouble."

"You're being a silly boy," she said as she dipped her head and strode over to him. "I'm not fucking you, not yet, but I want to." She trailed her hand around his neck, across his chest, and over his shoulder while circling him.

Diegert's face revealed his conflict and confusion, but he stood fast as she finished her circle and drew herself close to him.

"Honestly, what has a girl gotta do to show a guy she's hot for him?" She held his gaze, exuding sexual desire. Stepping back one pace, she undid the belt of her combat pants and lowered her zipper, revealing white panties with a red waistband and a little yellow flower on the front. She reached out and pulled his hips to hers. She smiled up at him with warmth and assurance. She squeezed his butt with her left hand, and with her right, she hit him in the chin with a palm heel strike.

Diegert's head snapped. She grasped his right arm, kicking him in the hip sending him sprawling on his back to the floor. She stepped on the biceps of his right arm, causing his hand to lie flat on the floor, palm up. She slid her foot out to his hand and placed her heel on his palm.

Diegert was shocked but quickly realized what a fool he had been. The pain in his palm was more intense than he'd ever imagined. Fatima dropped her right knee into the meat of his thigh; he rotated the leg, and her weight exerted extreme pressure on his femur. This, too, was far more painful than Diegert had expected. From her position, Fatima easily punched Diegert in the ribs. The excruciating pain of the injured bones took his breath away.

"Do I have your attention now? Do you recognize who your superior is? Will you realize that I'm better at what we do than you are? I have tools you will never have, and I know how to use them to disarm those who should be able to recognize a ruse."

Diegert was in so much pain from so many places he was having trouble listening to her. She reached down and slapped his face. "Hey, are you paying attention? Do you realize how vulnerable you are?"

She slapped him again. "Answer me."

Diegert had both his left arm and leg free. His eyes darted to her right side, planning a countermovement. "I see...you want to try to get free."

Fatima pressed her weight into his right palm and drove her left knee into his groin. The searing pain from the sudden strike on his testicles sent Diegert to a place of pain he had never experienced before. He was about to lose consciousness when she struck his ribs again. He thought she was speaking, but he could no longer hear her, and his world was closing in, his mind going gray. His face was slapped again and again, but he could no longer feel it, and soon he was in a black world of nothingness.

Fatima realized he was unconscious when every muscle in his body went limp.

"What a pussy," she said as she stood up and stepped off him. She looked at her watch: 07:42. She squatted back down next to him to confirm his heartbeat and breathing; he was still alive. She stood again and stepped away from him. She realized she had gone a little too far as she did up her pants and put her T-shirt back on. She reminded herself she was authorized to expose trainees to harsh treatment simulating that which they may encounter in the field. She reasoned he would now know his limits and operate accordingly.

When he came to, she would treat him nicer and brief him on the upcoming mission. 07:45. She had to admit that she had never applied this much abuse before. She was certain that waterboarding and stress positions were worse, but the sustained application of pain, with escalation on areas that had already been traumatized, could be considered excessive in a training program. Yeah...this was bad. 07:50. She gently tapped his face and rubbed his forearm, softly saying, "Diegert... David."

When he remained unresponsive, she stepped away and crossed to the far side of the room. She nervously brought her hand to her chin as she thought that she would have to keep a lid on his reactions so that the full story never left the room. Perhaps he'd have amnesia. 07:54.

Diegert coughed. He brought his hands to his face and rolled onto his side. He tucked into a fetal position.

Fatima asked, "Are you OK?"

"Fuck you."

"OK, well, if you're all better, I want you to sit up and listen to the mission briefing I have for you."

Diegert propped himself on his right elbow, saying, "What the fuck was that all about?"

"You're vulnerable to the seductive powers of women. You need to be able to see beyond the end of your prick and realize how disarming a woman can be. If you and I squared off directly, you would never end up like this. But throw in the possibility of getting laid, and you turn to putty."

"You're a fucking bitch."

"Yeah, I know. Don't ever let another woman do this to you. And don't tell anyone what happened here today. Now if you're ready to focus, there is a mission coming up, part of which is going to be assigned to you."

"Whoa... Whoa... Whoa. You just treat me like shit with your backhanded seduction, and now you're going to brief me on a mission?"

Fatima's fiery personality ignited, and she exploded at Diegert. "You want to cry about your treatment, go right ahead, but there is no one to listen to your complaints. If you are not able to produce what's requested, there are plenty of law enforcement agencies that would love to get their hands on you. Do you understand me?"

Rolling back onto his side so he wouldn't have to look at her, Diegert said, "What part of the mission do you want me to do?"

"Reconnaissance. A British national, a young boy, has been taken hostage and brought to Romania. Barovitz, the mob boss in Bucharest, is holding him. We've been tasked with locating the subject and then formulating a rescue plan. Obviously, we don't want the boy hurt, and it will be a team mission to retrieve him."

"You mean we do hostage rescues as well as assassinations?"

Raising her voice, she said, "When we have the opportunity to do something that will directly help an innocent person, we'll do it."

"How do we know he's innocent?"

Stepping over to him and rolling him onto his back, Fatima's fiery eyes locked on as she said, "He's an eleven-year-old choir boy. I think that qualifies as innocent."

"Alright, what have I got to do?"

"Blevinsky has identified three likely locations where the boy might be held. You will perform reconnaissance on a casino. The schematics of the building have been sent to your phone. When the boy's location is known, his extraction will be carried out by a strike team. Why don't you go rest up; the recon mission is tonight. Study those schematics and learn them a lot better than the shitty job you did learning code."

Diegert looked at her with disdain and distrust as he struggled to his feet and left the room.

33

In the free weight area of the fitness center, Blevinsky addressed Strakov, "Alexi, I want you to make certain all the men on the strike team realize that the mission is to rescue the hostage. You must use restraint. Your team is not to fill a room with dead bodies."

"When do we deploy? Do we have time to practice?"

"You have time. I have reconnaissance missions underway to locate the boy and gather intel."

"Alright, we'll practice selective shooting."

"Good, I'll keep you updated."

Blevinsky left Strakov, but the big guy cut his workout short so he could get his team prepared.

* * * *

As darkness fell, Diegert was driven to Barovitz's Casino Placere. The gambling establishment, located in an ancient palace, had long since lost its luster. The place was big and old with two floors of gambling. Roulette wheels, blackjack tables, and slot machines dominated the first floor, with the noise, lights, and smoke giving it both an exciting and a depressing feel. The second floor had poker and other high-stakes card games, which were played on well-lit tables in darkened rooms. Barovitz generated huge profits from this facility, and although there were occasional winners, the house dominated, and the mobster used both the profits and individual's debts to his advantage.

If a person was unable to pay, Barovitz often found some dirty job for them to do or took whatever property or valuables they had as payment. Barovitz considered young women an acceptable commodity. Several daughters of debtors now worked for Barovitz to pay for the losses of their fathers. The period between Christmas and New Year's was an especially busy time as people celebrated the holidays by feeding their desires for easy money.

The parking lot was full, and people were dressed in their best for an evening in the old palace. Diegert entered the casino with the rest of the gamblers. He was not interested in trying to win money. His objectives were far riskier than losing a couple hundred euros. On his smartphone, he checked the schematic of the area in the basement he was to reconnoiter. At the far end of the corridor, near the men's room, was a door to a staircase that led to the basement. Diegert found the door locked, but using a pick tool, he opened it and stepped inside. Descending the stairs led him to another locked door. Using his tool, he had it open in thirty seconds. Before entering, he reexamined the diagram on his phone, which revealed that on the other side of the door was a very large storage space. There was also a ground-level exit door on the opposite side of the building. The intel he was given indicated that this was the place where Barovitz held hostages.

Diegert opened the door a crack, peering into the cavernous space. In one corner, there were dozens of aged slot machines stacked horizontally and covered in plastic. There was no movement, but a light shone from the far side of the large space.

Diegert withdrew his HK45 tactical pistol from its holster. The gun was equipped with a laser sight and a flashlight. He affixed his suppressor and was now armed with his favorite weapon. Very cautiously, he stepped out from behind the door. On silent feet, he crossed the room and proceeded to the end of the row of slot machines.

From this vantage point, he could see an area lit by several hanging fluorescent fixtures. In the center of the space was a table with four chairs. The table was littered with food wrappers, cards, ashtrays, and liquor bottles. Flanking the table in an L-shaped arrangement were two dingy couches. Beyond them was a curtain strung between two hooks that were attached to the ceiling. The place showed signs of recent occupation, but at the moment it was deserted.

Diegert, dressed in black, carefully crossed the space, passed the table, and peered behind the curtain. There was a boy with his hands tied through the back of a sturdy chair. He was dressed in navy slacks and a white shirt, with a red tie and a dark-blue blazer displaying the shield of the Westminster Abbey. His right eye was bruised, and he had a cut on his left lower lip, but his eyes made direct contact with Diegert's from under his tousled mop of blond hair.

Stepping forward, Diegert said, "I'm here to take you home."

Diegert unraveled the duct tape binding the boy's wrists. The instant the bonds were broken, the boy took off running. Diegert chased after him into the open space and saw the boy rush around the corner of the stacked slot machines. When Diegert turned the corner, he was confronted by a very large, very bald bodyguard who held the struggling Andrew Cambridge by his right arm. The boy kicked and punched the big man. Annoyed by the boy's violence, the guard backhanded the lad across the face, turning him into an unconscious heap. The guard faced Diegert, who pulled the trigger of his HK45, firing a sound-suppressed bullet into the big man's chest. The round delivered a solid body blow, but the guard's Kevlar vest stopped the bullet, and he came forward, bringing the fight to Diegert. Stepping behind the slot machines, Diegert eluded his enemy. He sprinted back to the table and behind the curtain, drawing the guard away from the boy. Listening carefully, Diegert could hear the angry guard coming. When the big, bald man lifted the curtain, Diegert's laser sight marked the spot on the guard's forehead where the bullet entered his brain. The big guy's body collapsed with a powerful thud, and Diegert sprinted back to Andrew Cambridge.

Lifting the unconscious boy over his shoulder, Diegert headed for the exit down the hallway on the south side of the building. As he moved down the hall, Diegert texted Fatima.

I have the boy. I need extraction at the south end of the casino.

Fatima's response was immediate; she called, saying, "God damn it, you were only supposed to do reconnaissance. What the fuck is going on?"

"We'll argue later. Right now, I need help getting the boy out of here."

"There is no help. Nothing is organized."

"Fuckin' get it together. Call me back."

* * * *

The elevator descended and opened up not far from the door that Diegert had used to enter the basement. A second bodyguard exited the elevator, stepped around the defunct slot machines, and walked to the area where he was to relieve his associate. When he entered the area formed by the table and couches, he did not see his comrade and shouted, "Boris?"

When there was no reply, he moved to the curtained-off area, pulled back the cloth, and saw his dead comrade. Dismayed as he was by his dead associate, the boy's absence quickly rose to prominence, and he began searching for the missing prisoner.

* * * *

Fatima realized she had to do something but deploying a rescue team was out of the question and would certainly fail without thorough planning. Checking the map, she noticed a large water tower south of the casino that was serviced by a dirt road. If Diegert could get there, she could extract him with a vehicle. She texted him the plan.

Extract at the water tower in 30 mins.

Diegert checked the map on his smartphone. The water tower sat on a hill across from the parking lot surrounded by thin woods and a fence. He recalled seeing a toolbox on the floor near one of the couches. He made Andrew as comfortable as possible, turned off the hall lights, and went back to get a cutting tool for the fence.

After searching all the many hiding places in the big room, the bodyguard headed down the south hallway. Diegert could see the long shadow cast by whomever was backlit as he walked down the hall. From the cover of darkness, Diegert sprinted forward, placing a vicious choke strike on the trachea of the bodyguard. The shock and force of the strike cracked the man's larynx, triggering a disabling coughing fit. Diegert slugged the guy in the gut and then chopped him on the back of the neck, felling him to the ground.

Diegert didn't want to shoot this man in front of Andrew. He stepped back down the hallway to check on the boy. When he turned on the lights, the brightness startled the boy, who was suddenly awake and aware. Diegert approached the boy in a manner he assumed was friendly and reassuring. "Andrew, everything is going to be okay. Stay here, and I'll be right back to take you to safety. Okay?"

To the boy, none of it made sense, and Diegert looked like just another tough guy dressed in black.

Diegert drew his pistol and returned to the sputtering guard. He hauled the guy to his feet and pushed him back to the big room. He made him open the toolbox and dump the contents on the table. A hammer, screwdrivers, nails, screws, washers, but the closest thing to a cutting tool was a pair of needle-nose pliers and a wood-handled rasp. He stuck these two tools in a pouch pocket and looked back up to see the bodyguard reaching for the hammer. Diegert pointed his pistol at him, saying, "Touch it and I nail you."

Suddenly, a blaring alarm startled both men. The bodyguard looked past Diegert down the hallway. Diegert turned instinctively to the sound, giving the bodyguard the moment he needed to grab the hammer and swing at Diegert's right arm. The strike on his radius was intense, and Diegert lost the grip on his pistol. The bodyguard swung the hammer at his head, and Diegert leaned back as the head of the hammer passed within millimeters of his face. Diegert stepped in and used his arm to block the bodyguard's return swing. He struck him in the temple with three quick jabs. The bodyguard stumbled to his left, and Diegert delivered a full-force kick to the hip. Having fallen on his left side, the bodyguard flung the hammer at Diegert, striking him in his already injured ribs. Diegert gasped for air as the cage of protective bones was once again tested.

The bodyguard got to his feet, grabbed a screwdriver, and slashed at Diegert. The boy's would-be rescuer dodged the swipes and swings the big guy made with the pointed tool. Diegert stepped back up against one of the couches and felt the rasp he had in his pocket. The bodyguard thought he had his enemy trapped against the furniture and strode forward to impale him. Diegert flipped backward over the couch, extracting the rasp from his pocket. Holding the wood handle, he watched as the bodyguard prepared to climb over the couch. The moment the big guy's foot was on the unstable cushions, Diegert rushed forward and slashed the rasp across the bodyguard's face. So destructive was the sharp surface of the rasp that the guy's right cheek flayed open, revealing his molars. The blood poured out of his lacerated face, escalating his anger.

Diegert stepped out into an open area and squared off with his determined foe. With the screwdriver held forward, the bodyguard lunged at Diegert, who was able to avoid the thrusts. Eventually, the frustrated attacker charged, and Diegert struck him with the rasp on the back of his arm, shredding his shirtsleeve and turning it crimson from his ripped triceps.

Diegert struck again, this time hitting his opponent on the back of the head. The bodyguard was stunned from the blow, and Diegert hit him again and again with the rasp until the vertebrae in his neck were severed, blood erupting from the spinal arteries. The big bodyguard's body slumped forward, collapsing on the floor as his life-sustaining fluids pulsed out of his neck.

Diegert found his H&K just as the elevator doors opened and two more men stepped out. With the slot machines as a barrier, Diegert turned and sprinted down the hallway. Andrew was no longer there, and he raced through the open door. Outside, he noticed a pile of pallets. Grabbing one, he wedged it under the doorknob, making the exit inoperable from the inside.

34

From the door, Diegert saw tracks leading to the parking lot. The poorly plowed gravel space had at least a hundred cars in it, and Diegert had no idea where Andrew might be. He started searching the lot, looking down the aisles between cars. Finding nothing, he wondered if Andrew would've taken off into the woods, but there were no tracks in that direction. As his frustration grew, Diegert heard a group of kids shouting and laughing not far away. He moved in their direction and could see a group of six teens standing in a circle. The hoodlums surrounded Andrew and were taunting and teasing him. The boy was standing his ground as his tormentors threw snowballs and insults at him. Diegert stepped in front of Andrew and told the punks, "Get the fuck out of here." One look at the menacing face of David Diegert was enough to give them pause, but the gun in his hand made the group of troublemakers quickly disperse.

Diegert turned to Andrew, saying, "I know you don't know me, and you've been through some terrible things, but for your safety and survival you have to come with me. Now."

Diegert had moved to the fence at the base of the water tower hill. The wire-cutting jaws on the pliers were completely inadequate to cut through the fencing. Diegert used them, though, to untwist the chain link diamonds. As he struggled with the metal, men from the casino spotted them and came running. The guys were taking pot shots at Diegert, and he had to stop untangling the fencing and return fire. Each time they stopped firing he went back to work dismantling the barrier. Soon he could hear the men's voices growing closer. The chain links were almost untangled enough for them to slip through.

Diegert looked back to see one of the men ten meters away sighting his assault rifle on them. Covering Andrew, he looked up to see the man's head explode off his shoulders. The beam of a laser sight was briefly visible in the bloody spray before the lifeless body collapsed to the ground. The next man in the lot was similarly vanquished, and Diegert quickly pulled the fencing apart so that he and Andrew could crawl through.

They ran a short distance through the woods and began ascending the hill. Two more men were firing on them as they were exposed on the hillside. The sniper fire was not able to take them out but did keep them pinned down long enough for Diegert to pick Andrew up and shoulder haul him up to the top of the hill. Fatima directed them to the SUV while she placed an incendiary round into the chamber of her rifle. She aimed carefully at the gas tank of the car the men were hiding behind. The shot entered the tank, igniting its contents and taking out the last two men who knew where the boy had gone.

Diegert sat in the driver's seat, and Andrew was buckled in the back. Fatima put her rifle in the back of the vehicle and jumped into the front passenger's seat. She reluctantly handed Diegert the keys, saying, "You're in deep shit. What the fuck were you doing? I had to pull a favor to get the rifle, and you owe me."

"Thanks for coming. I'd like to introduce you to Andrew Cambridge, but I request that you control your profane tongue."

Fatima's anger hung on her face until she turned to Andrew. When she looked at the traumatized boy, she became warm and gentle. Her smile was loving and comforting. Diegert drove down the hill heading back to

Headquarters. She spoke to Andrew softly. "It's all over, you're going to be OK. You're going home to be with your family. Don't be frightened, Hamni, we'll be in a safe place very soon."

She reached her hand back and caressed the boy's forearm. He closed his eyes, and the tears squeezed out of his lids and down his cheeks. Fatima pulled a handkerchief out of her pocket, unbuckled her seat belt, and climbed in the back to hug Andrew in her arms. "Shhh..." she said as the boy took comfort in her embrace.

When Diegert neared the Headquarters, he looked back and saw that Andrew was asleep in Fatima's arms. She looked content and more peaceful than he had ever seen her. With less than a mile to go, Fatima told Diegert, "I don't want you telling anyone about my involvement with this operation. You understand?"

"Who's Hamni?"

"What?"

"Hamni? You called him Hamni when you spoke to him. His name is Andrew."

"I know his name, and I didn't call him anything else." Her pissed-off face was back, but it now had shades of surprise and perplexity.

"I'm just saying, you called the kid Hamni, so I was just asking who that is?"

"Shut up, just make sure you don't tell anyone I was involved at all."

"You sure? Because you were awesome."

"Tell no one anything. Pull the car over here."

Diegert parked the SUV on the side of the road.

"You're going to get out of the car and carry Andrew into Headquarters. I'll return before you. Using the car is no big deal as long as I return without you. Returning the rifle,

I have covered, but I owe Lindstrom a big favor which you are going to repay."

Diegert looked at her and shrugged.

"Now think up a lie about how you got away and how you got back here with the boy and stick to it. Don't mention me."

"Yeah... Yeah, I got it, you were never there."

Diegert stepped out of the vehicle, opened the passenger door, and lifted Andrew into his arms. Fatima drove away, and Diegert was left to walk the three quarters of a mile to Headquarters.

The gate opened automatically as Diegert approached with the boy. Inside, he went straight to medical as people in the halls and offices looked to see what was going on. A child in the facility was a very rare occurrence. Once Andrew was secure in the hands of the medical staff, Diegert reported to Blevinsky's office. The terse bald man stood in his doorway watching Diegert's approach. As the younger man got closer, Blevinsky stepped back into his office, never breaking eye contact until he was on the other side of the door. Diegert walked in as Blevinsky rounded his desk and took a position standing in front of his chair.

"Close the door. In some sappy Hollywood movie I would be saying something to you like 'Even though you broke protocol, you saved the day, you little rascal.' But this is not Hollywood, and the only thing that concerns me is that you broke protocol. I don't care about the outcome, you disobeyed, and now your training requires additional supervision."

"Sir, I was just trying to improvise as the situation developed."

"Improvisation! This is not some fucking comedy club. Is that what Fatima is teaching you?"

"Sir, aren't you even interested in what transpired before you judge it as wrong?"

"No, I am not. I was developing an extraction plan that was waiting on your intel. But your dangerous and careless actions have made that plan obsolete while exposing the hostage to even greater danger."

"He was already in great danger that he may not have survived if I just gathered intel and left him there."

Blevinsky shouted, "That's your judgment, and you are not qualified to make such assessments. In the future, you will follow orders when they are as explicit as these were." The angry man slammed his fist on the desk.

"Now you're dismissed. Tomorrow Alexi Strakov will have a training mission for you."

Diegert rolled his eyes and let out a sigh before leaving the office.

On the other side of the door stood Alexi Strakov. Diegert was surprised and had to step around him to keep from colliding with the big Russian.

"Guess you just can't wait, eh, Liberace?" Diegert said.

Looking around, Diegert realized the hall was full of Strakov's strike team. Strakov pounced on his statement.

"What the fuck was that? Are you insulting my homosexuality?"

Diegert looked at the imposing man and the expectant stares of the guys in the hall. He was reeling from the fact that his insult was not at all disarming but rather infuriated this combat-capable man who was backed up by a group of the toughest men Diegert had ever seen.

"That's right, I'm gay. You got a problem with that, then you got a big fucking problem."

"No, man, it's cool."

"You fuckin' phobe. The training session I have planned for you tomorrow will be just right for a single superman like you. You don't need anyone's help? You don't need to be part of a team? We'll see tomorrow how well you operate all by yourself."

"Hey, I'm sorry if your assault plan didn't happen."

Gesturing to the men in the hall, Strakov said, "You hear that? He's sorry we didn't get to be part of a well-planned and practiced operation. Well, your apology makes all of us feel so much better. We're really grateful you saved the day, even if it almost got that little kid killed."

Diegert looked at him quizzically.

Strakov went on, "Be ready for the mission at 1600 tomorrow, you selfish puke."

Strakov walked down the hall, passing between the six men leaning against the walls. As he passed, each man looked disapprovingly at Diegert and fell in line behind their leader. Diegert wondered to himself, *Are they all gay?*

35

As Diegert left his office, Blevinsky took a call from Kellerman.

"My good man, do update me on the situation."

"Sir, I can report that we have Andrew Cambridge safe and secure here at Headquarters."

"What?"

"Yes, sir, he was recovered just an hour ago."

"That's splendid; that's incredible. Arthur and Elizabeth will be so relieved. However did you manage it? Were there casualties? How many men were on the team? I must see to it they are rewarded."

"There were no casualties on our side, Mr. Kellerman. We were lucky to locate the boy quickly, and he's a tough little guy."

"Why, I'm sure he had to be. Give me details? How did the team extract him?"

Blevinsky ran his fingers through the gray band of hair on the back of his head and struggled to find a way to answer the questions. "He was…extracted from the location where he was found."

"Yes, of course, but how many men took part? Was there fighting?"

Blevinsky squeezed his eyes shut and banged his fist against his head as he listened to the question. Throwing his head back and tilting his chair, he fought against his reticence to tell Kellerman the truth. "Sir, there was no team in the rescue of Andrew Cambridge."

"No team? What do you mean? How many men were involved?"

Tapping the phone against the crown of his smooth head, Belvinsky answered, "Just one man."

"A single man…against a Michka Barovitz crew? That's incredible. Who is this man?"

"His name is Diegert, David Diegert."

"Well, very good for you, Aaron, training men who can operate on their own. I'm so very pleased. I'll see to it that Mr. Diegert is financially rewarded. You and he have returned the holiday spirit to the season along with young Master Cambridge. Thank you, old chap."

"Certainly, sir, I hope you and your friends can get back to enjoying your festivities."

"Oh, very well, good man. I thank you again and good night."

When Blevinsky hung up, he dropped his head in his hand, let out a sigh, and thought how unfair luck could be.

* * * *

Back in his room, Diegert was watching *Mission Impossible III*. Diegert's phone rang, interrupting the movie just as Tom Cruise was sliding down a glass building.

"Hello?"

"Is this Mr. David Diegert?"

"Yes."

"Good evening, sir, my name is Wendall Bishop. I am your account manager from the Royal Bank of the Caribbean in the Cayman Islands. I'm calling you regarding your account."

"OK."

"Sir, I'm calling, as stipulated in our customer service policy, to inform you that there has been a substantial deposit into your account. We have checked the depositing agent's source and confirmed the transfer. We suggest you check your account and verify the activity. Please contact us with any issues you may have with the account. Good night, sir."

Diegert stared at his phone skeptically, as if what he'd just heard had to be a prank.

Before he could check his account, his phone rang again, and he saw it was Fatima calling. "Yeah," he answered.

"You didn't let my involvement slip, did you?"

"No, everyone thinks I did this on my own, and it pisses them off."

"Too bad. This is the way I want it. Tomorrow morning, 0730, you're to report to the armory where you will do what Lindstrom tells you. You'll be fulfilling the debt I owe him. The armory is in Room 135. You know where that is, right?"

"Yeah, I know. I'll be there. Hey, are all the guys here gay?"

"No... Why does that matter? Some are, I suppose. Strakov is, but you already knew that. What are you pursuing?"

"Nothing. It was just on my mind from some things I've observed."

"Look, you gotta crawl out from under your year 2000 rock and recognize that people don't care about that anymore. We're not the ridiculous US military. If Strakov gets the job done, then who cares if he loves men. I'm glad he's gay.It's one less guy staring at my ass every time I walk by. Be at the armory at 0730."

After hanging up, Diegert had a hard time believing that such an obvious Alpha male, who led the men so powerfully, was gay. The values, or rather the prejudices, of his rural Minnesota upbringing just didn't allow for that combination. It seemed as though it was time to update his perspective. *Update,* he thought, remembering to check his account. There on the phone screen was his account balance with an additional ten thousand dollars in it. He now had $155,000 in his personal account.

36

The placement of the armory away from the living quarters was not only due to the noise of the shooting range, but its remote location reduced the danger associated with the storage of several tons of explosive gunpowder. Diegert liked the armory. It was clean and orderly; Carl Lindstrom, a man of Norwegian ancestry, made certain of that. Carl was a thin, wiry, energetic man in his early sixties. He spiked himself with a constant cup of coffee, using the caffeine to fuel his management of the ordnance and arsenal of the Headquarters. The six foot, 150-pound man with a full head of gray hair and glasses greeted Diegert's arrival. "Good morning. You must be David Diegert."

Shaking his hand, Diegert replied, "Yes, sir."

"So you're here to fulfill Fatima's debt?"

"Is that really how it works? If you supply us with what we need for a mission, we owe you?"

"If your mission is official, I will receive a requisition with a detailed list authorized by administration, and I'll provide you with everything you need. But if you arrive at 2230, waking me out of bed with a desperate demand to be given a sniper rifle and ask that the release not be logged, then, yeah…you owe me."

"Okay."

"Fatima can be a very forceful person, but she's also very fair. I knew she would keep her word, and I trust her with weapons. I know she helped you get the kid, but apparently I'm the only one."

"That's how she wants it."

"Appearances are very important to her, and she walks on eggshells because she's the only woman operator in the whole facility. Frankly, we would be more effective with more female operators, but it's a rare woman who can kill and live with herself."

"What do you want me to do?"

"Bullets!" said Lindstrom as he turned and walked through the armory into a workroom. Diegert followed, though he lagged as he passed the gun lockers and the fascinating arsenal of assault rifles, submachine guns, combat shotguns, handguns, and sniper rifles. Within the metal mesh lockers were all the accessories that gave the weapons greater lethality. Scopes and laser sights, extra ammo clips and enlarged ammunition dispensers, different styles of buttstocks for the assault rifles and the submachine guns, and a wide variety of sound suppressors, sights, and integrated lighting systems for the pistols. The hardware excited Diegert, and when he infiltrated areas where discovery meant death, these weapons gave him the confidence to proceed.

"We shoot a lot of bullets in this facility. Training new guys and keeping the active operators sharp requires a lot of practice, both in the range and out in the field. So I keep a very active inventory of ammunition. I like to assure quality in the projectiles we work with, and I don't like to see resources wasted, so I collect the spent shells and lead from the range and reload bullets."

Lindstrom had been moving while speaking, and now he positioned himself in front of a workbench with a large wooden box filled with shells, a smaller box filled with formed projectiles, and a large, funnel-shaped canister with a hose leading to the work space at the center of all these items.

"My dad believed the same thing, and he had me reload ammo all the time."

"Excellent! Then I'll just familiarize you with the process and let you get reacquainted with a part of your well-spent youth."

Diegert was very aware of what a boring and repetitive job this was, and now he knew why Fatima was so eager to subjugate him for the payback.

Soon Diegert was well into the six-step process of resizing the shells, decapping the old primer, expanding the inside neck of the shell with a small lathe, repriming with a new cap, loading the powder, and seating the new projectile. When all six steps were complete, the bullet was placed in a large tray that held a hundred individual rounds. Lindstrom was cleaning and repairing weapons that had been used recently and looked like they'd been dragged through dirt, mud, and sand. He had a workbench on wheels, so he was able to roll it over to where Diegert was doing his boring job. "Hey, what happened to that case of weapons I gave you when I arrived?" asked Diegert.

"Those are some very nice weapons. I have them down here."

"Did you know the guy to whom they belonged?"

"Shamus McGee? Yeah. He was the nicest guy. Always smiling and laughing. He was such a funny guy. Not really telling jokes but just adding humor everywhere he went. He was the best shot I have ever seen. Calm and steady. He could place the bullet exactly where he wanted it over and over again. His accuracy and consistency was absolutely deadly."

"What happened to him?"

"I can't tell you. I mean, I don't know."

"Which is it? You can't tell me, or you won't tell me?"

"I won't tell you. But I will tell you the rifle you brought in was the rifle I gave Fatima to help you last night. Since you just brought it in, it's not really in my inventory.

That's why I could loan it out without having to falsify any records."

Looking at the big box with thousands of shell casings, Diegert asked, "So maybe I don't have to do all these bullets."

"Yes, you do. You and she still owe me, besides, I don't get much company down here."

"Can you tell me what you know about Crepusculous?"

"The men of Crepusculous are so wealthy that they finance this whole operation on the lint from their pockets. Money is so available to them that expenses we incur represent the smallest decimal point on their balance sheets. I don't even know if they bother with balance sheets. Wealth is not the most important thing to them, though; they seek and desire power. They want to influence the world to turn in their direction, and then their wealth is assured without having to chase dollars."

"You seem to know a lot about them."

"I know a lot about their intentions and philosophy. I know what they're after, although I don't always know the means to their ends. I know life on their side is so much better than it would be fighting them."

"This all sounds diabolical and mysterious."

"It is, and it is also deadly. Be sure to conduct yourself carefully now that you're in the shadows of Crepusculous."

"Do you know the members of the Board?"

"No," deadpanned Lindstrom before posing his own question. "Was your father a big-game hunter?"

"Ahh…he was a deer hunter. Three or four a year to fill the freezer. We ate venison in so many different ways. God, I haven't had venison in so long."

"What did he hunt with?"

"A 12-gauge Remington on a drive, a Winchester 30.06 from a tree stand."

"Did you hunt with him?"

"No, but my brother did."

"Was he an older brother?"

"Yeah, three years older. His name is Jacob—Jake actually. He and my father just got along so well. He looked, acted, and sounded like my father: round, foolish, and loud. They were more like best friends than father and son. I just wasn't invited—ice fishing, snowmobiling, hunting. There was no explanation for it. I was just left home with my mom. She got me into other things, karate and strength training at the Y. I was on the wrestling team at school and did pretty well. My dad never came to a single match. Jake wasn't that big, but he played football. My dad was in the booster club. He never missed a single game."

"That doesn't seem fair," said the thoughtful armorer.

Diegert continued, "Jake would pound on me whenever my mom wasn't around, which was quite a lot, because she worked as a waitress in a busy restaurant. Eventually, the weight lifting, karate, and growing paid off, and when he couldn't physically dominate me anymore, he would harass me in other ways."

"Sibling rivalry, sometimes it never ends."

"One time he asked me to go fishing. I didn't have my own rod, so he told me to use my dad's. I knew Dad was very protective about his equipment and would be angry, but I took it anyway. We walked on the train tracks toward Sandy Creek. The creek is at the bottom of a steep ravine. The train tracks cross over on a very high trestle. Jake told me we should cross the trestle because the hillside was not as steep on the other side. The trestle has holes between each railroad tie. You must walk very carefully, and there are no rails on the sides. I was very frightened of the height and the holes and the whole thing."

Diegert set his tray of completed bullets to the side and placed a new tray in position.

"Out in the middle of the trestle, he stops and grabs my dad's rod from me. He takes it and starts pulling the line out of the end of the rod. He pulls out about ten feet of line. Then he says, 'Let's see how brave you are?' With the ten feet of line lying coiled in front of him, he tosses my dad's rod over the side of the trestle. I see the line quickly uncoiling over the edge. I knew my father would kill me if the rod was damaged. As the line is disappearing, I knew I must stop it from falling, but I was frozen with fear. At the last second, I lunge for the line, but it is thin and slick and so hard to get a hold of. I'm on my knees at the edge of the trestle extended over the side, but the thin plastic line slides through my fingers, and the rod plunges down into the depths of the creek. As I'm hanging over the edge, Jake grabs my feet and lifts them off the rail ties and scares the shit out of me. Only my chest was in contact with the rail. I grabbed the end of the ties to keep myself from falling. He dropped my feet and ran off the trestle back to the side we came from.

He said, 'I don't really feel like fishing. I'll see you later.' He started walking away. I got up, got off the trestle, and ran after him with the intent to kill. He heard me coming, and as I approached, he spun around with his fish knife in his hand.

"He said, 'Go ahead give me the reason to cut you out of this family. Do you know why Dad hates you? Because he's not your father. Mom was fucking some guy from the Deerfield Lodge when she was catering and got pregnant. Dad didn't kick the bitch out like he should have, and then you were born. You're a bastard. The product of a fucking affair, and Dad should've drowned you like a runt pup. Now he's gonna know how you lost his rod, and I'm glad you know the truth about yourself.'"

Diegert stopped for a moment from his process of reloading bullets. When he realized he'd stopped, he quickly started up again.

"My brother turned and walked away. I sat there a while, then went home, got all my money, went to the tackle shop, and bought the best rod and reel they had, and when Dad came home, I told him I lost his rod in Sandy Creek. I was sorry, and I gave him the new one. He was surprised I'd taken his rod, but I told him Jake had invited me to go. He was even more surprised and pleased to see the brand-new rod I'd bought him. He recognized it was the best rod they had in the shop. He wasn't pissed, and he forgave me.

"When he and Jake were next out of the house, I went to my mother and hugged her. I started crying, and I just kept crying. All the pain and sadness and rejection I had felt for so long had to come out. She soothed me and caressed me and asked me what was wrong. I looked at her with my tear-filled eyes, and said, 'I know, Mom. I now know the truth about me.' Her eyes grew round as saucers and she hugged me closer so she wouldn't have to see my face. I cried till I fell asleep, and when I woke up I was alone on the couch and she was in the kitchen. We never talked about it again."

Diegert turned his half-filled tray of bullets around so he could fill the other side.

"That's a real sad story," said Lindstrom. "But all you guys got sad stories. I often wonder if it's the sadness that lets you kill like you do."

"What I find sad, Mr. Lindstrom, is to have lived so long in a world of deception. Perhaps not lied to, but to live with—without the truth."

Diegert sat quietly for a moment, contemplating the impact of his realization. He reached into his shirt and stroked his leather amulet between his thumb and forefinger. Lindstrom sat quietly as well, not running away from Diegert's emotional turmoil.

"It's three o'clock, Mr. Lindstrom. I got a training mission at four, and I'd like to get something to eat."

"Alright, you've done enough. Good luck on your mission. It was nice having you down here."

37

Fatima knew there was no one in Headquarters who cared less about her success as an operator, a trainer, or any other role than Strakov. She wasn't surprised to find him in the weight room.

"What have you got planned today for my trainee?"

"Trainee? What a dorky word. You mean, what am I going to do to your superman?"

"Look, I'm his trainer, and you should consult me before you do anything with him."

"That's not what Blevinsky told me."

"Regardless, you know you should consult me."

"I think I should ignore you. I think you've been doing a lousy job training a guy who already has a lot of skills but no discipline. I think he needs to be reminded of the importance of teamwork. Blevinsky thinks so as well. So if you got a problem with that, take your sweet ass and go complain to him."

Strakov lay back down on the bench press, lifted the bar over his chest, and started another set. Fatima stood there fuming and counting Strakov's repetitions. When he approached ten and started to struggle, she stepped forward and put her hand on the bar. She pressed down as he strained to keep the bar moving up. Eventually, he could no longer resist her and the bar. His arms gave way, and the bar, with 230 pounds on it, collapsed onto his chest. He howled in agony as she walked away, leaving him screaming for help.

* * * *

Diegert went to the locker room after getting something to eat. At his locker was a bag with a pair of padded punching gloves. As he inspected the gloves, Gregor and Pierre, two of the guys who were part of Strakov's strike team, entered the locker room. Gregor was from Sweden and Pierre from France. Gregor continued a story he had been telling Pierre. "Then she climbs on my lap in the hot tub, even though there are three other couples in the tub. She pulls down my suit, slides her bikini bottoms to the side, and inserts me into her. Her movements were very gentle, but eventually I explode. Two of the couples leave, one couple stays, and we were all fucking in the hot tub for quite a while."

The guys visually acknowledged Diegert and started changing. Pierre said, "The wildest sex I ever had was with this Belgian girl. We were driving to Nice, and she said she wanted to suck my dick, while driving! She started in, and it felt great. We had to go through a tollbooth. I told her to stop, but she refused. All these booths are automated now, and they have cameras. The camera caught us with her head in my lap. The person who watches the cameras sent a message to the police with my license plate number. So we are driving along, she's still sucking me, and I look over to see the cop is driving right next to us watching. He turns on his lights and pulls us over. She makes me come just before the cop steps up to the window. He tickets me for distracted driving and her for public lewdness. He tells her, I got your number. She says, call me."

"What about you Diegert, ever have any wild sex?" asked the Frenchman.

"A drive-in movie in a convertible, doggie style. We were in the backseat with her bent over the front passenger seat. She was moaning so loud that we attracted a lot of attention away from the movie. Someone shined a flashlight on us, and I shouted I was going to charge them double the admission price if they didn't shut off the light.

Management came and kicked us out. She was really wild and loved the public spectacle of the whole thing."

"Women. How quickly we are willing to help them with their strange sexual desires," observed Pierre.

After they changed into shorts, T-shirts, and sneakers, they walked up to Room 240. In the padded room, Enrique, Jaeger, and Strakov were stretching and warming up. Diegert started limbering up and watched as the rest of the guys joked around, smiled, and basked in their camaraderie. Strakov was particularly jovial and inclusive of his team members.

"Alright, guys, bring it in."

When the guys had gathered around their leader, Strakov began.

"As a strike team, we know the value of teamwork and that when we work together, we can achieve things we could never do on our own. Today we are going to share that lesson with Mr. Diegert as we practice our defensive tactics."

All eyes cast looks upon the new guy. "Mr. Diegert's individual accomplishments are well known, but he will never be a member of a strike team without learning and practicing teamwork. Later this week, Mr. Diegert faces a mission in the Urban Zone."

All the guys chuckled and shook their heads at the memory of this training mission. Diegert was surprised by the reactions of such a tough bunch of men.

"You all know the challenges of the Urban Zone, but let's see how Mr. Diegert does with DTs."

Again the men laughed, sighed, and look at Diegert with pity.

"To demonstrate the value of teamwork, this is what we are going to do. Mr. Diegert will assume a defensive stance, and we'll attack him in a serial pattern. Each of us needs to take Mr. Diegert to the mat."

Diegert stabilized his feet, tugged on his new gloves, and faced Curtis Jaeger.

Jaeger stepped forward, throwing a flurry of high punches. Diegert defended them, but Jaeger utilized the focus to sweep the legs out from under his opponent, flattening Diegert on his back. He concluded his attack by placing fatal force on his opponent's throat. When he released the choke hold and stepped back, Diegert coughed and sputtered but stood up to face the next attacker.

Pierre had long legs and used them effectively. He threw a series of roundhouse kicks, landing blows on Diegert's hips, thighs, and ribs. His fourth strike was a spinning kick that struck Diegert in the head, snapping his neck to the side, sending him crashing into the wall before he crumpled to the floor.

Enrique was a very solid man with powerful muscles, which he used to generate painful blows to Diegert's head and face. The strong man drew blood from above Diegert's eye as well as his nose and mouth, before a right cross to the jaw put his opponent back on the mat.

Diegert felt like a foolish punching bag and resolved to get some strikes of his own in on the next opponent. Gregor stood ready as Diegert brought the fight to the big Swede. Diegert's first combination was deflected, and Gregor nimbly switched his position, causing Diegert to have to shift his stance. The frustrated American threw a jab, and the Swede grabbed his arm and, with just enough force, pulled Diegert off balance, pitching him face-first into the mat. Diegert's battered face left a bloody imprint in the mat and pain in his nose and teeth.

Strakov was next. Diegert wiped the blood from his face and found a renewed strength for the opportunity to hit the big Russian.

Strakov moved forward while Diegert stepped to the side to avoid him. The big guy's movements were awkward, and Diegert saw winces of pain each time Strakov threw a slow, ineffective punch. Like a wolf that selects the injured member of the herd, Diegert realized his opponent was hurt. He aggressively took the fight to Strakov, moving fast and landing punches on the face and body of the big Alpha male. Diegert saw the panic in the face of his nemesis but was unprepared when the big Russian bull-rushed him, tackling him like a linebacker. Strakov groaned when Diegert hit the mat with him on top, but he had fulfilled the requirement of taking Diegert down. As he struggled to his feet, Strakov said, "This phase is over."

Diegert stood by himself while Strakov handed weapons to the rest of the operators.

"Now," stated the big Russian, "if Mr. Diegert disarms one of us, he does not have to complete the mission in the Urban Zone. Ready? Attack."

All five operators, armed with weapons, attacked Diegert simultaneously.

Enrique had a two-foot truncheon with which he struck Diegert on the shoulder blade as the American ducked to avoid a blow to the head. Jaeger, armed with a knife, stabbed at Diegert, who had to twist his torso to evade the sharp blade. He countered Jaeger's strike with a punch to the temple, stunning the German enough so that he could focus on Gregor's attack with a six-foot staff. As the Swede swung the big stick, Diegert took the hit, grabbed the shaft, and shoved it forward, impaling Gregor in the abdomen. Pierre stepped forward, swinging a length of chain. The first swing was inches from Diegert's head, and the return required Diegert to jump above it. For the next swing, Diegert positioned himself so that when he ducked, the chain collided with Strakov's ribs. The big Russian gasped for air as the metal links concussed his chest, making it easy for Diegert to grab the pistol from his hand. As the leader of the strike team reinflated his lungs, Diegert kicked him in the hip, knocking him to the ground, and stood above him with the pistol, saying, "Too bad it's not loaded."

Strakov was furious. The situation was awkward, since no one, least of all Diegert, had expected this outcome. Strakov was in serious pain but struggled to his feet. He was gasping and at a loss for words, but his anger was visible, and Diegert told him, "I'm still gonna do your Urban Zone mission. I don't want to become an operator just because I beat you assholes."

Strakov wasn't prepared for this reaction, and with a look of disdain, he said, "Meet at the armory tomorrow at 1800."

Strakov, wincing in pain, walked away, not wanting the guys to see just how badly he was injured.

Pierre came up to Diegert, saying, "Very clever. I hope I get to work with you on a team someday." Pierre punched Diegert in the shoulder and went to the locker room.

* * * *

Outside the locker room, Fatima was waiting for Diegert and walked with him as he headed back to his room. "I heard about your self-defense training."

"I heard about your failure spotting Strakov on the bench press."

"Looks like we are always finding ways of helping each other."

"Yeah, what can you tell me about the Urban Zone?"

"It was a very gutsy call, and a wise one, because you don't want to have the reputation of being excused from the tough stuff. Strakov's arrogance just backfired on him, and it'll take a long time to live it down."

"What I meant was, what do you know about the details of the mission?"

"Just roll with it—they change them all the time—and be very skeptical of anything that looks obvious. I think you'll do fine, which is to say, you'll survive."

"Have there been others who have not?"

"Of course, how many times do I have to tell you? We don't train by the sissy safety rules of the US Army. If you don't win out there, you die. That's why your decision to do the training when you had a pass was so gutsy."

Fatima smiled at Diegert, tapped him on the shoulder, and left.

Holy shit, thought Diegert.

38

The next day at 1800 hours, Diegert reported to the armory.

"Back so soon?" said the wiry Lindstrom.

"Is this my stuff?"

Laid on a table in the armory was the equipment being issued to Diegert.

"The Urban Zone mission has several demands and hazards. This equipment will help keep you from becoming a casualty."

Diegert surveyed the equipment on the table.

"First you should put this on."

Lindstrom picked up the top piece of a protective body suit.

"This Kevlar-weave combat suit won't make you bulletproof, but it is bullet resistant. If it can resist bullets, then just imagine how good it is at resisting everything else." Diegert thumped the Kevlar with his kuckles, and Lindstrom continued, "The pants have reinforced panels on the thighs and around the hips. Here are your Viper tactical boots. We think they're the best. You also have Viper gloves. Scissors are here too, should you want to customize your gloves with an exposed finger or two. This outer shell vest will protect you from shrapnel and other projectiles. It has pockets filled with useful things such as explosives, listening devices, and other items. Take some time to check out each pocket."

Diegert counted the pockets with his fingers.

"This belt also has many items that you will find helpful. Your vest, belt, and body suit integrate to form an internal web harness so that this clip ring here on the belt can be used to secure you when climbing or rappelling. For weapons, you will have the HK VP9 tactical pistol. You can see it has the underbarrel flashlight and laser sight. There is a silencer, which will be in a pouch on the holster."

Diegert held the gun and felt the weight and balance of it. He nodded approvingly before setting it back down.

"Go put it all on and come back for a systems check."

When he returned, Diegert looked like a deadly operator capable of stealth and violence. The suit was snug and formfitting, projecting an appearance of fitness and mobility. Its shades of gray and black would allow Diegert to disappear into the shadows of the night.

"Looks good," said the experienced armorer. "Very crepuscular."

He handed Diegert a black backpack. "This is your climbing kit. I want the contents returned."

"Okay."

Dressed and ready to go, Diegert sat outside the room from which his mission would be controlled. Strakov arrived with a sour look on his face. "Let's review your mission. In the Urban Zone, you're to ascend the building marked 'H7.' You will then rappel to the fourth floor, recover a laptop that contains critical information, exit the building, commandeer a motor vehicle, and return here to base. You must accomplish this mission in twenty minutes. We have transportation for you to the Zone. I don't care if you have questions. I'm not answering them." With a shake of his head to the right, he said "Jaeger will drive you."

Diegert and Jaeger climbed into an open-topped jeep and drove down the road from the armory. After the first turn, the jeep encountered a row of orange cones across the road. Puzzled, Jaeger brought the vehicle to a stop. From the bushes on the driver's side, Fatima stepped out with her Sig Sauer P320 pistol pointed at Jaeger.

"Get out," was all she said. His hesitation produced a drawback of the hammer on Fatima's pistol. Jaeger released the steering wheel and put his hands up as he stepped out of the jeep.

Fatima took Jaeger's position in the driver's seat and flattened the rubber cones as she drove over them, leaving Jaeger behind.

"Is this my rescue?"

"Shut up. I'm here to warn you that Strakov has a hit planned on you. He's using your mission as a training mission for a counterstrike team. The team's mission is to prevent you from completing yours, and they are authorized to kill."

"I'm walking into a trap."

"Yes, you are, but if you didn't know this, you'd be walking into your grave." Fatima brought the jeep to a halt and looked beyond Diegert.

"There it is. It's totally wired with closed-circuit TV so they will be watching everything, and the clock starts when you first come into view. You'd better survive."

Diegert stepped out of the jeep. Fatima accelerated and left him standing in the dirt road on the edge of the Zone. The place was like an abandoned city block being reclaimed by nature. Just beyond the tall pine trees around him was a high chain-link fence with a gate marked "Urban Zone." The gate was unlocked and had an eight-foot crossbar above it. Diegert recalled what Fatima had said about things that looked too obvious, and he did not walk through the gate; rather, he stole through the woods adjacent to the fencing. As he moved, he pulled a folding multi-tool with wire snips from a vest pocket. He cut through the fencing and entered the Urban Zone away from the gate.

When he stepped through the hole, he set his watch for a twenty-minute countdown. It was uncanny how urban the

Zone looked. It had city streets, manhole covers, streetlights, traffic signs, and buildings of various different heights and architectural designs. The eerie thing was, there were no people. These streets looked like they should have people on them, living the urban life, but there were no inhabitants. When he found building H7, it was a six-story apartment building, gray concrete with rectangular windows. He pulled the climbing gear from his backpack and used the folding grappling hook and a length of rope to climb the side of the building from one floor to the next until he was on the roof. There he could find no suitable place to anchor the rope. He had to use valuable length to secure it to the back side and run the rope the width of the building so he could rappel down the front side. Once it was secure, he clipped in and rappelled down to the fourth floor.

The fourth floor was illuminated, and like the rest of the building, the hallways were exterior balconies. He stepped onto the balcony hallway. As he did so, he was ensnared in micro-mesh netting, which clung to him like a spider's web and entrapped him more and more as he tried to get out of it. His struggling triggered a mechanism that cinched a system of cords, retracting the netting, with Diegert in it, pulling him thirty feet to the western wall and depositing him on the floor. The netting had him entangled, and there was no way he could reach his knife. He was, however, able to reach a cigarette lighter in a pocket on his outer vest. He struck the lighter, and the netting ignited quickly, burning to ash with very little flame. His tactical suit protected him from harm, and he was free of the netting and surrounded by gray ash. He looked to the ceiling and saw the cords that ran through a tracking mechanism that were designed to entrap trespassers.

He drew his weapon, aware now that activating the trap would alert the hit squad to his location. A check of his watch indicated that he had seventeen minutes and thirty-five seconds remaining.

He moved down the hall, searching for the target. The first door he tried was locked, and so were the second and the third. The fourth door opened. Diegert gradually eased the door open; looking in, he saw four men sitting at a table playing cards beneath a bare bulb. He entered the room, firing lethal shots. As the bullets entered, stuffing flew out of the men. Plastic shells cracked and facial expressions remained unchanged while no blood spilled. The men were mannequins.

On the far wall, there was a doorway leading to another room also occupied by a mannequin. A laptop sat on a table in front of the mannequin. On the floor was a computer case. Diegert used the keyboard to shut the computer down. As the shutdown began, a message on the screen read: *25 seconds to explosives activation.*

Diegert's eyes grew wide, as he did not know if the message meant the computer would explode or the building. He ripped the cord out of the computer and placed it in the case, zipped it shut, and slung the strap over his shoulder. With the computer case across his back, he headed back to the hallway. His watch read 16:45. As he proceeded down the hallway, passing one of the locked doors, it exploded with a concussive force that blasted Diegert against the opposite wall, spraying him with splintered wood and plaster dust. Once again, the tac suit saved him, but his hearing was shocked. He stumbled forward, disoriented and confused. The dust and smoke made vision unreliable, but he knew he had to keep moving to the western part of the building to access the staircase.

At the stairwell, Diegert grasped the outside railing with his left hand and descended the darkened staircase. He rounded the landing, continuing on to the third floor.

Crossing the third floor landing, he stepped forward and his foot dropped into open darkness. As he fell, he twisted his body 180 degrees, catching the edge of the landing with his fingers. He struggled with his grip, desperately holding on as his legs helplessly flailed in the air. Realizing what was happening, he raised his left elbow onto the ledge. Looking up, he could just make out the position of the handrail about three feet away. He pressed hard with his left arm and reached for the handrail. He was so surprised when he missed it that he almost lost his entire grip on the stair ledge. Regaining his left elbow position, he swung his left leg up and got his knee on the stair ledge. With both a leg and an arm over the edge, he rolled himself onto the flat surface of the landing. "SHIT!" he shouted as the frustration and relief combined into an emotional outburst.

Rolling onto his stomach, he peered over the edge. In the patchy darkness, he could see that the stairway had collapsed, and all the material was in a pile of rubble three stories below. Climbing back up the stairs to the fourth-floor balcony, he found his rappelling rope was gone. Stepping back from the balcony, he realized that others were in the field and someone had removed his rope, making his precarious position even more dire. He remembered the micro-mesh netting and the cords in the tracks on the ceiling. He reached up and pulled the lines out. He kept pulling until he had all the available line. He knotted the sections together into a substantial length of strong cord. Deploying the line from the edge of the balcony left about a twenty-foot gap between the end of the line and the ground.

Dejected, Diegert rolled up the cord and descended the stairs to the dark abyss of the third floor. Securing the line to the handrail, he rappelled down to the rubble pile of the old stairwell. The darkness and the uneven surface of the pile made it a struggle to find secure footing. Soon, though, he was standing in the entrance to the stairs on the first floor. He stepped through a door that opened into the entrance lobby of the building. Light filtered in from the street, and Diegert pushed on the crash bar located on the front door. The bar was inoperable, and the door wouldn't budge. Looking at the casement and the surrounding structure for the door, he realized it was load bearing and blowing it open would destabilize the front of the building. The adjacent window was thick double-paned glass, but the casement was not load bearing. C-4 charges at all four corners blew out the window, shattering it into thousands of shards of sharp glass.

Diegert peered out the hole and looked across the weed-infested parking lot to see four vehicles. He also noticed the movement of a dark figure taking cover near the vehicles. Holding his position, he waited and saw the first figure make a hand signal, and two more weapon-carrying personnel moved forward into shooting positions around the parking area. He had 8:38 left to complete the mission.

Taking stock, Diegert had a full clip of twelve rounds in his pistol. Attached to his vest, he had four more twelve-round magazines, two flashbangs, and two frag grenades. As he inventoried his equipment, a canister flew in through the window, clanged off the back wall, and landed on the floor in front of him.

Instantly, Diegert dove back to the entrance of the stairwell. Just as he crashed through the door, the explosion ripped apart the area between the window and the front door, and a great fireball erupted from the front entrance, propelling the door ten feet from the building.

Diegert was fortunate the force of the blast went in the opposite direction of him. The kill team was sure to come forward. Trapped in the stairwell, he found a piece of metal handrail in the rubble and used it to barricade the door.

Holding his pistol ready for whomever broke through the door, he stepped forward, peering through the wire mesh–enforced glass window of the stairwell door to see if the hit squad was coming.

The three men approached the building cautiously, seeking to confirm Diegert's status. The first looked in the window and could see the crater in the floor the grenade had made, but he didn't see Diegert's body. He signaled to the other two to move forward and check through the front door. As they approached, the load-bearing walls buckled and six floors of concrete facing sheared off, collapsing to the ground. The two operators were crushed as tons of material fell on top of them. The third operator was partially buried in debris. Both of his legs were trapped, and his left arm was impaled by a piece of rebar that pierced his biceps and pinned his arm behind him.

Diegert was fortunate to have been in the stairwell, which was constructed independently of the front wall and had withstood the collapsing debris. He removed his barricade and climbed over the rubble of the front wall. To his left, he saw the third operator. He was a pitiful sight and would not survive many more minutes. Diegert looked at him and mercifully removed his combat helmet. The guy was delirious and suffering incredible pain. David Diegert stood back, aimed his weapon, and fired a round that brought peace to the wounded warrior's tortured body. He had 4:04 left.

Beyond the debris field, parked in a row was a motorcycle, a Hummer, and a sedan. Diegert approached the Hummer first. He opened the door and heard a faint growl. In an instant, the growl erupted into the vicious snarling of a ferocious dog. Diegert slammed the door shut as the powerful beast lunged into the truck's door. With a sigh of relief, he stepped away from the Hummer as the dog continued to attack the window with intent to get blood from any intruder.

Diegert straddled the motorcycle and kicked the starter. He noticed an electric crackle as an overloaded wire sent a surge of electricity from the starter to the gas tank. When the gas tank exploded, the force hit Diegert directly in the protective chest plate of his outer vest. The force lifted him clear off the motorcycle, propelling him through the air until he ended up sprawled on his back in the dirt. Debris from the motorcycle lay all around him. He struggled to get his bearings. His face was burned, his hair was singed, and his ears were ringing. He sat up and wobbled to his feet. He stepped over to the sedan to find the front passenger tire pierced by a metal shard from the motorcycle. 3:15 remaining.

Back to the Hummer. He grabbed a shaft with a twisted metal end on it from the motorcycle debris. He climbed on the Hummer's roof and used the elongated metal piece to open the driver's door. The dog blasted out the door ready to attack. He ran forward snarling, but there was no one to bite. The dog realized Diegert was on the roof and launched into a relentless assault on the side of the Hummer, leaping up trying to reach Diegert. After watching for a moment, Diegert drew his pistol and fired a bullet into the dog's chest. The beast staggered and fell to the ground. Diegert descended and stepped toward the wounded animal, which continued to snap and snarl. Sighting down the length of the barrel, he fired into the dog's head, permanently ending his aggression. He slipped the computer case off his shoulder, climbed into the truck, and drove the Hummer back to the armory, arriving with fourteen seconds remaining.

Strakov, Jaeger, Blevinsky, Lindstrom, and others had been watching on the television monitors. They saw it all, and still Strakov sat stunned when Diegert pulled up to the armory and walked into the monitoring room.

"I guess you're going to have to do a little building reconstruction, and you'll need some body bags." Diegert placed the computer case on the table and took off his backpack.

Turning to Lindstrom, he said, "You'll have to ask one of these guys what happened to the contents, because I sure as hell didn't lose them."

Pulling his gloves off and removing his outer vest while looking at Strakov, Diegert said, "You couldn't beat me in DTs, and now you've failed to kill me."

Strakov stood up. "You still have to survive the tournament."

Diegert stepped right up to his face, saying, "I'll not only survive, but win the fucking tournament, you shadow of a man."

The two men stared into the hate simmering in their souls. Diegert stepped back without breaking eye contact, wiped the blood from his head, and said, "I'll be in medical."

39

As the adrenaline wore off, the shock from the trauma began to eat away at Diegert's strength and even his consciousness. The medical staff recognized the symptoms of slowed speech and an awkward gait. They immediately got him out of the tac suit and into a gown and on a hospital bed. Using IV sedation, they forced his injured body to rest. Fatima arrived and sat by his bed for a long time. Eventually, the medic had to leave the clinic, saying, "I have to go for about fifteen minutes. Will you be staying with him?"

"Yes, I'll stay until you get back, and maybe even longer."

When the medic had left, Fatima went to the medicine locker, picked the lock, and searched until she found a vial labeled, "Multisystem Performance Enhancer." The medicine was a booster. It enhanced neural function, increasing strength and reaction time. It improved sight and hearing while facilitating faster reflexes. It improved aerobic capacity, allowing for greater endurance as well as anaerobic energy supply, creating greater speed. The fluid also had the capacity to reduce the experience of pain by blocking pain receptors in the brain. The medicine would give Diegert an advantage and allow him to recover quickly. Fatima filled a syringe and injected it into the side port on Diegert's IV. The fluid flowed unimpeded into his bloodstream and was distributed throughout his body.

For Diegert, there was no sudden reaction; in fact, he didn't wake up. The influence on his systems would create no visible changes in appearance, and the performance enhancements would only be functional as a result of use. If he didn't practice, the stuff wouldn't make any difference.

He wasn't going to become Captain America, but with practice, he would be a better David Diegert.

Fatima closed up the medicine locker and disposed of the syringe. When the medic returned, she was sitting right where she had been. She stayed another thirty minutes and then said to the medic, "I have to go, but please call me as soon as he wakes up."

Walking down the hall, she was pleased with herself for giving Diegert an advantage. In this dangerous business, any advantage had to be utilized.

When Diegert awoke two hours later, Fatima was called. She stepped into the room and drew the privacy curtain around the bed, shielding them from the medic's view. She had a very happy, energetic, and, Diegert thought, sexy smile. She seemed genuinely glad to see him. She could still turn him on with her beauty, energy, and charm, even though he had been so wronged by her beguiling ways before. She picked up on his reactions, saying, "Keep your gown on, big boy. I'm not here for any of that. I'm just glad you did so well in the Urban Zone."

"You make it sound like I just won a blue ribbon at the fair. Three operators died while trying to kill me, and a building is lying in ruins, and I'm supposed to celebrate this as a success? It's fucked up!"

"Oh, stop your sniveling. You were brilliant. You got by every obstacle they threw at you. Maybe no one else is telling you how well you did, but I am."

Looking at her, he didn't know if he should thank her or call the medic for a psych consult. He just looked down and asked, "When do I get out of here?"

"Right now," replied the bossy dark-haired lady, shouting, "medic!"

The startled medic rushed in. *"What?"*

"Please remove the IV and release the patient." The medic looked bewildered. Fatima provided clarity, snapping, "Now!"

After a late meal and a comfortable night's sleep in his own bed, Diegert felt good the next morning. Following breakfast, Fatima had a full day of activities for him: shooting in the range, including both sniper rifles and mobile handgun practice, and hand-to-hand combat, using defensive tactics against assailants with weapons.

Pierre served as his opponent, and he showed Diegert some very effective takedown maneuvers, using the legs while on the ground. Diegert practiced the moves, surprising Pierre with how quickly Diegert learned to master the complex maneauvers. Diegert was surprised as well. He wasn't one to tire easily, but today he felt like he was never going to get tired, and it felt great. Pierre attacked with knives, clubs, a hatchet, and even a long-handled pike, and Diegert learned quickly how to respond to the variety of weapons.

Finally, Pierre shared some methods of disarming an assailant with a gun. The key to success was proximity. If the assailant was within six feet, then the probability of success went up.

Diegert practiced moves that allowed him to strip the gun from the assailant and use the weapon against him. None of this was new to Diegert, but practicing the techniques refreshed his reflexes, improved his reactions, and boosted his confidence. He spent the rest of the week practicing the skills of combat using the extensive facilities and guided by the expert personnel of the Headquarters.

"You've spent your time well," remarked Fatima. "The tournament is in two days, and I can tell you a little about your opponents."

"Oh yeah, are they some of the guys who've been training here?"

"No, these men are arriving from other facilities. I don't know how extensively they've been trained, but presumably they have the same skills and abilities you do."

"So what's the point?"

"The tournament's goal is to expose operators to the challenge of facing opponents who are as deadly and lethal as they are. This gives each operator the chance to see if they can face the most dangerous and violently skilled assassins in the world and prevail."

"How many guys are in the tournament?"

"There will be four of you in total."

"So four of us go into the area you walked me around, and then we try to kill each other."

"The four participants will enter the Proving Grounds, and you will win by assassinating all of them."

"Okay, tell me what you know about these guys."

"Brutus Orilius is a Bulgarian who completed his Army service and was a decorated security officer. He wants to work for the Crepusculous Board as a bodyguard, and his military background got him into the program. He's big, six four, two hundred thirty pounds, and he was the Bulgarian army's judo champion for three years."

"That's it? An MP who knows how to grab you by your shirt and roll you to the ground?"

"Hey, these guys could've gone through the same training program we put you through."

"Well, if they did, it wouldn't make any fucking difference. This program sucks; it's not about learning, it's about surviving."

"You want to hear about the next guy?"

Diegert nodded.

"Shioki Wong is a former member of the Chinese special forces."

"The People's Liberation Army Special Operations Forces," clarified Diegert.

"What a mouthful. He was an explosive specialist, and apparently, he mistakenly killed some comrades with charges. He was court-martialed, but his sentence was purchased by a powerful individual, and Wong has been trained for service with Crepusculous."

"Okay, now we got a guy who can't safely light his fire crackers, and his admission to this death match has been purchased by some rich prick?"

Fatima looked at him not wanting to acknowledge his sarcasm. "The third participant is Deiobo Mogales. He comes from Brazil, where he was convicted of murdering two sons of a cocaine cartel boss. In prison, he killed three more men who were apparently instructed by the boss to kill him. For a sum, his sentence was purchased, and he was released to a member of the Board. Deiobo is skilled in capoeira, the Brazilian martial art. He killed the cocaine sons with a gun, but the three men in prison were killed with his hands."

"Alright, this guy sounds like a challenge. Someone worth going up against."

"You can shove that arrogant attitude. If you underestimate your opponents, you're sure to lose."

"Did you read that on the bumper of a truck or a car?"

"You fuck this up, and all that I've invested in you will be for nothing."

"I see you want all that's been invested in these other guys to be for nothing. Training operators and then sending them to be killed seems stupid and wasteful. Why do they do this?"

"Failing on a mission is the real waste we are trying to avoid. The Board has enough resources that it can afford this process to develop the best operators."

"Yeah, as long as the lives of the guys are worthless."

"You're in this way too deep to start with that kind of sanctimonious shit. The resources of Crepusculous make the expense of this a total nonissue. Now get your head straight and be ready for these guys on Tuesday."

"What else is in it for me if I win?"

"You mean, what else besides the rest of your life?"

"Yeah, Yeah, what else?"

"You'll get to operate alone, carrying out clandestine sanctions in remote locations."

"That's not a reward, that's a continuance of service. I mean is there money, a vacation, a new car?"

"It's not a fuckng TV game show."

Diegert's crestfallen look drew a smile from Fatima before she told him, "There is however a monetary inducement. If you win you will be given $100,000 dollars."

The stoic face of David Diegert looked like a little boy just given a Christmas toy. Fatima's smirk blossomed into a smile as she watched him beam with excitement. 100K would solve his Mother's problems allowing her to pay off the house and stay in the only home she ever loved.

"Now this whole stupid thing has a purpose."

"Money? Your purpose is money?"

"It depends what's done with the money."

"And what's that?"

"I'm not telling you."

Fatima withdrew from the position into which she had leaned. She realized that no matter if she felt like she and Diegert were growing closer, this place was no substitute for the real world. Their hidden pasts preserved the dearth of intimacy that this business required.

"Very well." Fatima handed him the file with the mug shots of each participant as she stood and walked away saying, "You only get the money if all three of them are dead."

Diegert opened the folder, looked into their faces to see strength and ruthlessness. He imagined facing them, visualizing what he would need to do to kill each one.

40

Three vehicles arrived at the Headquarters Monday night. Each transported a man who was capable of killing others and living with himself. Each man found that violence was within his comfort zone and was willing to take people's lives at the request of others without having a personal dispute with the victim. An assassin's work was to be a purveyor of death as a service to those who wanted to kill but were unwilling to take a life themselves. These men possessed that capacity and were now coming to the Proving Grounds to test their skills, strength. and determination— not against innocents and unknowns, but against men of the same breed.

Diegert's breakfast was brought to him in his room. He had never had breakfast in bed, and, in fact, he sat at his desk and ate his meal in his chair. He dressed in his combat blacks and placed his gloves with the padded knuckles and open fingers in a cargo pocket. Fatima came and walked with him to the Proving Grounds. "Use your head when you're in there. Look for weapons and tools dispersed throughout the area. They'll be on the ground, in the trees, hidden behind objects. Keep whatever you find, or at least make certain it is unavailable to the others."

"Thanks. Mom, I wrote my name on the waistband of my undies too, anything else?"

"Fucker. When you take a man down, check his pockets to see what valuables he's carrying."

"Alright, step back," a big guard said, moving between Fatima and Diegert. "Trainers must go to the monitoring area. Participants will come with me."

Diegert followed the big guy to the gates of the Proving Grounds. Standing outside the gate were his three opponents, each escorted by a pair of Headquarters-assigned guards. The Bulgarian MP was big and looked very strong, but he stoically looked above everyone and avoided eye contact. If Diegert had to make up a name for him, he couldn't have done better than Brutus Orilius.

The Chinese man, Shioki Wong, looked straight ahead like the soldiers of China on parade that Diegert had seen in *National Geographic* magazines. He was unwavering in his absolute discipline, remaining detached and focused on his mission.

Deiobo Mogales, however, leaned against the post of the gate. His hair, braided in cornrows, was covered by a tight black do-rag. He had tattoos on his arms and neck, which continued under his sleeves and the collar of his black T-shirt. He had a thin mustache, and his jaw was dark with the stubble of yesterday's growth. With a tilt of his head and a dismissive smirk, he looked Diegert right in the eyes and had that crazy kind of stare that people use to make others feel uncomfortable. Diegert held his gaze, raised his fist to eye level, and extended his middle finger. Deiobo's surprised chuckle produced a devious smile that revealed his crooked yellow teeth.

The guard opened the gate, and each man and his guards moved in. They were then escorted to the four corners of the fenced in area. Diegert recalled that the swampy area was to the north, while the field of concrete blocks was in the center, and the urban movie set was to the south. Diegert was taken to the southeast corner, passing behind the buildings of the movie set.

In this far corner of the Proving Grounds was a ten-by-twelve-foot concrete block building with a shingle roof. There was a door in the center of the front wall but no windows. Diegert hadn't seen this structure when he was here with Fatima. The guards directed him toward the building. Standing in front of the structure, one of the guards unlocked the door, opened it, and motioned for Diegert to step inside. The interior of the building was pitch black, but Diegert could smell water—or rather, the foul smell of stagnant water. His hesitation at the threshold earned him a powerful shove. He fell several feet, landing with a splash in waist deep water.

The door closed, and the complete darkness robbed him of vision. Being blind was disorienting. Diegert extended his hands out in front of him and tried to get his bearings. The walls were slick and straight. He didn't know how far below ground level he was, except that he had fallen quite a ways after being shoved. Touching the wall again, he recognized the feel of plastic used to create a liner for a backyard pool. He stretched and reached as high as he could along the wall, and his fingers touched a wire. Immediately, he felt an electric shock, and deafening acid rock music blared out of unseen speakers. Diegert withdrew from the side wall and stood in the middle of the waist-deep water.

He slowly walked forward but was startled when he bumped into a solid structure in the middle of the water. He tested it with his hands, feeling around it to get a sense of its shape. It was a square wooden box that was just barely under the water. If he stood on the box, he would be out of the water. He climbed on the box and stood up on it. When he reached his full height, and all his weight was on the center of the box, he heard a great gushing sound of a large volume of water flowing into the pool. It sounded like the water was flowing in from the corner behind him, but worse was the smell. His nose was assaulted with the stench of untreated sewage. He jumped off the box and back into the water, but the flow didn't stop. He walked toward the sound of the water, and the powerful volume of disgusting waste splashed him as he sought a shutoff valve. He reached up to explore the pipe and received another electric shock and an unrelenting blast from an air horn. The eardrum-splitting sound lasted a long time. When the sewage finally stopped flowing, it was up to his armpits. He stood in it as the foul stench assailed his nostrils. He made contact with pieces of shit whenever he moved his arms and hands.

Diegert started to feel an irritation and a wriggling sensation at his ankle just above his boot and below his pants. He kicked his leg and shook his foot, but the wriggling only grew more intense. Soon he felt more and more wriggling motions against the skin of his legs. Creatures were crawling up his thighs. He put his hands under the water and pressed against his legs. He tried to stop the invaders, but when he had isolated one and tried to squish it, it delivered a bite that was sharp and painful. Diegert pulled his hands out of the water, only to feel the wriggling beings now on his arms. The slimy attackers moved up his sleeves and onto his chest and back. They didn't wait to be driven off before biting, and soon Diegert was suffering multiple bites from these aqueous aggravators.

Focus was difficult to find, but he located one of the tormentors on his forearm. He palpated it and determined he was being besieged by aquatic leeches. Their bites hurt at first, but then the pain subsided. The problem was they were blood sucking, and without counting, Diegert was afraid he already had over a hundred bites. If they all sucked a hundred milliliters of blood, he would soon lose a liter. The longer he stayed in the water, the more leeches he would be hosting.

He reached up the side of the pit again and flattened his hands so he was just able to slide under the shock wire, which was held out an inch or so from the wall by spaced insulators. With his fingers under the wire, he found the top edge of the pool liner. The plastic sheeting had been nailed to a wooden top piece, but Diegert was able to claw at the very top edge of the plastic. He curled the plastic over and pulled on a small piece of it with all the strength in his fingertips. The plastic cracked, and he pulled on one side of the separation, tearing the plastic and forming a vertical split. He managed to pull the strip of plastic below the shock wire, and then yanked it with both hands, rendering the lining and revealing the earth underneath. He kept pulling until the tear was below the waterline and the ground began absorbing the water. The liner was pushed away from the earthen wall as water widened the space between it and the underlying dirt.

The water level fell, and when it reached his waist, the flow from the corner pipe restarted. There must have been a float valve somewhere in the darkness that regulated the water level. As the surrounding earthen walls became saturated, the water level rose again, soon reaching his neck.

Diegert felt the earth through the torn plastic and discovered a section of shale rock. Shale was a sedimentary rock that formed in layers. It was very strong in one plane and quite brittle in the perpendicular plane. He dug into the softened earth and extracted several pieces of shale. One piece was rectangular, about eighteen inches long and one inch wide. Another piece was a twelve-inch triangle with a very sharp edge on one of the lengths. Diegert took the eighteen-inch piece and broke it perpendicularly on the edge of the wooden box into two nine-inch sections.

He searched the wall of the pit to find a span between insulators. Cutting the wire would break the circuit, stopping the shocks, and provide eight feet of current-carrying capacity. The wire lacked insulation, so it had to be kept out of the water, yet the bare wire would be useful.

He reached up, and after shocking himself a couple times, managed to impale the sharp point of the triangular piece of shale into the wall above the wire. He took the two sections of rectangular shale and placed them on either side of the wire. Using the lace from his boot, he tied the two pieces together so the wire was held firmly and could be safely handled. He then pulled down on the triangular piece, severing the wire with the sharp edge.

Now he held the live wire with the tied pieces of shale and had to make sure it didn't fall into the water. With a four-inch piece of wire extending from the shale, he touched a blood-filled leech on his arm. He felt a shock, but the leech got the worst of it and released its blood-sucking grip as it died. Diegert electrocuted leeches on his arms and neck above the waterline.

With the electric circuit broken, he investigated the sewage pipe again. Putrid sewage continued to flow, but the pipe was no longer electrified. It was very strong and extended out from the wall far enough that he could climb up onto it. He took off his belt and affixed it around the pipe. He needed to climb up while holding the live wire out of the water. Using his left arm to hoist himself, and holding the wire in his right hand, he lifted his upper body over the pipe. He shimmied forward and was able to swing his right leg around the pipe, and suddenly he was sitting on the pipe like a horse. His feet were still in the water, but he could raise them out.

What qualified as a victory depended on the circumstances of the struggle. Diegert felt like he'd just won a world championship, even though he was still trapped in a cauldron of shit. The stench did not subside, and he still was losing blood to leeches, but he had foiled his captors and found refuge from the tortures in the midst of their trap.

It was the first moment Diegert had to consider the other tournament participants, and he hoped they had it worse than him. Fatima had never mentioned anything about this, and Diegert reasoned that the tournament would continue as planned just as soon as the sick fuck who'd thought this up decided they'd weakened the contestants enough to now let the killing begin. Meanwhile, Diegert sat on his pipe electrocuting leeches.

After twenty-four hours in his private cesspool, a bottom drain opened, and the water started to drain out of the pool. A light high up in the rafters came on, and when the water was gone, the door opened and a ladder was tossed into the pit, providing a route to the exit. Diegert tested his live wire; it no longer carried a current. He relaced and tied his boot before climbing off the pipe. The bottom of the pool wriggled with the movements of thousands of leeches. It disgusted Diegert to walk across them but crushing them under his boots felt like evening a score. When he stepped outside, it was sunny and warm. Greeting him with assault rifles was Strakov and Jaeger.

Standing in his sewage-drenched clothes, several blood-swollen leeches hanging from his skin, he looked at his dual nemeses who offered nothing but a bullet if he didn't comply. Diegert said, "I'm done with the shithouse, if either of you have to go."

Strakov plunged the butt of his rifle into Diegert's gut, doubling him over. Strakov drove the end of the rifle up under his chin, cracking his jaw, sending him sprawling onto the pine-covered ground.

Diegert lay there, lost consciousness, and remained prone while Strakov and Jaeger chuckled on their way back to Headquarters.

41

An air horn blasted, and the three other contestants, also released from twenty-four hours of torture, began actively searching for quarry. Diegert didn't hear a thing as he lay on the ground unconscious. His awareness began to return when he felt a heavy object jabbing his left shoulder. A mass was driven under his left hip, and he felt a powerful force roll him onto his back. Opening his eyes, he saw the big Bulgarian cop standing over him. He was not only imposing but hideous. His torture session must have involved fire, because he was burned over much of his body. His hair was singed back from his face. His cheeks and jaws had second-degree burns, but his lower legs, hands, and forearms were all burned to the third degree. Diegert could see the bare muscle of his appendages where the skin had been destroyed by fire. How he was able to hold on to the heavy machete in his right hand, Diegert couldn't understand.

"Brutus," Diegert exclaimed. The man was amazed that Diegert knew his name, and at that instant, Diegert realized Fatima had shared with him information the others didn't have.

"I'm glad you found me," he said as he slowly rose to his feet.

"What?" asked the confused giant.

"God damn, wasn't that the worst thing ever? What the fuck did they do to you?"

"Whatever I touched, it burned me. And fire"—the big guy gestured upward with his charred hands—"came up through the floor."

"Sounds like a live barbeque."

Brutus was bewildered by Diegert's sarcasm. The big guy stared at the side of Diegert's neck. Diegert followed his eyes and placed his hand on the side of his neck, where he felt a fat, fluid-filled leech. He pulled it off, leaving an oozing sore.

"I had hundreds of these things on me in that house. There's a deep hole they filled with sewage. I almost drowned in a pit of shit."

Brutus sneered at the thought, but then looked at Diegert menacingly from beneath the place where he used to have eyebrows.

"We can plan our team strategy now," Diegert said matter-of-factly.

"What?" questioned the big man, who had to put the brakes on his intent to kill.

"I think with your police skills and my communication and negotiations, we can win this thing."

"It is kill or be killed," belched Brutus.

Diegert could see the perplexed look on the man's scarred and disfigured face. "Oh, come on, you're not falling for that. That's misinformation. They're just testing to see if we are smart enough to realize that we can accomplish a whole lot more working together than apart."

"No, kill everybody."

"Oh really? Now does that make sense? Put a group of the world's most highly trained assassins together and then have them kill each other. When did that plan start making sense to you?"

"Never," said Brutus as the release of that thought unweighted his shoulders.

"Exactly! They want us to think. To demonstrate that we can use the resources available to us to do more than we could ever do alone; right now, those resources are each other."

"So what now?"

"Come here."

Diegert knelt down and brushed away leaves and pine needles clearing some dirt. He drew with his fingers in the dirt. Brutus kneeled down next to him with his machete blade in the dirt upon which he leaned for support. Diegert watched how slowly the big guy moved and how each point of contact brought a wince of pain from the charred hands and arms. He could also see large sections of clothing were burned off the guy's back.

Pointing with his fingers to his drawings, Diegert began, "We're right here, and I think the other guys are over here. Now, if they are coming this way, we can isolate them in these buildings and try talking to them, and if that doesn't work, then this is a very defensible position."

"I don't know. This is very different from what they told me."

"Really?"

Diegert swung his hand back and knocked the machete out from under the weight Brutus was placing on the weapon. He grabbed the back of the big guy's neck and drove his face forward. Brutus let out a scream of pain as his sensitive skin hit the dirt. The big Bulgarian swung a powerful left arm out at Diegert, but when his fist made contact, the pain was so severe that Brutus fell to the left and rolled on his back, covering his injured left hand with his burned right one.

Diegert grabbed the machete while Brutus writhed in pain. He stood above the pitifully damaged man. Brutus swung his right leg and shrieked when his burned shin collided with Diegert's stable leg. He closed his eyes and grimaced as the pain from the bare muscle exploded in his brain.

Diegert watched the suffering and could only imagine the infection he would develop as a result of rolling in the dirt. His skin would never grow back, and he would need several square yards of grafts to be whole again. The former police sergeant stared at Diegert with the only two spots on his face that weren't burned and said, "Kill or be killed?"

Diegert nodded his head as he held the machete to Brutus's throat. "Don't move."

Diegert checked the man's pockets for valuables. In the left front pocket, there was a circular metallic object. Diegert pulled it out and pressed a button on the top, opening the cover to reveal a timepiece. On the inside cover was a photo of Brutus seated with his young wife and two children. Diegert looked at the boy and girl and slowly closed the watch, putting it back in the man's pocket.

"Nice family."

Brutus clenched his teeth, saying nothing.

Checking the cargo pockets on the legs, he found a fully loaded ten-round magazine of 9 mm bullets. Not much good without a gun, but he put it in his pocket. With the machete still pressed to the throat of Brutus, he stood back up.

"Get up," he told the pain-ridden Bulgarian.

With a lot of struggle, Brutus stood, stoop shouldered and wincing. Diegert motioned with the big knife, directing Brutus to the door of the brick shithouse.

"Get in." Brutus kept his gaze on his captor as he entered the dark interior and descended the ladder into the pit. Diegert withdrew the ladder and slammed the door, locking the man inside.

42

On the north side of the grounds, the blast of the air horn left Deiobo particularly unmotivated to move. He remained immobile in the northeast corner. The acid burns on his face, head, and body were painful and pissed him off.

Shioki could not be so patient. He was compelled to venture forth because he had endured twenty-four hours of refrigerated cold. Frigid unrelenting temperatures made worse by saturating water sprays whenever he searched for an escape route. When he stood still, a great fan came on, creating a deafening wind chill. He had frostbite on his fingers, ears, and nose. Heading south, he soon encountered a murky swamp, which quickly became impassable as he sank to his waist in the soft-bottomed ooze. Retracing his steps, he regained solid ground and proceeded to the east, moving with as much stealth as his saturated boots would allow. He kept an eye out for objects with which he could improvise a weapon.

Deiobo, by remaining still, hoped to be able to detect movement around him. When he employed this technique hunting in the jungles of Brazil, he was rewarded with a monkey or a capybara, his favorite bush meat. To his mind, there was a lot less wildlife in these woods than in Brazil, but he wasn't looking for animals. He did, however, painfully recall his imprisonment in the concrete hut with the acidic shower that forced him to move from one square area to another. Each attempt to escape was greeted with nozzles spraying sulfuric acid on his hands, arms, and clothing. The burns were persistent, and he had no way of removing the noxious fluid from himself. It was a relief to be out of the hut, but he would be in pain throughout the tournament.

While motionless, Deiobo sensed the movement to his right. He riveted his eyes on the moving patterns of lines in the woods, and soon he was able to see shadow and form slowly progressing toward him.

Shioki had poor orientation to the grounds, but he believed he was approaching the northeast corner. He was unaware of the width of the fenced in area. Each step taken to the east brought him closer to the place from which his opponent began this deadly game. Shioki was getting more and more anxious; he didn't want to walk into a trap. Deiobo felt he was adequately concealed up in the big-trunked tree. He realized there was a risk being elevated, but he reasoned the visual advantage was worth it. The canopy of the tree also created a cleared space under its branches so the trunk couldn't be approached without exposure. He wished he had a weapon with which to shoot his enemy.

Shioki continued east until he reached the eastern fence, at which point he was afraid he'd crossed the path of his opponent who might now know his location. He turned suddenly with a sense of panic that he may have lost the advantage.

Deiobo watched as Shioki passed his tree. The Chinese special forces soldier never entered the clearing underneath the tree but kept to the south of the open space. Nevertheless, Deiobo was able to observe his movements, and he realized the Chinese man did not have a weapon and he distinctly heard the squishing of sodden footwear. After the soldier passed, the convict climbed down from his tree and followed on silent feet.

He saw the soldier reach the eastern fence, and he closed the gap. As the soldier turned from the fence, the convict struck him in the chest with a driving head butt. The power of the blow stunned the soldier, evacuating his lungs, and thrusting him into the eastern chain-link barrier. The convict followed with punches to the ribs and face. The soldier took the punishment, but his training had instilled in him a series of practiced reactions. He thrust up his arms and rotated his torso, blocking the strikes to his face, allowing him to see his opponent and counter with strikes of his own. The convict was close enough that the soldier used his legs to kick his attacker in the shins and stomp on his foot. The pain forced the convict back.

The two men now squared off, remaining in their defensive stances, circling each other seeking advantage. The soldier had suffered the worst. He was breathing heavily, and the strikes to the face had created a wound above his right eyebrow. Deiobo's right foot was sore, but his boot had prevented broken bones. He dropped his hands and moved in the wide-ranging fashion of capoeira. The soldier remained with his fists raised and his feet perpendicular, vigilant of his enemy's movements.

Suddenly, the convict let out a loud, piercing scream, frightening the soldier, who stepped back from the strange man. The convict took the moment of surprise and ran off to the west. The soldier stood alone, looking around trying to make sense of this erratic behavior. Needing to continue his pursuit, the soldier passed under the tree canopy and found a large fallen branch. He placed the branch between two trees and, using leverage, snapped it. He now had a club as a weapon, and he moved west in the direction of the convict. Soon he found the narrow wooden bridge without side rails that traversed the swamp. He noticed wet footprints on the boards. He stopped. There was swamp water on both sides of the bridge, and the closest vegetation that might support weight was several meters to either side. His enemy must have crossed, he reasoned, and began to make his way over the bridge.

The convict remained motionless, suspending himself above the water, clinging to the underside of the bridge. Tracking the footfalls passing over him, he reached out from under the bridge tripping the soldier. The instant the soldier fell to the surface of the bridge, the convict pulled him over the side and into the dark water. He placed his hands on the struggling soldier's shoulders, pressing down on him with all his weight. He kneed the soldier in the groin several times, inflicting not only great pain but making the man gasp for air. Those gasps sucked in the dark swamp water, which quickly filled the soldier's lungs, drowning him within twenty seconds.

Deiobo quickly grabbed the bridge as the soft organic matter of the swamp entombed the soldier's body. He climbed back onto the bridge, completely saturated but eager to find and kill his next opponent. Heading south across the bridge, he left the swamp behind as he walked up onto dry land. Just past the bridge, he spied an object he could hardly believe he had the good fortune to find. In the dappled light of the woods lay a Beretta 9 mm pistol. He stepped to it quickly, then hesitated. Was it a trap?

Being so obvious and inviting, he realized he might be in the crosshairs of an enemy. Pulling back, he lay down behind a fallen log. He remained still for several minutes. All was quiet. Using a long, sturdy branch, he reached out and pulled the gun to him. No booby trap. He held the gun and was delighted to have such a powerful weapon, but his happiness faded when he realized it was not loaded. Dejected, he reasoned it was better for him to have it than someone else, but it was not the lethal advantage he'd thought he'd found. Deiobo's disappointment left him when he saw another weapon lying in the weeds. With much less caution, he stepped over to a sinister-looking item, and sneering with menace, picked it up.

Diegert, carrying his machete, had completed an exploration of one of the movie-set buildings. Finding no enemies, he exited and crossed the street to the structures on the other side and crept around to the back. He looked north, searching for his next opponent. Beyond the buildings, there was a sparsely wooded area and then the concrete block field, which held about forty blocks of concrete, each about five feet high and four foot square. The blocks were lined up in rows forming a grid. It was a big space with weeds growing up through the gravel between the blocks. Diegert thought it a very strange thing to have constructed, but maybe the tactical teams used it for some kind of specific combat training. He was about to double back and head west when he saw a man moving on the far side of the block field.

Diegert watched the man move left and pick up an object that looked like a giant silver-gray lollipop. As he observed him swinging the object, Diegert realized the man had found a weapon. It looked to be a metal shaft with a cross tube at one end upon which was affixed a sprocket gear from a bicycle and a circular saw blade. The man ducked back down, looking around.

Diegert continued to monitor the block field, seeing weeds between the blocks swaying and shaking in spite of the lack of wind. He figured the man must be crawling between the blocks, and he tracked the man's progress through the field by watching the weeds. Diegert moved north, entered the field, and then moved west to intersect with the southern path the man was taking. Moving very slowly, Diegert was careful not to disturb the weeds as his quarry was doing. When he saw the weeds wobbling just north of the intersection where he stood, Diegert raised his machete over his head.

Deiobo, crawling quickly forward now that he could see the end of the field, heard the crunch of gravel to his left. He turned and saw a figure lunging toward him. He rolled to his right and raised his weapon. Diegert's machete made a metallic clang as the blade struck the shaft of the junkyard mace. Deiobo crouched his legs and kicked out with as much force as he could muster, taking the feet out from under Diegert. The assassin fell forward, landing on top of the convict. His face was inches from the saw blade, but his machete and his weight disallowed the weapon to be swung. Diegert put his hand on the back side of the machete and shoved the blade forward, catching the cross tube of the mace and forcing it out of the hands of the convict.

Once the weapon handle had left his grasp, the convict kneed Diegert in the thigh and punched him in the ribs. Diegert pushed the weapons away and sought to choke the convict, who rolled to the right and pushed up off the ground, elbowing Diegert in the gut. The convict stood up, and Diegert staggered to his feet as well. The convict lunged forward with a kick to Diegert's midsection, which Diegert blocked with his hands. The convict swung his fist, and Diegert ducked under the blow. The assassin jabbed the convict's chest and crossed with a punch to the face. The convict fell back against a concrete block, and Diegert pinned him against the block, hyperextending his back with a chokehold on his throat. Diegert began to apply crushing pressure to the convict's throat, when he felt a cold steel ring on his temple. The convict had a pistol to his head.

He released Deiobo and stepped back. Deiobo coughed and sputtered as he struggled to breathe, but he kept the gun pointed at Diegert and followed his movements.

"Go ahead and shoot, you pussy, I don't give a fuck."

The convict was still struggling to breathe and couldn't say a thing.

"Come on, you lousy prick. Get it over with!" Standing with his arms wide open and his chest fully exposed, Diegert shouted, "Go ahead shoot me, you shithead. Shoot me, you punk ass bastard."

Seeing the indecision in the convict's eyes, Diegert said, "If you don't have the guts to shoot me, then I'm gonna kill you right now."

As Diegert approached, Deiobo tossed the gun up in the air, grabbed the barrel, and threw it. The gun hit Diegert on the forehead, gashing the skin and toppling him to the ground. Deiobo ran back and grabbed the mace. He turned to go back to Diegert, who had picked up the gun and stood back up. Deiobo looked at him, laughing.

"What are you doing, you dumb shit? The damn thing's not loaded."

"I know," said Diegert as he reached into his cargo pocket, pulled out the clip, and jammed it into the Beretta. Deiobo stood in shock with his junkyard weapon as Diegert prepared to pull on the slide to chamber a round. Diegert pulled, and the slide wouldn't move. The slide was jammed, and the gun wouldn't load. Deiobo smiled as he drew his arm back and charged with his dual-disc weapon. Realizing the gun was jammed, Diegert reacted to the attack. He swerved his upper body as the mace whizzed past his face and chest. He was not quick enough, though, to avoid the saw blade digging into his right thigh. The jagged cutting tool lacerated the muscle as blood sprayed from Diegert's leg.

Deiobo tried to pull the weapon back, but it was caught in the fabric of Diegert's pants. Standing this close, Diegert crushed Deiobo's nose with the pistol. The blow dislodged the nasal cartilage and cracked the bones of the convict's nose. Blood spewed out, and Deiobo was in more pain than Diegert. With the Beretta still in hand, Diegert again pulled on the slide, which slid back and snapped forward, chambering the first round. As Deiobo staggered with blood all over his face, he looked up to see Diegert pointing the gun again. He smiled, revealing his crooked yellow teeth, just before two bullets hit his chest and a third entered his head, ending his participation in the tournament.

At that instant, Diegert didn't know if the fourth participant was still active, but having a loaded gun gave him a lot more confidence. He started to move west when the air horn, which had begun the competition, sounded. Diegert removed his belt and used it as a tourniquet on his bleeding leg. The gates opened, and teams of men entered with body bags. He was the only one going out. Outside the gate Strakov, Blevinsky, and Jaeger looked at him but offered no congratulations. Strakov barked, "You left one alive."

"With his injuries and the shit he's in, he'll be dead by morning."

Pierre and Gregor's smiles said much more than words. Pierre slapped him on the shoulder as he passed, and Diegert felt the camaraderie, even though he realized it was awkward for the Frenchman to be so positive in front of Strakov.

Fatima waited beyond the others, and her warm smile told Diegert that she was pleased. Also finding words difficult, she held out her hand, saying, "I'll take that."

Diegert handed her the gun and was placed in an ambulance. Fatima climbed in for the ride to medical. "I'm very proud of you."

"Killing those men was pointless. I get that it is part of this process, but those guys being dead doesn't accomplish anything."

"It showed us who is the best new operator in the world."

Diegert thought she sounded like a schoolgirl with her cheery assessment. She accompanied him to medical, where he got a shot of morphine and his thigh wound stitched up.

"One thing this did accomplish is the fulfillment of your training phase. You are no longer a trainee but an operator with all the rights and privileges ascribed to the role."

"You mean I'll be assigned to kill more people."

"You'll be an integral part of Crepusculous security."

Snorting, Diegert said, "Yeah right. What about the 100K?" he asked while getting his head wound cleaned.

"That'll be deposited in your account, but David there's more where that came from. You will be well paid for completing missions."

At the mention of money, Fatima could see she had Deigert's attention.

"Eventually you can be assigned to a regional location and operate independently at Headquarters' direction."

"Now that sounds like a good thing so I can get the fuck out of here."

"Right now, no one but Blevinsky can tell you what to do, and until assigned a mission, you can conduct yourself as you wish within the facility."

"You mean I get to have a staycation."

Fatima patted him on the forearm, saying, "I'll see you around, but I won't be coming to your room again to wake you in the morning."

As she walked out of medical, Diegert still couldn't deny the desire he had for her to come to his room for a completely unofficial visit.

With his wounds bandaged, Diegert returned to his quarters. Checking his numbered account, he found the additional 100,000 dollars was there. He now had over a quarter of a million dollars, more money than he could ever imagine. Transferring $167,000 to his mother's account, he sent her a text:

Mom, I love you, and I want you to be safe, secure and happy. Use this money I transferred to your account to pay off the mortgage, so you own the house. The money was earned through hard work and determination, so you don't have to ever worry about being without a home.
Love David.

THE END

Blood of the Assassin
The David Diegert Series, Book 2

Preview

1

Broward County Sherriff Michael Lowery pulled his Ford Explorer Interceptor into the lot of the Moose Jaw Inn. The bright colored lights of his vehicle remained off as he parked the white, black and gold SUV next to the rust accented Toyota Camry of Tom Diegert. Watching for the last customers leave at 2 am on a Wednesday, Sherriff Lowery knew where to find the man with whom he wanted to speak.

Standing with the bar door open, Tom Diegert leaned back and shouted past his son Jake, "Hey Brad."

The bartender looked up from cleaning glasses.

"Hey, thanks for a really good time," slurred Mr. Diegert.

"Right, Fuck you, Tom, just pay your full tab next time."

"Hey, I gave ya what I could..."

"Come on Dad, let's just go," said Jake as he directed his father out the door and down the stairs.

"Christ, it was only one or two beers, I paid for the rest," bitched the man in whose home David Diegert had grown up.

Jake tapped his father's shoulder when he noticed the police truck parked next to theirs.

"Judas, what the fuck is he doing here now? He knows we're going to be drunk. What the hell's he doing, check'n?"

Straightening their gaits, they continued approaching their formerly gold-colored sedan. The paint had dulled to a tarnished beige with oxidized corrosion on the wheel wells and door jambs. Sheriff Lowery stepped out of the Interceptor. "Hello, Tom."

"Evening Officer."

"Morning, Tom."

Tom nodded. He stood with his hands folded in front of him like a pious Quaker.

"I was hoping I could have a word with you two about David."

"David?! I got a word for ya, Fuckin Bastard. That punk ass bitch up and left the family months ago. We don't even know where the fuck he is."

Lowery looked from Tom to Jake, who nodded agreement.

"What the hell's going on? Why the hell are you out here in the middle of the night asking about that fucker?"

Lowery found himself a bit off guard, but he asked a critical question anyway. "Did you know that David joined the Army?"

Tom's ruddy red cheeks blanched. He stammered to say, "No fuck'n way. He left a note saying he was leaving. He didn't want to live with us no more. He never said he was joining the Army." Looking at Jake, they both nodded. Jake spoke up, "He would've told me something like that. He was my brother."

Lowery let that sappy, past tense, line pass. He knew neither of these two douche bags ever gave David any reason to trust them. He regretted asking the question, but the investigation into a violent incident in Austin required him to collect background information. He had to ascertain if these guys might be hiding the man wanted for questioning in the murder of a Mexican citizen outside a bar in Austin Texas.

"When was the last time you saw him?"

Jake replied, "February."

"Yeah right, it was cold as a bitch. Fuck'n snow everywhere," added Tom.

Pushing for more information, Lowery asked, "What were the circumstances when you last saw him?"

"Aah, he was taking Denise to the doctor. He dropped her off and was long gone when she came out."

Lowery's suspicion intensified in the red glow of the Moose Jaw's neon sign.

"He left a note," blurted Jake.

"Yeah, it said he was sorry for being a fuck–up and he was going away," shared Tom. "He didn't say where, so I suppose he could've joined the Army once he ran outta money."

"But you haven't spoken to him since February?"

"Nope," said Tom, shaking his head.

Lowery wanted to cut his losses with these losers, but Tom started asking questions.

"What kinda trouble is he in?"

"What makes you think he's in trouble?"

"HA, You do. You're not going to hang out here and talk to us in the dark unless something serious has happened."

Lowery held his tongue, but he couldn't stop staring at these guys. He knew what an abusive man Tom Diegert was, and Jake was complicit in the domestic domination and violence of the Diegert household.

"Sherriff, did David kill someone?"

The stoic lawman struggled to control his reaction to this blunt question. He also reasoned if they knew something, he might as well get it out of them now.

"A man was murdered in Texas, and David is a person of interest wanted for questioning."

"Texas? He ain't never been to Texas before," exclaimed Tom.

"Who did he kill?" asked Jake.

"We aren't sure he killed anyone. We just want to speak with him."

"Down in Texas, is the dead guy a spick?"

Lowery glared at Tom, his features made all the more intimidating by the flow of red neon over his stony expression.

Tom retreated, "I mean if he killed a spick, that's different then if it was a white guy, right?"

Lowery could barely contain his rage as he listened to the ignorant bigotry of Tom, reinforced by the head nodding of Jake.

Bringing his 6 foot 4-inch frame closer to the squat man and his chubby son, Lowery handed them each a card. "The taking of any human life is murder. Please call me if he contacts you, we need to talk with him."

"OK, Sherriff," said Tom, "but if that bastard shows up, I'll save Texas the trouble and just shoot him myself."

Lowery's anger popped. "You're a pathetic excuse for a father. Whatever David may have done, you are culpable." Stepping closer as his eyelids narrowed. "The hateful way you treated him sickens me. I should've arrested you a long time ago."

A sadistic smile crept on to Tom's face. "But you can't, and you know it. You can't do shit to me. Besides Jake here, is a fine son." Broward's local drug dealer smiled at the Sherriff as his father patted him on the back.

Looking at the pair with disgust, Lowery realized Tom was right.

"Get in your car and drive home. I'll be following you."

Tom gave the Sherriff an awkward salute before climbing in the Camry and letting Jake drive.

Driving the deserted streets of Broward with Lowery right behind him Jake thought back to when David was, maybe 12 years old. They had a chicken coop out back that was regularly being raided by a clever vixen. Tom wanted to kill the fox, but the persistent canid always eluded his 12 gauge attacks. Staying up late one night Jake sat in a blind near the coop. He watched as the bright red killer stole a chicken and ran into the woods. Following the thief, he discovered the lair where this young mother had a litter of kits.

Six baby foxes waddled out of a hole under a log and shared the bounty of chicken their mother had provided. Waiting until the mother left to hunt again, Jake dug out the pups, stuffing them in a canvas bag. In the morning he showed his father what he had. Tom was so proud of Jake. He beamed with his yellowed tooth smile as he gave the 16-year-old a can of beer for breakfast.

"You know what we're going to have to do with them don't ya?" asked Tom.

Jake sullenly nodded his head.

"I think you've done enough," said Tom, "it's your brother's turn."

Tom called David out to the barn. The kits had been dumped into a cardboard box. David looked in and saw the cutest little creatures he'd ever seen. The six of them huddled together, frightened in this strange place as they tried to comfort one another. Their big dark eyes peered from their tiny little faces with curiosity and trepidation. David knelt down, reached in and picked one up. The soft, warm body felt so small as it trembled in his hands. He gently stroked the fur on the top of its head as the bright orange bundle, with its little black paws, curled into his palm.

Tom stepped forward slapping David's arms, sending the kit tumbling back into the box.

"These aren't fucking pets."

Falling back on the ground, David looked up at the rage on his father's face.

"They're our enemy." Pointing across the barn at Jake who sat impassively blank-faced, Tom continued. "Jake captured them. He did an important thing for this family. You know the mother of these little runts has been killing our chickens. The fox is stealing our livelihood," shouted Tom as he thrust his fingers at the box of babies. "Now we're going to even the odds and reclaim our power by eliminating the enemy." Striding between his two sons, Tom took center stage as he barked, " Protecting the things your family needs to survive is the job of a warrior. Being strong, and not letting others take what you have requires guts and toughness. Jake stayed up all night to find the home of the thief and capture these terrible, vicious threats." Tom leaned forward as he glared at David. "It's now your turn to protect this family."

Tom reached into the box grabbing each kit and stuffing them, squeaking and yelping, into the canvas bag.

"You're going to kill them," he commanded as he handed David the bag with the wriggling little bodies desperately clambering over one another. Their pitiful yelps and mews emanating through the fabric, made David cringe with despair.

"You can either drown them in the rain barrel like a pussy, or you can use the sledge on them."

Tom hefted the sledge hammer and dropped it on the barn floor next to David.

"A warrior makes sure his enemy is destroyed. He takes the life of those who steal from him and does it with brute force. Those little pups will grow into thieving foxes. We stop that right now. Smash 'em and prove that you deserve to be part of this family."

Jake felt sorry for his brother, David loved nature, he studied animals and knew way more about them than either he or his father. Killing animals was all Tom Diegert knew, and he took pride in any successful hunt. The Warrior stuff he was prognosticating about always came out whenever they so much as shot a squirrel. Still Jake was on the upside, and he remembered how there was no way he was going to let any sympathy for his brother cause him to act against his father.

"Stand up," shouted Tom. David rose from the floor, quivering. The bag of wriggling little fox kits at his feet.

"Pick up the hammer and smash'em," ordered his father.

David hesitated, looking from the bag to the hammer.

"Don't be a pussy like your Mom. These fuckers need to die."

David placed his hand on the hammer. The sledge had a 36-inch wooden handle with a 10-pound octagonal head. He closed his fist around it, lifting it very slowly. Tom's eyes widened with delight. David held the tool turned weapon in both hands. He looked at his father and saw wretched anticipation in the ugly man's face. He saw the thirst for violence and the bloodlust the old man held for these infants of the forest. Broadening his stance, as he had been taught to do when chopping wood, David lifted the hammer, looking at the canvas bag with its little bodies struggling within. Holding the hammer aloft, he started to tremble, the hammer looked as though it was going to fall out of his hands behind him.

"Do it," shouted Tom.

David's tears broke over his lids, falling to the barn floor like the first drops of an unexpected rain shower. Turning away from the bag of pups, he dropped the hammer and broke into uncontrollable sobbing.

"Oh no you don't, you wuss. You pick up that hammer, and you finish the job."

David collapsed to the floor curling into a fetal position.

"Oh my fucking God," exclaimed Tom. Turning to Jake, he said, "Can you believe this fucking pussy is crying like a little girl over these foxes?"

Jake recalled how bad he felt for David, but he just nodded his head.

"He is not the son of a Warrior. He's an injun bastard, who doesn't have the strength to protect his own family."

Tom drew close to David, "You're a no good pussy who doesn't have the guts to kill his enemies. Well, you just keep your fucking eyes open."

Tom stepped back grabbed the hammer swung it high and brought the ten-pound mall on to the canvas bag. The yips and mews turned into screeches of terror as blood stained the fabric. Tom swung the hammer, again and again, each blow ceasing the wriggling of the little bodies. After striking the bag a dozen times, the short, ruddy man panted as he paused. Seeing one body still moving he swung the hammer, flattening the bag, darkening the canvas with more blood.

David watched the massacre from eye level as he remained on the floor throughout the ordeal. Struggling to catch his breath Tom said, "You don't deserve to be in this family since you aren't willing to fight for it. I won't forget that."

Dropping a shovel in front of David, Tom said, "Since you're so fucking sympathetic about these runts, you bury 'em."

Leaving the barn with his father, Jake recalled feeling like shit, but glad that he was not the one his father hated. David took the shovel and the grisly cloth bag and disappeared into the woods for three days. Their mother, Denise went crazy not knowing where he was, but Tom didn't care. When he eventually returned, Tom didn't say a thing, and Jake remembered David never confided in him ever again. As the years passed and David grew much bigger and stronger, Tom always sided with Jake, isolating David, so he had only the friendship of his Mother.

Reaching their driveway, Jake parked in front of the garage. He watched Lowery's Explorer pass on by. Tom had passed out, so Jake reclined the seat and covered his father with the blanket he kept in the car for just such occasions. At the kitchen door, he stopped to look at the barn. He wondered if his father had really made a killer out of his brother.

Thank you for Reading

Please post a review on Amazon, or the site of your choice. A review need not be long. A sentence of two is sufficient.

Thank you.   *Bill Brewer*

ABOUT THE AUHTOR

Bill Brewer writes to engage his readers. Using imagination and research, he creates compelling characters whom he thrusts into dangerous situations. To thrill his readers, Bill sets a blistering pace and keeps the action coming as the plot explodes across the pages. The story reveals its secrets as the characters experience triumph, betrayal, victory, and loss. While you're reading, look for passages filled with anatomical details that this University Professor of Human Anatomy & Physiology uses to bring realism into his story.

When not teaching or writing, Bill can be found seeking adventure, peace and camaraderie, hiking, biking and paddling near his home in Rochester NY.

SOCIAL MEDIA

Please visit my website and subscribe for e-mail updates.

billbrewerbooks.com

Also, please follow me on

- <u>Facebook</u>: Bill Brewer Books
- <u>Twitter</u>: @Brewer Books
- <u>Instagram</u>: billbrewer434

9 781734 507713